VIC

"*Her Perfect Life* is the perfect read. From the very first
sentence, I was hooked by this engaging and heartfelt story of
a woman's journey through danger, adventure and romance."
—National bestselling author Susan Wiggs

"Katie Slater's whole life is a war story,
literally and figuratively, and her only weapons are her wits
and her soul. To fight her way to freedom, she dons an
emotional armor that only love can pierce."
—Joyce Holland, *Northwest Florida Daily News*

"Hinze has a knack for combining compellingly realistic
characterizations with suspense and a romantic plot line."
—*Publishers Weekly*

"Hinze is clearly one of the leaders of military romances that
emphasize action, suspense, and romance."
—*Affaire de Coeur*

"Dynamic author Vicki Hinze guarantees her readers
an edge-of-the-seat thrill ride."
—*Romantic Times BOOKclub*

"Hinze grabs the reader on the first page
and holds their attention to the very end."
—*Rendezvous*

Dear Reader,

Spring is on the way, and the Signature Select program offers lots of variety in the reading treats you've come to expect from some of your favorite Harlequin and Silhouette authors.

The second quarter of the year continues the excitement we began in January with a can't-miss drama from Vicki Hinze: *Her Perfect Life*. In it, a female military prisoner regains her freedom only to find that the life she left behind no longer exists. Myrna Mackenzie's *Angel Eyes* gives us the tale of a woman with an unnatural ability to find lost objects and people, and *Confessions of a Party Crasher,* by Holly Jacobs, is a humorous novel about finding happiness—even as an uninvited guest!

Our collections for April, May and June are themed around Mother's Day, matchmaking and time travel. Mothers and daughters are a focus in *From Here to Maternity*, by Tara Taylor Quinn, Karen Rose Smith and Inglath Cooper. You're in for a trio of imaginative time-travel stories by Julie Kenner, Nancy Warren and Jo Leigh in *Perfect Timing*. And a matchmaking New York cabbie is a delightful catalyst to romance in the three stories in *A Fare To Remember* by Vicki Lewis Thompson, Julie Elizabeth Leto and Kate Hoffmann.

Spring also brings three more original sagas to the Signature Select program. *Hot Chocolate on a Cold Day* tells the story of a Coast Guard worker in Michigan who finds herself intrigued by her new downstairs neighbor. Jenna Mills's *Killing Me Softly* features a heroine who returns to the scene of her own death, and *You Made Me Love You* by C.J. Carmichael explores the shattering effects of the death of a charismatic woman on the friends who adored her.

And don't forget, there is original bonus material in every single Signature Select book to give you the inside scoop on the creative process of your favorite authors! Happy reading!

Marsha Zinberg

Marsha Zinberg
Executive Editor
The Signature Select Program

SPOTLIGHT

VICKI HINZE

Her
Perfect Life

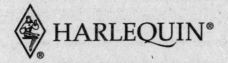

HARLEQUIN®

TORONTO • NEW YORK • LONDON
AMSTERDAM • PARIS • SYDNEY • HAMBURG
STOCKHOLM • ATHENS • TOKYO • MILAN • MADRID
PRAGUE • WARSAW • BUDAPEST • AUCKLAND

ISBN 0-373-83692-9

HER PERFECT LIFE

This edition published by arrangement with Harlequin Books S.A.

® and TM are trademarks of the publisher. Trademarks indicated with ® are registered in the United States Patent and Trademark Office, the Canadian Trade Marks Office and in other countries.

www.eHarlequin.com

Printed in U.S.A.

Dear Reader,

I am so excited that *Her Perfect Life* is being published! This story has haunted me for years, ever since I saw a TV news broadcast on the Gulf War and heard an anchor say that "no man is left behind." That was the goal, of course, but Scott Speicher *had* been left. I started wondering what it would be like for a woman to be held a prisoner of war for an extended length of time, then rescued and returned home—only to find home was different. *Everything* was different. How would she cope? Rebuild? What would her challenges be and how would she meet them? That's the core story in this novel.

Sometimes we think we have it all. Katie Cole Slater did, too. But it's in losing everything that we gain most. Katie realizes that in *Her Perfect Life.*

Blessings,

Vicki Hinze

Acknowledgments

As always there are many to thank for a completed work, and only me to blame for any challenges anyone finds with it. I'm grateful for the contributions of:

Evan Fogelman, my agent, champion and secret weapon. You are the stuff of heroes.

Susan Litman, an amazingly gifted editor, who sees the vision in my head and helps me translate it clearly onto paper.

Sandie Scarpa, my assistant, master research whiz and resident guardian angel. Thanks for keeping me on track, Sandie, and for the million things you do I never slow down long enough to acknowledge. I do notice, and I am grateful.

My family, who know my every flaw and yet somehow manage to love me, anyway.

Lorna, Marge and Bill, friends and blessings that enrich my life.

All those who serve in our Armed Forces, who take the risks and make the sacrifices, and all those at home who do the same and await them.

Dedication

To Scott Speicher and his family.

And to my son, Iraqi War veteran

Raymond Hinze.

I love you, Ray.

Thank you for the privilege of being your mother.

And thank you for coming home.

PROLOGUE

LIFE SHOULD COME with warning labels.

Warning! At fifteen, you're going to be tempted to give your virginity to Donald Simoneaux at Mel Ott Park behind the baseball bleachers. Don't. He's an arrogant idiot with a big mouth and, if you do it, you'll never hear from him again. You won't anyway—it'll be a one-date train wreck—but if you sleep with him, you'll feel you wasted your first, you'll be down on sex for the next decade and ticked off about it forever. If you don't, you'll thank the gods for sparing you from a second date with the jerk, you'll meet a great guy at eighteen who has finesse, and the first time you two twist the sheets, you'll totally understand all the fuss about sex.

Warning! At seventeen, avoid the Pink Daisy. It's a cute club with cool people, but you'll get busted because Marianne Demsey will stuff her dope in your purse when the place is raided, and she won't admit that it's hers. You don't smoke anything, including pot, but you'll never convince your dad—or the police—of that. On the up side, you'll test clean, get community service and your mom will know the truth. She's psychic, remember? She knows everything. But she won't be able to convince your dad she's not covering for you, and he'll choke you nearly to death trying to keep you on a tight leash until you're twenty-one. You will *not* be a happy leashee.

And oh, while we're talking about twenty-one, skip the Mardi Gras frat party at the Louisiana State University campus in New Orleans. You'll save yourself an ex-husband. That's where you'll meet Wonder Dick, who considers fidelity a rule just for women.

Warning! At twenty-four, you'll be a pilot, just as you've always dreamed. Air Force all the way, baby. And right after pilot training, you'll meet a jock who makes you weak in the knees. You'll marry him three years later, have two great kids—a girl and a boy—and you'll love your life.

Okay, so over the years you'll get a little wistful now and then because your relationship could be better. Jock—aka Dr. Sam Slater, leading gynecologist in Willow Creek, Florida—isn't perfect, but unlike Wonder Dick, he's worth keeping. He's a faithful husband, a decent if uninspiring lover, a good dad so into having the perfect image he still hides flaws from his parents, and if he's a bit selfish and seemingly unconscious about what's important at times, well, you're not perfect yourself.

Actually, his faults are relatively minor compared to those of the spouses of many of your friends. If you looked at vaginas and dealt with hormonal women all day, you probably wouldn't get overly enthused on nights at home, either.

As compensation, you'll have the coolest copilot in the Air Force, C. D. Quade, who is a walking violation to the libidos of women everywhere. He's totally irresistible: gorgeous, sharp, funny, sensitive and straight. You two will be great friends, nuts about each other, and on occasion you'll wonder what it would be like to be with him instead of the jock, but loyalty and vows keep your wedding band on your finger and your panties up around your hips. C. D. Quade isn't the kind to trespass on another man's turf anyway, so it's just as well you keep your blood cooled to a simmer around him. Regardless, with the jock, the kids and your beloved garden at home, and C.D. at work, you'll be reasonably content. That's not bad for real life.

Now for the grand slam, kick-your-ass-and-pad-your-knees-because-you're-going-to-be-on-them-for-the-duration warning:

Love your family so fiercely that it almost hurts, and do all those things you keep saying you'll get around to someday—like finding a way to make a living with your gardening, taking that Alaskan cruise you've dreamed about since your eighteenth birthday, and making that pilgrimage you promised your grandmother you'd make to Scotland to see where your dad's ancestors lived. Don't wait.

Do it all now.

All of it.

Because if you don't, when you're thirty-four, you're going to be assigned to fly a mission in Iraq, and on June 23rd your plane is going to get shot down. You'll be with your devoted sidekick copilot, C.D., who will still be incredibly sexy and single, but…well, the bottom line is he's going to be rescued, and you're going to be dead.

At least that's the way it's going to seem for a long, long time. And many times during this dark period of your life, you'll remember the little list you made when you were eight, the one that detailed all the things you wanted when you grew up. Remember? You wrote it shortly after you completed the magical leap from the fat pencils you conquered in first grade to the brand-new, Number 2, slim-and-sleek writing machine.

This list was the most important document of your life, and to mark the rite of passage in creating it, you pulled out your most prized possession: the black ink, clear barrel, comfort-grip, Bic medium-point pen you'd been saving to use on something really, really special. This was that life-defining moment. That momentous occasion you would forever recall as the one instant in time when you knew exactly what you wanted in order to be content.

You felt it the moment the tip of the pen touched the page and you printed in bold, broad letters:

KATIE COLE
AND
HER PERFECT LIFE

I'm sorry to say that many times during these trials you'll have to fight hard to not lose hope and heart and let your spirit be broken. It won't be easy. It will be hell. You'll curse that list and your life, and you'll wish you were dead.

Oh, yeah. Life definitely should come with warning labels.

But it doesn't.

And that, Captain Katie Cole Slater, is the most important *Warning!* of all.

CHAPTER ONE

Six Years Later

HER PRISON CELL WAS DARK and dank.

Weak moonlight cut through the tiny barred window, barely casting a thin strip of shadow on the hard sand floor. The air lay still, silent and heavy, yet compared to the days of hundred-twenty-degree temperatures, it seemed blissfully cool.

In just a few hours, dawn would come and the desert heat would again turn her cell into an oven. Trapped between the walls in this armpit of hell, the heat swelled and seemed to suck all the oxygen out of the air. Day or night, Katie felt choked. Midday, she often spent strangling, and when the sandstorms came, the misery increased tenfold.

That which is endured is conquered.

She gently held the photo of her husband, Sam, and their children, Molly and Jake. It was far too dark to see it, but that didn't matter; she'd memorized every detail. Though it made the ache in her heart so acute she swore it would kill her, each night she forced herself to remember every quirk and expression and sound they'd ever made, terrified if she missed even one night she'd forget and never again be able to recall them. She relived each memorable moment and the way it had made her feel, the way *they* had made her feel, at least a million times, and prayed it would be enough to last her the rest of her life.

Eyes are unnecessary to view what is stored in the heart.

The photo's edges were frayed and the images worn smooth in places—one on Molly's hair and one on Jake's nose. Katie had always done that—stroked Molly's hair, and dragged her fingertip down the slope of Jake's nose. Back then she'd been comforting them. Now she stroked their photo, trying to comfort herself.

In the last six years, there had been little comfort.

But there had been an abundance of nightmares.

Nightmares of the crash, of her injuries. The pain of setting her own broken bones. When she'd discovered she'd gone down in a lawless tribal area, she'd known that there would be more pain to be suffered. And there had been. Much, much more.

Despite the warlords' bets that she wouldn't last a week, she had endured and conquered every single violation. She had survived. Yet each abuse had created horrible images that didn't fade from her memory on awakening. Images that ignited resentment and anger and made it burn as strong in her as the loneliness of isolation and the constant fear of what the sadistic bastards holding her prisoner would do to her next.

General Amid had been a godsend.

Still, it'd taken a couple years to come to grips with being left behind. C.D. had to be dead, or he'd have found her by now. She still mourned him. Mourned losing Sam and their kids. Mourned having her life stripped away from her and being left with…this.

It'd taken a couple more years to give up hope of ever being rescued. But on the fifth anniversary of her crash and capture, she'd reached critical-crisis point: accept it or go insane. That night, alone in her cell, she had slogged her way through a minefield of emotions and faced the truth. No one could reach her here. No one would even try—not anymore, if they ever had. Too much time had passed, and living in this cell, cleaning General Amid's home, shopping for his household at the market—that was her life now, and likely that's all it would ever be. She refused to think about his leaving. Without his protection, the guards would revert to the way they'd treated her before he'd stepped in, and that incited more nightmares, more withdrawing deeper and deeper inside herself, closing even more shutters in her mind, locking away the memories of torture to stay sane.

Yet on still nights like this one, where she lay alone in her cell on a bare cot with but one thing of her own— the photo—she silently wept inside, crushed under the weight of her darkest fears. She *would* die in this god-awful place, still wearing her tattered flight suit because it made the guards feel superior and powerful to hold her—the U.S.—captive.

She would never again see Sam or Molly or Jake.

She'd never again know the joy of watching them play while she worked in her beloved garden. It, too, likely stood as withered and overgrown as the day they'd first moved into the house. Sam was not a master gardener. He wouldn't even remember to water the lawn if it wasn't on an automatic sprinkler system. She'd worked two years on that garden. But… Reality hit her. Every-thing in her life ceased to be when she had ceased to be.

Except for Sam and the kids.

Yet even with the most heartfelt and resolute rationalization, she couldn't convince herself that they weren't gone from her life forever.

On her cot, she curled on her side, pulling her knees to her chest, trying to shut out despair. *God, how long must I endure this? Why can't I die, too? Please, just end this pain....*

For the hundredth time that long, sorrowful night, she swallowed a sob and buried her hopelessness. The guard was apt to come in at any time, and she didn't dare let him see her in tears. She'd made that mistake once early on and would kill herself before doing it again. He and the other guards had tortured her for six hours straight.

Shaking head to toe at the memory, she crossed her chest with her arms and squeezed. The sensation of pressure swept sweet relief through her body. She was awake, not asleep, not dreaming those haunting dreams. She had survived.

That which is endured is conquered.

Rubbing the faded U.S. flag patch on her sleeve, she wondered. What were the children doing? Was Sam home from the hospital, tucking them into bed, singing them night-night songs? Did he notice that Molly showed signs of being as psychic as Katie's mother? Did he remember that she hated the crust on her sandwiches, and Jake had to have orange juice every morning to jump-start his blood sugar level? Did Sam remember to kiss them good-morning as well as good-night? How often did he remember to tell them he loved them? He'd seldom slowed down long enough to tell Katie herself, but love had always been there in his eyes. Always there in his eyes. Molly would sense that. But would Jake?

A tear splashed onto Katie's cheek and her heart

ached. *God, how can I keep taking this, day after day? Please, please let what happened today matter. Please let that French doctor report seeing me.*

He *had* seen her. Hadn't he? He definitely had made eye contact, been startled and quickly covered it up, then pretended not to have seen her at all.

General Amid, who ran the prison camp, had sent her to the market for his fresh vegetables. There was no danger of her running away. There was nowhere to run and no one to run to, and anyone foolish enough to try would die in the desert or be slaughtered by the warlords hiding out in the region. In the market, there had been a small group of medical workers treating the sick, passing out medicine…. That's where she'd seen the French doctor. He *had* to have reported seeing her….

But nothing happened that night to verify it.

Katie consoled herself. It took time to notify people. Time to identify her and to debate the options and decide what to do. Warning herself she was being a damn fool, she couldn't seem to stop hope from flickering to life inside her.

Nothing happened the next night, either, and doubt seeped in. Maybe she'd just seen what she'd wanted to see, and the Frenchman hadn't noticed her at all. Or maybe it was just taking a little longer to get the wheels moving. It *had* to be taking just a little while longer….

But a week later, when still nothing had happened, her certainty disappeared. The Frenchman hadn't seen her, or if he had, he'd chosen to ignore it or he'd thought nothing of it.

The most important glimpse of her life—but to him it'd been too insignificant to even notice.

You've got to stop this, Katie. Stop hoping. It's in-

sane. Nothing is going to happen. Keep hoping, and how are you going to handle the letdown? Hope is a luxury you can't afford.

She paced her cell in the darkness, bitterness burning her throat, her chest so tight she could barely breathe. *Die, hope.* She pushed a fisted hand over her heart. *Die!*

And whether it did, or it was buried so deep she couldn't feel it anymore, she put the Frenchman from her mind, locking him behind the shutter to forget him, too, and then returned to stroking her worn photograph in the sweltering heat, missing Sam and the kids, mourning C.D., and scrubbing General Amid's quarters, longing for her weekly bath and swearing she'd trade her eyeteeth for a hamburger, soda or bottle of skin lotion. And conditioner for her hair. She squeezed her eyes shut and indulged in heartfelt longing. She'd give a molar for one squirt of conditioner. Just one...

While she hadn't dared to hope, she had put herself in General Amid's presence as often as possible, in case he wanted to send her back to the market. The medical workers still being around was highly unlikely, but it wasn't impossible.

Yet whether or not they remained close by quickly became a moot point. The general watched her with an odd look in his eyes, but he never sent her back to the market. Instead, just before she was to return to her cell one night, he stopped her. "Katie," he said. "I am to be transferred to a new prison soon."

Fear sliced through her heart like a knife and she had to fight to find her voice. "Will you take me with you?"

Regret burned in his eyes. "I am sorry. That is not possible."

Disappointment raised terror, and tears clogged her

throat. She couldn't speak, and so nodded. He would leave, and things would return to the way they had been before he had learned what was happening to her. *Oh, God. I can't stand it again. I can't.*

"I am sorry," he whispered. "I have done all I can do to protect you."

He had. Here, and maybe in sending her to the market. Maybe he'd meant for her to be seen. On the chance he had, she felt gratitude swell and her chin quiver. She cleared her throat to hide it. "Thank you."

He, too, had given up hope. She was lost. Lost, screwed and defeated.

Knowing it, she walked the dark pathway back to her cell. The defeat had her despairing, but even more than despairing, she was terrified.

Long after midnight that night—exactly two weeks after she'd seen the Frenchman in the market—Katie paced her four-foot wide cell until her feet ached, and then collapsed onto her cot, exhausted. Her stomach growled. She hadn't been fed since yesterday, and hadn't been able to steal anything from General Amid's. If he ever noticed food missing, he never mentioned it. But she didn't flaunt stealing his food in his face, either.

Holding the photo over her heart, she ignored her rumbling stomach and closed her eyes.

For the first night since she'd seen the Frenchman, she didn't drift to sleep seeing his face in her mind. Every other night, she had alternated between praying he'd think of her and the thought of her would nag at him until he did something to help her, and cursing him for not being more aware, seeing her and doing something to set her free. But this night, she didn't think of him at all. General Amid, the man whose protection had kept her alive and safe, whose food had kept her from starving to death, was leaving. A new commander would take his place and things would return to what they had been.

She would be dead within a month.

If God was merciful, sooner…

A SCUFFLE STARTED OUTSIDE her cell door.

Katie awakened abruptly. Every nerve in her body sizzled, hyperalert and warning her to hide, but she forced herself to stay still. For her own protection, and until she discovered what the hell was going on, she best served herself by not letting anyone know she was awake.

"Colonel Katherine Slater?" a man said in a crisp, sharp voice.

Colonel? She didn't respond. It could be a setup for torture.

A second man's hushed voice carried through the bars to her. "Call her Captain. She doesn't realize she's been promoted."

Katie stiffened. As a POW she would automatically be promoted, but the enemy knew that, as well. And Americans considered her dead. Unless the Frenchman… She stifled a gasp. *Oh, God! Was it possible?*

"Captain Slater," the first man said, then recited her code word that only she and her superior officer knew.

American! He had to be an American! She sat straight up. "Yes? Yes, it's me." She strained to see him, but it was a moonless night, and she could barely make out his silhouette. What did this mean? Had they engaged the tribal warlords in the lawless area and been taken prisoner, too?

"Captain Daniel Wade, ma'am," he said, his husky voice catching. "We're here to take you home."

CHAPTER TWO

"YOU SEEM IRRITATED, Colonel."

Katie turned from the window to look at Dr. Green, the major and chief physician who had been poking and prodding her physically and mentally for three damn days. "I'm fine."

Thin and lanky, with glasses he wore low on his long nose, he dragged a hand through his gray hair and let out a frustrated sigh. "You won't discuss what happened to you from the time of the crash until you saw the Frenchman. You refuse to answer questions, other than in the most general terms, about your treatment while held captive. You won't respond at all to questions regarding torture or rape." He leaned forward, clasped his hands on his desktop. "We can help you, Colonel Slater, but only if you allow us to do it."

"With all due respect, Major, I haven't asked for help. I've had six years to deal with all of that, and I did. I'm fine." She didn't dare lie, and she couldn't tell him the truth; she'd never get out of the hospital. But he needed a bone to chew on or he'd never hush. "I don't want to discuss those things because I'll relive them again, and once was more than enough. The one thing I do want to discuss, no one will talk to me about." She walked across the office and leaned over his desk. "I want to talk to my husband and children. Now. Please."

"Colonel, we've discussed this. Your debriefing isn't complete—"

He wouldn't break her. Frustration had tears choking her, but she would *not* break. No one would ever break her again. "The military left me behind. Is it any wonder that I don't care about its debriefings? I realize you're just doing your job, so when I say what's on my mind and in my heart, understand that it isn't personal. The truth is I couldn't care less about anything of interest to anyone but my family and me, and I am particularly un-interested in any concerns of anyone in uniform. Men in uniform left me for dead. I suffered the consequences. They went on with their lives."

"They rescued you, too," he softly reminded her.

"After six years."

"I've explained that." He sighed. "You were reported dead and we verified your death through human intel-ligence contacts on the ground."

"Yes, you've explained that. But your explanations haven't changed my consequences. I've still lived them." She nearly had died, had been in a coma for days. Had spent six years in hell. "You know what? Screw those verifications and contacts. I'm here, I'm breathing and my tour of duty expired two years and six days ago. I'm free now, I'm done here and I want to go home."

"You will, Colonel, in due time."

"Isn't six years long enough?" She reined herself in, swallowed her anger. "Listen, I appreciate your concern, but you really don't want to know how I feel."

"Yes, I do." He folded his hands atop his desk, leaned

forward, and his watch twinkled in the light streaming in through the slats of the window blinds. "I really do."

"Okay." She pulled up courage and tried hard to express herself without leaving herself more vulnerable. "I'm angry," she admitted. "I'm so angry I can barely breathe." Perspiration at revealing that much gathered on her skin. She sucked in a sharp breath, fought to keep her voice steady, her resolve strong, and pressed on. "For six years, not one person did a damn thing to help me in any way. Nothing. Now the entire military is falling all over itself to do everything it can for me, but I know the truth. All anyone here really wants is to coerce me into not saying anything antimilitary to the press. The honchos want to avoid a public relations nightmare they can't win."

He looked her right in the eye. "I won't insult you by denying that."

"Then thank you for acknowledging that this *help* isn't about me at all." Sarcastic, she pulled her lips back from her teeth in a frozen smile.

"Colonel, you must be cognizant of the potential ramifications and impact on the military as an entity—and on all of the other people in it. You must see the rationale for—"

She held up a hand and interrupted. "I can't afford to care about the military's rationale or its nightmares, Major. I have all I can hold, with far too many of my own." Weary of the battle of wills, she frowned, then softened her tone. "I want to go home, Dr. Green. I want to see my husband and children."

He slumped back in his chair. "I know that, Colonel. And you will, just as soon as—"

"You're doing it again. You're patronizing me. Please

don't do that. I've earned the right to better." She had a trump card, and it was time to play it. "I've been patient and I've been forced to play by other people's rules far too long already. Send me home now, Dr. Green, or tell your superiors that I *will* talk to the press. And if they force me to do that, I promise all of them, they will *not* like what I have to say."

He stiffened. "Do I need to remind you that threatening your superior officers is a crime?"

She stood up straight. "No, you don't. I'm well aware of rules and regulations. That was not a threat, it was a promise. If they choose to interpret it as a threat, fine. Tell them to court-martial my ass. Put me in jail. Won't that make for lovely headlines?" Rage rolled over Katie in waves. "Abandoned POW rescued and jailed for wanting to see her family." She glared back at him, keeping her voice calm and steady. "Go ahead. Tell them to do what they have to do, but to do it knowing that I'm going to do what I have to do, too. And you might remind them that I've had a lot of time to think about what that will be."

"Colonel," he said, then paused, masked his expression and took a more personal tack. "Katie, as hard as it might be for you to accept, we do have your best interests in mind as well as the military's best interests. What happened to you could happen to anyone. We'd like to prevent that."

"So long as there are wars and pilots, there'll be risks, and everyone involved knows it."

"True. But we need to know what happened to you after the plane went down. You can help us lessen the odds of a recurrence," he said. "You can rely on us, Katie."

"Listen, I'm grateful that you're trying to figure out

what went wrong. It was bad intelligence, pure and simple. But if you want advice for those who follow me, here's the best I can give them—if you're taken captive, you're on your own. Deal with it."

"Katie." His sigh heaved his shoulders.

"Major, I'm not being flip. I'm being frank. I learned a lot while I was being held captive. One of the most important lessons was that I must never rely on anyone else for anything. Never need or want anything."

"That isn't a healthy teamwork attitude."

"It is when you're a prisoner and you *are* the team."

He paused, his gaze sweeping back and forth across the room. "It's not in your best interest—"

She held up a staying hand. "Thank you, but I'll mind my own best interests, Dr. Green. And I'd appreciate it if the honchos would leave me to it."

"Look, I understand why you feel this way—"

"Great," she interrupted, then sat down and relaxed in the chair. "Then let's cut to the chase. Just tell me the truth. That's all I want. Easy enough, right?"

"Of course." He seemed baffled.

"Good." She nodded, then tilted her head. "So tell me, Doctor. What are the honchos so afraid of?"

Decidedly uncomfortable, he paused and removed his glasses, then set them on his desk blotter. "You lived through hell, Katie," he said, softening his voice and choosing his words very carefully. "I don't need for you to tell me what they did to you, I see it in your eyes. You survived that, and I expect that makes you a very strong woman. I just want you to survive the homecoming."

That surprised her. She took in a deep breath and slowly expelled it. "What is so bad that you fear it'll drive me over the edge? Because I'll tell you, Doctor, if I didn't lose it in the tribal prison, I'm not going to lose it now. The bastards have gotten all of my life I'm going to give them. For that matter, so has the Air Force. The rest of my life is mine. And I'm going to spend it with my family, doing…I don't know what, exactly, but something I *want* to do." An image often relived, of her in the garden with the kids, filled her mind. She'd love doing something with her gardening. It'd always brought her solace and peace. "Only things I *want* to do." She shrugged. "What in that do the honchos fear?"

"Nothing." He looked down at his desk, then back at her. "A lot has changed during your absence, but we can learn from your experience and insight."

After all she'd given, they wanted more. Always wanted more. What about her? Sam and the kids? What about what they all wanted? She paused and looked deeply into his eyes. "Dr. Green, are you a father?"

He nodded, clearly aware of where she was about to go with this. "Yes, I am."

"Then for God's sake put yourself in my place. I want my husband and children. I need to see them. How can you not realize that?"

"I do realize it." Worry wrinkled his brow. He paused a moment, obviously thinking, then went on. "All right," he said, dread lacing his tone. "All right." He held up a hand. "But you need to realize that things are not as they were when you were at home last. Things are very…different…now."

"Excuse me?"

"Your family mourned you, and then they went on with their lives."

Fear buckled her knees. She slid down farther in the

chair. That sounded ominous, pregnant with chilling things left unsaid. "What are you telling me?"

"You'll be flown to Paxton Air Force Base tomorrow. Sam will be there—I spoke with him personally again this morning. He'll explain."

Were the kids dead? Injured? What was wrong with them? Were they safe? Oh God, she couldn't have endured and conquered only to come home to that? She couldn't stand it. "Dr. Green, please." She risked letting him see her fear, her raw pain. "Don't you torture me, too. Tell me what's wrong with my children."

"No. No, nothing is wrong with them, Katie," he said quickly, reassuring her. "But they aren't the same as when you left them. Children change significantly in six years, you know?"

Shocked, Katie went still. Dear God, how had she missed that? She'd thought of little else but getting back to the children, and yet she'd pictured them in her mind exactly as they had been the last time she'd seen them. Not once had she imagined Molly or Jake a day older, a bit different....

She leaned forward, supported her head with her hands, elbows on her knees. Molly had been three. She was nine now. And Jake had been six. Good God, he was twelve. Twelve! Nearly a teenager!

She tried hard but just couldn't wrap her mind around it. She sifted through the years and her own changes, then forced the facts into her mind and tried to imagine the kids at the ages they were now. She couldn't do it. Tried again, and again, and the truth slammed into her with the force of a head-on collision with a brick wall.

Nothing was the same.

Would the kids even know her? Would they remember anything about her being in their lives?

Panic seized her. Fear set in. But blissfully merciful, logic intervened. Surely Sam had told them all about her. Molly had been awfully small; she might not remember much about Katie. But Jake would remember the songs she sang to him, the games they'd played. Surely they would both remember her love.

How could either of them not remember her love?

"Katie?" Dr. Green stood to look into her eyes. "Are you all right?"

"I'm fine." She lowered her hands and stood up, trying hard not to let the shaking inside her show on the outside. "I don't expect we'll be seeing each other again. Thank you for your candor, Dr. Green."

Resigned, he stretched out a hand. "It's been a privilege. I hope that things go smoothly for you, and you find peace. I really do."

She shook his hand, then went to the door. Pausing, she looked back over her shoulder at him. "I am angry, but I'm not ungrateful to you, Doctor. I'm sure you're very good at what you do and your intentions are good. Thank you."

In a moment of total honesty, he admitted, "In your position, I'd be angry, too."

"I appreciate your admitting that," she said, and meant it, then reassured him because his concern seemed genuine. "I do know what I need."

"Sometimes we think we know, but we really don't."

"I'm a wife and a mother. I love them." Her voice held a slight tremble. Still, she forced herself not to back off, to speak plainly and from the heart. "I need my family more than anything but air."

"You need to feel loved more than you need anything but air." Regret shone deep in his eyes. "Six years is a long time to be deprived of anyone who loves you." His voice caught. "I really do understand, Katie, and I'm very sorry for what's happened to you."

She nodded, let him glimpse her sadness. "Aren't we all?" She walked out the door.

Dr. Green watched her go. She was so fragile, clinging to control by a thread. And God forgive him, he was grateful he wasn't the one who was going to have to give her the bad news that was going to break it.

His nurse came around the corner. "How did her talk go with the president? Was she surprised to hear from him?"

"She didn't have much to say to him."

"Awestruck?"

"Not in the least," Green said, wishing that were the case. "Preoccupied. She's totally focused on seeing her family." A sigh he couldn't withhold heaved his shoulders. "She was badly abused, Helen. Very badly abused."

"I figured."

"But she has worked through it—at least far enough to know she needs to feel loved to heal."

"That's a long way to come on her own."

"Yes, it is." He looked at Helen. "And it makes what's to come all the more tragic."

Sadness filled his nurse's eyes, then surprise. "You didn't tell her?"

"I couldn't," he said. "She's very bright. She picked up right away that the honchos want a pass with the press from her."

Helen frowned. "Oh, no. You should have told her.

It's not right." She tugged on the stethoscope dangling around her neck. "She'll be crushed."

"I wanted to but I couldn't," Dr. Green repeated. "Her husband insisted he tell her himself."

"That poor woman." The nurse sighed, then swallowed hard. "She lived through hell all those years solely on the hope of going home."

"Yeah." Dr. Green blinked hard and fast. "Now, when she finally gets there, she's going to find out that there's not much ahead of her except more hell."

The nurse looked up at him sadly. "Sometimes life totally sucks."

He nodded. "And sometimes it's even worse."

"COLONEL SLATER." Dr. Muldoon, the physician she'd been assigned on returning to Paxton Air Force Base in Florida, entered the room with an entourage of six doctors on his heels.

It had been six days since her rescue, and a frustrated Katie sat in a chair beside the hospital bed. "Dr. Muldoon, I will not agree to one more vial of blood being drawn or one more test. I've had it."

He smiled, his blond hair short and styled in a typical military cut. "We're done with all that. While you're a little undernourished, I'm happy to report that you're relatively healthy."

"Finally." She stood up. "I'll see my family now, then." She'd arrived at Paxton night before last. And still no Sam. No children. No phone call to her mother. And the longer the honchos delayed her reunions with medical tests and intelligence debriefings, the angrier she got.

He frowned. "I'm afraid that we're pushing you to reorient too fast, Colonel. You need time—"

"No, I need my family." She caught herself, squeezed her eyes shut and forced her temper down. "I've cooperated. I've been debriefed by every intelligence organization in the U.S. arsenal. Now I'm done with cooperating and debriefing, Doctor. I've said my last word on this. I insist on seeing my family. Either you bring them to me, or I will escape from this facility and go to them."

Feet shuffled on the tile; the student doctors behind him were uneasy and backing away. Muldoon stood his ground. "Sam will be here this afternoon around four."

Her heart beat hard and fast and it was all she could manage not to burst into tears. "And my children?"

"First see Sam. Then the two of you can discuss how to make your reintroduction easiest for the children." Muldoon's frown deepened. "I don't mean to minimize how difficult this is, or how challenging it has been for you, Katie. You're my primary concern, but you aren't the only person impacted by your return. Remember, your death and sudden reappearance after six years has significant consequences for your loved ones, too. Sam and the children—especially the children—have a great deal of adjusting to do."

It was true. She blinked hard. They all had a lot of adjusting to do. "Of course."

Muldoon and his students left, and Katie leaned against the window and looked down on the parking lot. What if they didn't want to see her? Didn't want to adjust? What if they liked their lives without her so much they wished she'd stayed dead?

At this point, C.D. would have told her to knock it off. To quit borrowing trouble, and imagining things at their worst. He'd have told her that she was wrong, letting fear drive her over the edge and off the deep end. He'd have told her that they all loved her, and of course would happy to have her home.

But knowing it and hearing it were two different things.

"Damn it, C.D., why do you have to be dead? I need your support here." She fingered the glass. "Even dead, I'd support you."

"I'm glad to hear you two were that close," her nurse, a young and bright redhead named Ashley, said from behind her.

Katie turned, her heart in her throat. "Why?"

Ashley came closer. "Maybe you'd better sit down."

"Trust me, I'm beyond the point of anything shocking me."

"Okay." Ashley walked around the edge of the bed, stopped a few feet away. "C.D. is alive, Katie. He's here and he wants to see you."

So many emotions swamped her at once, Katie didn't know where one stopped and the next started. Disbelief. Mistrust—but why would Ashley lie to her? Relief. Joy. And anger.

He'd left her.

So much anger…

"Katie?" Ashley stepped closer still. "I'm sorry. I've been a nurse for ten years and there is no easy way to break news like that, but I thought you'd be happy…." Now she seemed unsure.

"I am." Katie swallowed. "Excuse me just a minute." She rushed into the bathroom, burst into tears and threw up. C.D. was alive. Gratitude swelled in her heart. But he'd left her. Left her to rot in a prison cell in the sweltering desert, to be tortured and tormented for six freaking years. Her heart shattered.

"Katie?" Ashley rapped on the door. "Are you all right?"

She rinsed her mouth at the sink, splashed her face. "I'm fine." She dried off, then opened the door. "Where is he?"

"In the waiting room, but Dr. Muldoon says Sam must see you first." She gave a little shrug. "C.D. says he was your copilot."

"Yes." Katie swallowed hard. "Yes, he was. I thought…"

"He was dead. I know. He told me. But he's not." She smiled. "He's very handsome."

"Yeah." Katie nodded, not at all surprised that C.D. still had the ability to turn heads and flip hearts. "Ashley, I look like a hag." Katie couldn't believe what she was saying. "I—I don't want them to see me like this."

"Well." Ashley smiled. "That's something I can fix."

"How?" Katie lifted a hand to her raggedly cut hair. "Short of putting a Stepford body in my place?"

She laughed. "Well—" she walked around Katie, looking at her hair "—you'd be amazed at what can be done with a pair of scissors."

"I didn't have any." In the bathroom mirror, it looked chopped, as if it had been hacked at with a knife. Had she had a knife? How had her hair been cut, and by whom? Odd, but she couldn't remember. Why couldn't she remember? Had she shuttered that, too?

That she might have scared her. She should know what was locked away in the closet inside her mind, shouldn't she? She should know it, just not think about it. Had she locked away so much she'd just forgotten it? If so, why didn't she recall it now? Odd. That'd never happened to her before. Had it?

"Well, you do now." Ashley smiled again. "I'm going on my lunch hour. I'll run over to the base exchange and pick up a few things. Do you have a favorite color?"

"Purple," Katie said, rattled by the memory gap. Uneasy, she grabbed for her mug of water and sipped strongly through the straw. Her throat was parched, raw. Maybe it was fatigue? The shock of being rescued? The grueling transport back to the States, all the medical tests and exams, and all the questions being thrown at her? That had to be it. With so much going on, who wouldn't be forgetting things? "But I don't have any money. They have to get my pay straightened out."

"I'll float you a loan. You've got six years' worth of money coming. I'd say you're good for whatever I spend."

"Can you spare the cash?"

"Uh, cash, no." Ashley smiled. "But not to worry. I have plastic."

Credit cards. Oh, yes. "I can't believe you're willing to do this. Thank you."

"Katie, you did a lot more. This is nothing."

"Not to me."

"Let's see." She checked Katie's bedside table. "I refilled your spare water mug, so you're set there. Need anything else?"

"No," she said without thinking. "As long as I have water, I'm fine."

Ashley paused. "Did they deprive you of water?"

Katie stilled, looked at her.

Ashley lightly shrugged. "I brought in the second mug because you were so upset about running out of water earlier."

"I was?" Katie didn't remember that, either. This was

getting weird. "Sorry if I worried you." Fatigue. Had to be fatigue playing games with her mind and memory.

"No problem." Ashley didn't push. "I'll be back in an hour with the treasures—and with a hamburger and a Coke. It's been a couple hours, and I'm sure your low-level light is on." She smiled and wrinkled her nose. "Be ready for your transformation."

Katie couldn't seem to eat enough hamburgers or drink enough sodas, and her low-level light was on. She smiled. Ashley had to be at least half as psychic as Katie's mother—another person in her life they wouldn't let her talk to until all their debriefings had been completed. Excitement bubbled in her stomach. "Thank you, Ashley. I—I..." Overwhelmed, she couldn't find the words.

"My privilege and pleasure," the nurse whispered. "These doctors just don't get it. A woman looks good, she feels good." Ashley winked. "We'll forgive them, though. They do have other assets." She lifted a fingertip. "Take a little nap. You're in for a busy afternoon and you've got to still be feeling the jet lag—oh, and I'll bring more water when I come back, too."

"Thanks." Katie wracked her brain, but didn't remember ever being upset about water. But she must have been... Had to be the jet lag. Between it and all the medical tests and the constant debriefings, it had to be that she just didn't recall it. *Lost in the shuffle.* It was pretty insignificant, considering the scope of things. "I appreciate it. Being in the desert turned me half camel."

"No problem." The redhead smiled. "We've got plenty."

Katie nodded but she was far too wired to sleep. C.D. was alive and here. Tears welled in her eyes. Sam was coming at four, and after his visit, she would be allowed to phone her mother. All that after such a long dry spell of no interaction with those she loved… It was just too much. The joy was bubbling over; she couldn't hold it all. And then for some reason, Ashley reaching out to her, doing more for her than anyone other than General Amid had in six years… Well, sometimes life was good. And after a long stream of tough, bad times, today would be a very good day.

A chill raced up and down Katie's spine.

Rubbing at her arms, she checked the thermostat. Seventy-eight; it was freezing in here. Wondering how long it'd take her body to adjust to nondesert conditions, she cranked the thing up to ninety, then crawled into bed and snuggled down under the covers to get warm.

C.D. was alive. Sam would soon be here. She would soon hear her mother's voice. And later she would see Molly and Jake….

These things rolled over and over in her mind and heart—and had dragons breathing fire in her belly because she didn't have a clue what to expect from them, or a clue what they would expect from her. Would they be happy to see and hear from her?

Surely they would. How could they not be thrilled she wasn't dead? They couldn't be, could they?

God, these reunions were going to be so sweet. She'd prayed for this for so long, and finally, finally, those prayers had been answered….

ASHLEY SHOOK KATIE'S shoulder. "Wake up, sleepyhead. I've got food, drink and treasures."

Katie was wide awake the moment Ashley had opened the door. *Always be aware, so you see attacks coming.* Silently, she sat up in bed, brushed her hair back from her face. The hamburger smelled like heaven.

Ashley passed it and the soda first. "You eat. I'll show you all your stuff."

Katie opened the bag, then the wrapper, and finally sank her teeth into the burger. The tang of tomato, the bite of onion, the taste of decent bread—she savored each texture and flavor separately. "Oh, you remembered extra mustard." She let out an appreciative groan.

"Of course, dahlink. You've gone through a quart of the stuff in two days."

"Am I being a glutton?" Katie frowned, covering her mouth with her fingertips to hide her chewing.

"No, not at all." Ashley pulled clothes and underwear from bags and tossed a shoe box onto the foot of the bed. "Shopping sprees are so much fun." She smiled. "There's a purse to match the shoes, and this." She passed over a purple velvet bag.

"What is it?"

"Essentials for non-hags," Ashley said, smiling. "Makeup and cologne, a hairbrush, lipstick and all that fabulous girl stuff we love so much."

Katie laughed from deep in her throat. "You're something else. I don't know how to thank you."

"Be well and happy, Katie," Ashley said, fingering the lilac dress she'd just bought. "With your silvery blond hair, this dress is going to look great on you. It's the exact same color as your eyes, and the fabric is to die for."

Katie touched it. "It's so soft. I love it."

"Well, I can see I'm not needed here."

Katie looked over at a doctor standing in the doorway. He was about forty, blond, thick and gentle-faced. "Who are you?"

"Dr. Firestone." He nodded. "Dr. Muldoon thought you might like a chance to chat with me."

"Why?" Katie dabbed at her mouth with a napkin.

Ashley whispered to her. "He's the resident psychiatrist, Katie."

Firestone ignored her question. "I understand you won't discuss what happened to you."

"I've discussed all I care to discuss," she said, bristling at his approach. The man could learn a thing or two about bedside—in this case, door-side—manners. "Don't worry, Doctor. I'm not in denial. In six years, I've had a lot of time to deal with it, and I have. I'm on my time now, and I'm not wasting a second of it focusing on something I can't change."

"Sounds healthy to me." Leaning against the frame, he gave her a lopsided grin that transformed him and her opinion of him.

Liking him, she smiled. "To me, too."

"I wouldn't mind a chat, anyway." He hiked up his eyebrows. "To ease my mind that your form of dealing with it is somewhere in the neighborhood of my form of dealing with it."

"Sorry." She didn't dare. How do you explain memory gaps you yourself don't understand? She'd be hospitalized the rest of her life. "I don't deliberately revisit. It screws up my aura." She wrinkled her nose.

He laughed. "Gotta protect that zen."

"Exactly." She exaggerated her nod. "I appreciate your concern, but I have what I need to move on with my life—at least I will, once I'm permitted to see my family—and I'm sure you have patients who really need you."

He seemed a little surprised, but not offended; his

eyes warmed. "I believe you might be right, Colonel Slater."

"Katie Slater. My tour of duty has expired. And I'm fine."

"I have to admit you do seem fine."

"I am. You can bank on it." Katie forced herself to look back at him over her shoulder. If little else, she'd learned to mask her fears. "Now, I don't mean to be rude, but I have to get gorgeous for a reunion with my husband."

"Ah, girl stuff." His eyes twinkled.

She lifted a hand, motioned from her head to her toes. "As you can clearly see, it's going to take some time."

"Less than you think, Katie Slater. But I'll leave you to it." Still smiling, he closed the door.

Ashley gasped. "Oh, my stars, Katie. I can't believe you talked to him like that. He's a god around here."

She looked at the gray shoes. They had a heel. Could she still walk in heels? Probably not. Honestly, she never had walked well in the damn things. "Not to me."

Ashley patted her on the shoulder and grunted. "You know, you probably did him good. Not that he's a bear or anything. He's actually pretty nice. But it doesn't hurt to remind gods that they're not God, you know what I mean?"

Katie did know. During their marriage, Sam had often told her that she kept him grounded and humble. Changing the topic, she swallowed her last bite of burger and washed it down with a healthy swig of soda. "Okay, I'm ready." She crawled out of bed. "Give it your best shot. How you're going to transform this scrawny body into anything resembling gorgeous—well, it'll take a miracle."

"Believe, Katie." Ashley giggled. "Miracles happen every day. You're here, right?"

That really was a miracle. "Which is why I don't dare ask for another one." She stretched and grabbed her water mug, squelching a twinge of panic at it being out of reach. "That'd be exceedingly greedy."

"Nonsense." Ashley shook out the dress, then laid it on the bed and smoothed the wrinkles from it. "Miracles aren't rationed. They're there for anyone with the guts to ask for them."

Sipping through the straw, Katie hoped Ashley was right. The dragons filling her belly with fire were sprouting wings. She so wanted Sam to be thrilled to see her, to feel she looked beautiful; she needed the confidence that came with that. So did that mean she wanted one miracle or two? Did it matter? "Okay, Ashley. You'd better be right about this multiple miracle business." Her heart felt light. Odd, it'd been so long. But it *did* feel light. "I'm asking—"

"You laughed!" Ashley's mouth rounded in an O. "Now, that's a miracle!"

It was, and Katie laughed again.

SHE STOOD BEFORE the full-length mirror at the nurse's station and stared at herself. The lilac dress fit well enough, but she was a good twenty pounds too light. The shoes felt strange after six years of flight boots and bare feet, but at least they didn't pinch. Though the heels were low ones, she felt off balance, but resisted the urge to reach for something to hold on to to stay on her feet. She'd adjust. Hadn't she'd learned to quickly adapt to whatever conditions she landed in? She had. She was alive, right? Of course she had.

"Gorgeous." Ashley met Katie's eyes in the mirror and beamed. "You got your miracle."

Katie smiled. Tapped her hair. Straightened her skirt.

Ashley checked her watch. "Oh, shoot. Hurry. Sam will be here any second."

"My water." The twinge of panic returned and she turned clammy. "Where is my mug?"

"Right here." Ashley passed it to her.

Relieved, Katie clasped it, took a sip and then a last look in the mirror. She looked good and felt good, and hurried back to her room. *Oh, please, don't let anything mess this up. Don't let me mess anything up.*

"HI, KATIE."

Sam stood near the door. His brown hair was tousled by the wind, his face flushed. He'd gained weight, aged easily, and all signs of the boy in him had disappeared and given way to the man. His eyes were red, and he was blinking hard.

"Sam." She choked out his name and rushed to him, closed her arms around his neck and pressed close. The sobs she never allowed herself tore at her throat, and she swallowed hard and fast, but couldn't keep that soft mewl from escaping.

He held her close, squeezing her to him. "Oh, God, Katie. I can't believe it. You're really here." He sobbed against her shoulder, his whole body shuddering, quaking. "You're really here."

"I can't believe it, either." She pulled back enough to smile up at him.

He wasn't smiling.

Dr. Muldoon came into her room, whispered something to Ashley, and she went pale.

"Sam?" Katie looked back at him. "What's wrong?"

"Everything is going to be all right." He patted her on the shoulder. "Come sit down."

Going to be all right. As in, things are not all right now. Something was definitely wrong. Something serious. Ashley still had no color, and Dr. Muldoon looked as tense, as if he were having a root canal. She walked to the bed and sat on its edge, stiff and more afraid than she'd been in the prison camp. There, she'd known to expect the worst. Here, she had no idea what was coming, but it had Sam's hands shaking. That wasn't something a surgeon did easily.

He sat on the chair beside her. "I'm very happy that you're alive, Katie. The news was just…"

"Shocking?" she finished for him.

He nodded. "But good." He clasped her hand, squeezed it hard. "Very good."

She wanted to pry out of him whatever was coming. He was being so careful, casting worried looks at Muldoon, silently asking permission to go on, and Muldoon was responding with equally subtle gestures. Ashley, while still pale, didn't look dead anymore, just as if she wished she were. Whatever it was, it was worse than serious.

Katie steeled herself for certain devastation.

"It is so amazing to be sitting beside you," Sam said. "I keep thinking about your funeral and how distraught I was that day. I prayed so hard for just one more look at you. One more chance to tell you how much I loved you."

Her heart filled with hope and the need for reassurance suffused her. "Then my coming home is a miracle for you, too?"

"Of course. You're the mother of my children."

She tried a smile, but he didn't return it. Just blinked fast, as if he was close to tears. Emotional was expected, but this kind of tension wasn't. She couldn't peg the cause. "How are the kids, Sam? You can't imagine how much I've missed them and you. You guys are all that kept me going."

That remark generated another worried glance at Muldoon, and another subtle message to continue. "I, um, brought some photos. Dr. Muldoon feels it's best for you and me to come to terms before the kids actually come see you."

"Come to terms?" Odd language. "What do you mean, honey?"

He looked at her and a tear rolled down his face. "Um, here's a photo of Jake." He passed it to her, ignoring her question.

Stunned, she let out a groan. "He's so big. Oh my, Sam." She stroked the photo, sliding a fingertip down the slope of Jake's nose, just as she had the photo that had been with her in the prison. "He's all grown up."

"He's twelve."

She tore her gaze from the photo to look at Sam, let him see the agony of all she'd missed in her eyes. "I know." She glanced back at the photo. "How long was I gone, Sam? Do you know?"

"Over six years."

"How much over?" She pushed to make her point.

"A little. I don't know exactly."

"Six years, two months, one week and one day," she said. "That's how long it's been since I've seen you and the kids."

He blew out a shaky breath that had his chin quivering. "Here's one of Molly."

"She's nine," Katie said, taking the photo. She smiled at it. Molly looked happy, her ponytails bound with a blue ribbon that matched her dress. "She has your eyes. And your nose." Katie smiled. "God, she's beautiful, Sam. She's…so beautiful."

He still didn't smile back. "Um, here's one of the three of us." He shrugged, increasingly uncomfortable and less able to hide it. "I tried to find the most recent ones."

This was taken outside someone's home. But it wasn't their home—no garden—and it wasn't a house she recognized. "Where is this?"

"Our new house."

"You moved?" The first spear of pain sliced through her heart. "Why?"

Again he looked at Muldoon. "We, um, needed a change."

A change? "You left my garden?" They'd planned to stay there forever. She'd worked so hard on it. Prepared every bed, pulled every weed, planted every bulb. She'd spent six months just planning it, and two years getting everything in place so they'd have color year-round. Now it was gone? He'd sold it as if it had meant nothing? "Oh, God."

"I'm sorry, Katie," Sam said. "There were so many memories…." His voice hitched. "We just needed somewhere we could have a fresh start."

"A fresh start?" She'd clung ferociously to memories of him and the kids. He'd shunned memories of her, and knowing it hurt.

He thought you were dead.

He had. That made it different, didn't it? Maybe it did, but it didn't feel different. It still hurt. Reasonable or not, it still hurt. "You wanted to forget me?" Hating the pitiful note in her voice, she stiffened and fisted her hands, then forced strength she didn't feel into her tone. "You wanted my children to forget me?"

He squeezed his eyes shut, paused a long moment and then finally opened them. The pain in him was raw, pounding off him in waves. "It—it seemed right at the time. It seemed healthy for the…family." There was an apology in his tone. Regret and shame, too. "I'm sorry, Katie."

She swallowed the hurt. "It's okay," she said, trying to make herself believe it. "You did what you thought was right. No one could ask any more of you."

He nodded, looked to the window, and the wistfulness in him proved he wished he could be out there. Be anywhere but here with her. That hurt, too. More than she could put into words. "They're good photos, Sam," she said, trying to set him at ease and get things between them back on a positive footing. "Thank you for bringing them to me." Such a surreal conversation. So polite and distant and different from anything she'd imagined. This wasn't as it should be. Not at all what it should be between a man and wife reunited after all this time.

Not sure what was wrong or how to fix it, she glanced down at the photos—and noticed something she should have picked up on right away and hadn't. Something that struck fear in her heart. "Sam?" She looked over at him. "Who took these pictures?"

He avoided her eyes and Muldoon's. "Sam?" She waited but he still didn't answer. "For goodness sake, Sam." She let out a nervous little laugh. "It's not a difficult question."

Muldoon cleared his throat, warning Sam off.

What was that about? Unsure, Katie pushed. What

could be so awful about who held a stupid camera? "Sam, answer me. Who took the pictures?"

Sam looked at her, his eyes riddled with pain and fear and dread. "Katie…"

"What, honey?" She clasped his arm, gave it a reassuring squeeze. "What's out there that we can't fix?"

Muldoon cleared his throat again. Louder. He definitely didn't want Sam going here. "I think that's enough for this first visit," he said. "Sam, let's leave it there for now, okay?"

"No, damn it." Katie glared at Muldoon, then at Sam, about out of patience with both of them. Whatever this was, she didn't want it to be a demon terrorizing her until his next visit. "Answer me." She softened her voice. "Whatever it is, Sam, it can't be as bad as anything I've been through in the past six years. Just tell me the truth."

"The person behind the camera—" Sam said in just above a whisper.

"No, Sam," Muldoon said, his own voice quiet but urgent. "You gave me your word."

Katie glared at the doctor. "Will you please shut up?"

"No, Katie, I won't." Muldoon stepped toward her. "Sam, it's time to leave. You can visit again…later. After I've talked—"

Katie shot him a glare and saw Ashley. She was crying. "What the hell is going on? Somebody tell me what the hell is going on!"

Haunted, Sam shook off Muldoon's hand on his arm. "She's my wife, Katie," he said, tears coursing down his face. "The woman taking the pictures is my wife."

CHAPTER THREE

KATIE FELL BACK on the bed, gasping and grabbing her chest. "I can't breathe. I can't breathe!"

Muldoon rushed to her side. "It's okay. You're okay." He handed Ashley a syringe. "Give her this."

Sam moved away from the bed, horrified at the sight of her.

Dr. Muldoon moved in close, whispered softly, reassuring her. "You're reacting to the shock, but you can breathe. You're fragile, which is why I wanted Sam to wait to tell you this. You're okay. Just breathe normally, Katie. Slow and easy. You're going to be fine. Just fine. Just breathe slow and easy…."

She felt the sting at her hip, but focused on Muldoon's words, the sound of his voice. It seemed forever, but finally she caught her breath.

"Stay with her, Ashley," Muldoon said.

She nodded and clasped Katie's hand. "I'm so sorry, honey."

A deep, gut-wrenching sob tore loose from the depths of Katie's soul, but she refused to let it out. She bit her tongue until it bled, and then escaped into a drug-induced sleep.

MULDOON FOUND SAM LEANING against the wall in the hallway, outside Katie's door. "Damn it, Sam. I specifically warned you not to tell her yet. I specifically warned you that her condition was too fragile for that deep a shock."

"I have a wife, Dr. Muldoon." Sam lifted an arm. "Ignoring that fact makes it no less true. I have more to consider here than Katie."

"I would think, under these circumstances, you owe Katie priority consideration, Slater."

"I am concerned, of course. I loved her. She gave birth to my children. But my priority now is and must be my family."

"She *is* your family." Muldoon frowned. "Is this how you practice medicine?"

"I beg your pardon?"

"You're a doctor, for God's sake. You of all people should know better than to traumatize a patient in Katie's condition. What were you thinking?"

"Do you honestly think that telling her later would make it easier? It would just be worse. She needs to know the truth before she starts making assumptions that just aren't true."

"When she is strong enough to deal with it, yes, she does need to know the truth. But as you clearly saw, she is *not* strong enough right now." Muldoon reined in his temper. "You did this deliberately. You never intended to keep your word." Anger hit, and sharpened Muldoon's tone. "I can't believe it."

"Don't judge me, Doctor." Sam glared at him. "I have a lot to consider here, and I'm doing what I think is best."

"For whom?" Muldoon lifted a hand. "Don't bother

answering that. I already know. Just listen to me. You've opened this can of worms now and it's your responsibility to soften the impact on Katie in any way possible."

"Me?" Sam looked genuinely shocked. "Get her a psychiatrist. I'm an ob-gyn. What do you suggest I do? A pap smear?"

Muldoon's jaw was so tight it ached. "Go get her kids and bring them to her—and if she has any friends, then bring them, too. She needs someone she knows who is completely in her corner now, because it's glaringly apparent to everyone that you're not."

"The children aren't prepared for this," Sam said.

"Neither was she," Muldoon insisted. "Get them here, Slater, or I'll get a court order."

"Tomorrow."

Muldoon nodded sharply, not trusting himself to say any more to the man.

Sam glared at Muldoon and turned to look right in the face of a furious C. D. Quade.

"I should've known you'd screw this up, too," C.D. grunted. "Some things never change."

"Back off, C.D.," Sam said.

"Back off?" He stepped closer, got in Sam's face. "You're lucky you're not eating my fist. How the hell could you be that cruel to her?" One hand on his cane, he dragged the other one through his hair, frustrated and outraged. "Stupid question. You've always put yourself first. Always. Just whatever it takes to make life easiest for Sam. Katie never saw it, but everyone around her did, and we couldn't stand you for it." C.D. glared down at Sam. "Just once, stop thinking about yourself and think of Katie, you selfish son of a bitch."

"Hey, I've had enough of you judging me—interfering in my life, checking up on my children—and I'm fed up with you telling me what to do."

"I'm interested, not interfering. I've been around the kids since they were born, Sam. You can't expect me to just forget them."

"I don't." Sam shoved a hand in his pocket. "But I haven't done a damn thing wrong in any of this and yet my whole life is suddenly in shambles." He took a breath. "I'm a widower, but I'm not. I'm married to Blair, but I'm not. My kids, who lost their mother, have Blair—the only mother they've known and the only children she will ever know—and they all love each other. Only all of a sudden she's not their mother anymore. Our worlds have been turned upside down and inside out, C.D. We didn't do anything we weren't supposed to do. Our lives were rolling along fine, and then I got a phone call saying Katie was alive and well and coming home, and from that moment until this, our lives have been tossed into chaos."

"*Your* lives are in chaos?" C.D. couldn't believe his ears. "Katie has lived through hell for six freaking years, Sam, while you lived a normal life. While you ate when hungry, and worked, and went on vacations and to ball games and swim meets, and did exactly as you damn well pleased. During that time, what the hell do you think was happening to her? Have you even *once* thought about what she was going through?"

Not liking what he saw on Sam's face, C.D. shoved his shoulder. "Get out. Just get out before I find the closest window and throw your ass out."

"You can't throw me out of here."

"*I* can." Muldoon stepped between them. "Go home,

Sam. Bring the kids tomorrow. Katie likely will be sleeping for a long while, if not until morning."

Sam slid C.D. a killer look, then turned and headed for the elevator.

C.D. glared at his back and told Muldoon, "You should've let me throw him out the window."

"I was tempted to myself," Muldoon said. "But he has a point—about his life and Blair's and the kids', too. I imagine that's what has him exercising faulty judgment."

C.D. muttered his thoughts on that. "If so, he's had it ever since I've known him."

"Are you by any chance Katie's first husband?"

"No," C.D. admitted. "She had too much sense to marry me. I was her copilot and her best friend."

A speculative gleam lit in Muldoon's eye. "Ah, I see."

"I don't think so. Katie was married, and we both respected that."

"But you obviously love her?"

His knee was stiff from all the sitting in the waiting room. He leaned heavier on his cane. "More than life itself."

Muldoon looked at him, long and hard. "She has no idea."

"Of course not. She was happily married to Sam." C.D. let him see the truth. "To her, we were a team. Friends. Nothing more."

"Well, right now she needs a friend desperately," Muldoon said, then took a risk. "Katie knows she needs to feel loved to heal and make the transition back into a life where she isn't a prisoner. I'm thinking you can give that to her."

"If she'll let me." Sadness filled C.D.'s eyes. "I was her copilot. I was rescued. She wasn't."

"Blame." Muldoon nodded. "I'm thinking the bond between the two of you is strong enough to overcome that, though she is admittedly angry. Still, it's obvious she isn't going to get what she needs from Sam."

"She never did." C.D. paused while a nurse rolled a cart down the hallway. "Funny thing is, I don't think she ever really noticed it."

"She's different now," Muldoon said. "She notices everything—and I'm seeing her situation a lot more clearly now than before today."

"What are you seeing?" C.D. asked, not following.

"Why you act more like her husband than her husband." Muldoon walked to Katie's room. "I had to sedate her. She's going to be out for a good while. Probably until morning."

"Doc, I've been parked in the waiting room for twelve hours. I'm not leaving without seeing her."

Muldoon's eyes gentled. Clearly, he recognized that C.D. was the man who would always be there for Katie to lean on. "Why don't you wait in her room? I think it'll do her good to see you when she wakes up."

"Be sure to tell your nurses. They wouldn't let me anywhere near her before."

"I'll take care of it." Muldoon nodded. "You go on inside."

"Thanks." C.D. didn't waste time. Leaning on his cane, he pushed through the door and saw her, lying on her side in bed.

Ashley came around. "May I help you?"

"I'm C. D. Quade, remember? We met at the nurse's station?"

"I remember." She smiled warmly. "Katie was so happy to hear that you were alive."

"I'm glad to hear that." C.D. sat down in the chair beside her bed. He couldn't look anywhere else. She was thin. Not gaunt, but she'd definitely been hungry. "Is she okay?"

"She was." Ashley said softly. "Sam really knocked the wind out of her sails."

The bastard. "He's good at that." Hair smooth and shiny, makeup, new dress. "She must have spent half the day getting ready for his visit."

"Yes, she did." Ashley sniffled. "She was so excited. I think she'd been dreaming of their reunion for so long, she never considered that he could be married to someone else."

Why would she? Her life had been on hold from the moment she'd been taken prisoner. All she'd thought about was getting home. C.D. hated knowing it, hating hearing it confirmed that Sam's news had come as a total shock. Kate looked far too frail for that kind of revelation; no wonder Dr. Muldoon had expressly forbidden Sam to tell her. But he had to have things his way. And poor Katie had to still be in love with the jerk to be excited enough about seeing him to spend her strength primping. *That's His Majesty. His way or the highway.*

C.D. had often called Sam "His Majesty," and fell back into the old pattern as easily as Sam had. In the old days, without fail, Katie had objected to it, too. But truth was truth, and Sam always had put himself on the throne and her below it. Even if Katie never saw it, Sam's wants and needs came first with him and ranked first and foremost in his mind at all times.

She deserved better.

"I've got some things to do," Ashley said. "But I

didn't want to leave her alone." She sniffled again. "After what happened, it just didn't seem right."

"It's okay, Ashley." C.D. did look at her then and saw the tracks of tears staining her face. His heart warmed to the woman who cared more about Katie than her own husband did. "I'm here. I'll be here as long as she needs me."

She smiled and warmed up to him. "You're a good friend to her."

He nodded.

"Well, C.D. Maybe you still can rescue her, too. Because if ever a woman needed someone at her side, Katie Slater does now. What happened today was only half the shock."

He frowned. "Half?"

"She's not yet actually seen her children—or their new mother. That's bound to knock Katie right back to her knees."

It would. Of course it would. And the saddest part of it was that as much as C.D. wanted to make everything in her life easy for her from here on out, there wasn't a damn thing he could do to shield her from that. She'd have to suffer the full brunt of it.

Not that she'd let him shield her, anyway. She never had. But she was vulnerable now in ways she hadn't ever been, and all things considered, he'd sure try to protect her. "What can I do to make it easier for her?"

Ashley walked around the bed and stopped beside him. "Hold her while she cries."

"YOU SON OF A BITCH." Katie looked at C.D., sitting on a chair beside her and bent double, his head resting on her thigh. His black hair had gone gray at the temples, but his face was the same familiar mix of strong angles and slopes that blended together to form one gorgeous man. "Wake up so I can kick your sorry ass."

"Katie." C.D. awoke with a start. "You're up? Ashley said you'd sleep through the night."

"Get off me, C.D." She whacked his shoulder. "I'm going to slug you and I don't want your blood getting on my new dress."

He straightened up. "Left or right jaw?" He pivoted his face. "Either or both is fine."

"Don't you dare patronize me. Don't you dare. You left me!"

"Honey, I was injured. I didn't even see you, and I couldn't walk to look for you." He pointed to his cane, leaning against her bedside table. "I blew out my knee."

"You should have crawled." She tossed back the covers and then whacked him in the shoulder again. "If I hadn't been in a coma, I would have crawled across that freaking desert to find you." She reared back to hit him a third time.

He caught her arm midair. "I'm sorry, Katie." His voice broke. "You have no idea how sorry I am."

She stared at him, feeling his fingertips on her wrist, gentle even now. "I hate you for leaving me."

"I know." He let her see that he had suffered, too. "But I'll tell you a secret, Angel." He reverted to his pet name for her. "No matter how much you hate me, I hate myself more."

She stilled. Staring deeply into his eyes, she knew he was telling her the truth, but she was too angry to care. Too full of her own pain to have room inside her for his. "Why didn't you come back for me?"

"Home base said you were dead." He leaned forward. "Your satellite tracker showed no signs of life."

"They cut it out of my neck and planted it in a dead chicken."

He blew out a long, shaky breath. "Intel also confirmed and verified you'd died in the crash with human resources on the ground." He let go of her arm and cupped her chin in his hand. "Katie, if I'd had any idea, if I'd considered you being alive even a remote possibility, forget the desert. Honey, I'd have crawled through hell for you." He blinked fast, but tears rolled down his cheeks anyway. "I'd have done anything. But everything and everyone agreed that you were gone."

"I wasn't gone. I wasn't…gone." Her chest heaving, she felt torn between anger and a despondency that ran so deep she didn't know where it started or stopped, only that it smothered everything else inside her. "I survived. And I kept on surviving because I wanted to get home. That's all I could think about." She talked fast and let the words tumble from mind to mouth unchecked, hoping that in releasing them, the tight grip on her chest would loosen and the deep pain would ease. "I thought, if I can just live today, just make it until dusk, or dawn, or through the next hour—at times, through the next minute—then I'll get home. One day I'll get home." The reality of Sam's second marriage hit her and stole her breath.

"Katie?" C.D. stood up. "What is it?"

"I can't breathe. I—I can't breathe, C.D."

"You can. Ashley warned me about this," he said, stepping closer. "It's an anxiety attack, Katie. Just calm down."

"Calm down?" She struck out at him again.

He ducked. Her fingers grazed his ear and air rushed over her skin. "That one would have hurt."

"I hoped to knock your block off."

"Katie, you adore me." He smiled and stepped closer still. "Did you forget that?"

Sobered, she knelt on the hospital bed and stared him in the eyes. They were such beautiful eyes. Smoky blue and rimmed in silver. Gentle. Teasing. Serious. But not innocent anymore. Now they carried regret and remorse. And she knew it was she who had put both there. "I didn't forget," she admitted. "I mourned you, C.D. I thought you'd died in the desert, and I mourned you until the moment I found out you were alive."

"Then you wanted to kill me."

"Yes." She lifted her chin, unapologetic and not hiding it.

"I mourned you, too." He let his hands slide over her shoulders, pulled her into a hug and buried his face at her neck. "Oh, God, Katie, I mourned you, too."

She fell against him, wrapped her arms around him and held on for dear life. "C.D." Her voice cracked. "Just because I'm talking to you doesn't mean I don't hate you."

"I know." He rubbed a circle on her shoulder. "You need to raise a little hell, and I need to do a lot of groveling to get us back on our usual ground. So go ahead. You first. Let's get started so we can get it done."

He was right, and that irritated her. "I don't want to raise hell," she said. "I don't want you to grovel, either."

C.D. looked her in the eye. "Then what do you want?"

She thought about it for a long moment, then answered the only way she could. "I don't know now." She sat back on her haunches. "I wanted to come home more than anything in the world. I thought about it all the time and it kept me strong. They were right about that in survival training, C.D. You do need a reason to keep fighting to live. Even with one, you honestly do still get to a point where you just don't care anymore, you just want it to end and be over."

"That is what they say."

But…" Her voice broke, and she paused, trying to sort through her feelings and shove them behind the shutters she could close. That proved impossible. She felt too much, and it overwhelmed and confused her.

"But what?" He smoothed a hand over her face.

No answer. She couldn't—and when she could, she didn't dare. She was too close to losing it.

"Tell me, Katie," he urged, stroking soothing circles on her shoulder. "We've always told each other things we'd never share with anyone else."

"I know, but this is…"

"Tell me."

Tears welled in her eyes. "Home's not here anymore, C.D." And as the words left her mouth, the dam inside her burst, and heart-wrenching sobs ripped loose from the seat of her soul. "They took that from me, too. Oh, God." She slumped forward, face to his chest, hands over her eyes.

And weeping with her, C.D. held her while she cried.

"KATIE, I TALKED WITH your dad. He and your mom are waiting for you to call," C.D. said. "But you need to know that your mom…well, your dad says she's getting forgetful." C.D. looked down, avoiding her eyes. "Dr. Muldoon spoke to her doctor, Katie. It's dementia."

Katie felt the blow and let it ripple through her. "How bad is it?" she finally said.

"It depends. Some days are better than others. Your dad just wanted you prepared, so it didn't blindside you."

She squeezed her eyes closed. Yet another change. An enormous one. "Will she know me?"

"If it's a good day."

Katie let that news settle, then dialed her parents' number, imagining it ringing on the table in the living room between their recliners.

"Hello?" Her mother answered.

A knot so huge it blocked her air settled in her throat. It took three swallows to clear it. "Hi, Mom. It's me, Katie."

"Katie… Frank?" she said to Katie's father. "Katie's on the phone."

Shuffling sounded in the background. "How are you, Mom?" Katie asked.

"I'm fine, honey. Are you sick? Do you need Daddy to come get you from school?"

Tears filled Katie's eyes. "No, Mom. I'm okay. You sound wonderful."

"Why are you calling, darling?"

Clearly it was not a good day.

"You're not cutting class, are you?"

"No. No, I'm not cutting class." She locked gazes with C.D., and he clasped her hand and gave it a reassuring squeeze. "Can I talk with Dad for a second?"

"Of course. He's right here."

There was a pause, then he said, "Hi, honey."

"Daddy." A little gasp escaped from her, and for a second, she was once again a little girl eager to run to her father for protection and safety.

"Are you okay, baby?"

"I'm fine, Daddy. A little skinny, C.D. says, but okay."

"Well, you tell him I said to feed you, and bring you to see us."

They still lived outside New Orleans, in the house where she'd grown up. Her dad hadn't been able to travel for over a decade due to his heart and crippling arthritis. Now, with her mother's complications, it was even more impossible for them to come to her. "Just as soon as I can, I'll come see you and Mom. Right now I'm, um, trying to get things straightened out with Sam and the children. It's been…difficult."

"I know, honey." Her dad's voice shook. "Sam hasn't been here since you died—you know what I mean. But Blair brings the kids to see us every three months. She's called every day since you were rescued to let us know how you're doing."

Surprised, Katie wasn't sure what to say. Yet another kindness Blair had done for Katie. One there was no reason for her to do; she had nothing to gain. Nothing. "She's obviously a good woman."

"Yes, she is," Katie's dad said. "We're grateful to see the kids. Your mom can't seem to remember them from time to time, but the visits with them mean a lot to me. Somehow Blair knows that."

Katie's dad owed her, too. "I'll be sure to thank her." Loud crashes and bangs and high-pitched grating sounds came through the phone. Katie winced. "What's all that racket? Is the house coming down?"

"Your mother's rearranging the furniture again. I don't know why. She does it a lot on bad days."

"I'd better let you go then." Katie resisted the urge to hold tight to the connection. "I love you, Daddy."

"I love you, too, baby."

Her throat went thick. "Tell Mom."

"I will." He paused, his voice cracking. "Katie girl, you come home to me soon."

Katie girl. His pet nickname for her, one she'd never thought to hear from his lips again. Her nose stinging, the backs of her eyes burning, she mumbled a noise she hoped resembled a reassurance that she would, hung up the phone, and then launched herself at C.D. Hugging him, she cried her heart out.

When she dredged up enough of a voice to speak, she still couldn't verbalize all the emotions churning inside her. The pain ran too deep, had too many tentacles. But the strongest of bonds released, anguish-ridden and raw. "Mom's gone, too."

Katie curled her fingers and sank them into his shoulders, doing her damnedest to hold on, and not even sure why. "Damn it, C.D. When is the bad news going to end?"

She asked the questions but didn't wait for answers; he had none. Instead, she wept out her anger against the injury inflicted to the bond she'd brought with her from the womb—and she worried that her mother's grief over her "death" had caused her dementia. Her mom saw too much. She knew what Katie was enduring; she'd always known everything. And futile and helpless, she could do nothing to stop it, not even convince anyone Katie was alive. The authorities had verified and confirmed her death. The file was closed, and she'd been forgotten. And her mother could do nothing.

Nothing except watch the horrors of what was happening to her daughter unfold in her mind.

THE NIGHTMARE WAS familiar, frightening.

Her plane clipped by a ground-to-air missile. Fire. Ejecting. The chute jerking, the wind rushing past her ears. Hitting the ground at an odd angle. Pain slamming through her body. And then darkness.

She groaned in her sleep, aware she was sleeping, but unable to wake up. *Don't put me through this again. Please. Please...*

But the dream didn't stop. After the crash, she came to in so much pain it hurt unbearably to draw breaths. She couldn't move. Strapped into a hospital bed...

You've been in a coma. Four days. The nurse's voice was clinical, crisp.

Katie wanted to ask what was wrong with her, but she couldn't find the strength to ask. The pain overwhelmed her, seemingly invading every cell in her body, and she took refuge in sleep.

Awake again. Whether hours or days had passed, she didn't know, but the pain remained intense, smothering her. She fought to localize it. Ankles. Both shins. Left arm. Ribs. Back. *Oh, God, she couldn't move her arms.* She cranked open an eye. It was broken. Her left arm was broken. Why hadn't they set the bone?

Voices. Doctors arguing at the foot of her bed. One wanted to amputate both of her legs from the knees down. The other wanted to give her time to heal on her own. She'd be crippled, but she would have more than stumps.

In a cold sweat, she moaned, but no one noticed. *Don't let them cut off my legs. Please, don't let them cut off my legs.* Sleep again claimed her.

The sound of the doctor's voice roused her from a drug-induced sleep. "We're taking her to surgery," he said to someone she couldn't see, "to amputate her legs."

A man in his fifties with weathered skin walked closer to the bed and looked down on her. He wore an enemy uniform, a general's rank, but the look in his keen eyes was full of empathy. "Captain Slater?"

She nodded.

He passed something to her. "This is significant to you, I believe."

She fought to focus. The photo of Sam and the kids. Her heart wrenched and she swallowed a lump from her throat. "Thank you."

He nodded, turned to the doctor. "You will not amputate her legs."

"Yes, General Amid," the doctor said.

"Why have her bones not been set before now?"

"We were waiting to see if she died."

Anger flashed across the general's lean face. "She will not die. You will set the bones in her legs now. I will observe."

To keep from crying, Katie bit her lip until it bled, and nodded in gratitude yet again.

You are not safe. You are not safe. Wake up, Katie. Wake up!

She awakened, but lacked the strength to move. Sharp, stabbing pain throbbed through her, making her sick to her stomach. She screamed, but all that escaped her was a puny mewl.

"She is conscious, General."

General Amid with his lean face and kind eyes stepped into her line of vision. And once again, he placed the picture of her family in her hand.

She couldn't speak, but she mouthed her thanks.

He didn't acknowledge her, just turned and left her bedside.

A woman in white—a nurse—spoke to the doctor. "Her arm is also fractured. Will you be setting it, Doctor?"

"I was instructed to set the bones in her legs," he said in a clipped tone. "I have done so."

Katie had use of her right arm. Her left throbbed as much as her legs and ribs, but the muscle spasms in her chest and back were so severe she couldn't tell for certain where her arm was broken, and it was underneath a white sheet. She couldn't see the damage. *Please, let it be simple. If it's a simple fracture, I can deal with it myself. Please...*

Where was C.D.? Why wasn't he here? He would set the bone for her.

The nurse stopped and looked down at her. She managed to croak, "C.D."

"Your copilot?"

Katie nodded.

"He's dead." Compassion flickered in her eyes.

The news sucked the air out of Katie's lungs, the will to survive out of her mind. *No. No. Not C.D. Please, not C.D. Oh, no...* She wept from the heart, wept until she couldn't weep anymore. Wept, and prayed for death.

CHAPTER FOUR

"HEY." C.D. clasped her shoulder. "Hey, take it easy, Katie."

Startled awake, she looked up, her heart beating hard and fast. C.D. It was C.D. He was alive. He was alive and she was…not home.

Home is gone.

A crushing ache seized her heart. Sam had remarried. The kids…

"You were crying in your sleep." C.D. sat down beside her on the bed and clasped her hand. "Bad dreams?"

She didn't want to talk about them. The horrible things that happened in her dreams were hell. Torture. Why did she dream them? Had those horrors happened? Was she remembering or imagining? Why didn't she know? She should know.

That she didn't know, and couldn't tell if they were real, terrified her. Maybe she'd slipped over the edge into insanity. If she had, would she know it?

Having no answer, she focused on what she did know. Talking about nightmares made them more real, and they were powerful enough, frightening enough without added fuel. She nodded, then reached to the bedside table for a glass of water and took a sip, focusing on the clock on the wall. "It's two in the morning. Why are you still here, C.D.?"

He smiled, charming even now, knowing she hated him. "You need me."

She did. Sam had deserted her. He'd moved on with his life and had left her behind. *Dead and buried.* "You've had a million women after you your whole life," she said. "Didn't you come home and marry one of them?"

"No, I didn't." He lowered his gaze to her chin.

She fluffed her pillows and leaned back against them, shaking off the vivid images trying to stay put in her mind. "What did you do—after you mourned me?"

"While."

"What?" The room was dark, except for the amber glow of the light above her hospital bed. It spilled onto them, but left the rest of the room in shadowed darkness.

"While I mourned you," he said. "I didn't stop, Katie. After the crash, I spent a lot of time in hospitals. Three surgeries, and then what seemed like a lifetime of physical therapy. The knee locks up, so I limp." He lifted the cane. "This helps."

"Can it be fixed?"

"No." He shrugged. "Once we knew that, well, there's not much use for an Air Force pilot in my condition, so I medically retired. Then I bought a little bar on the bay—Top Flight. It's right outside the base's main gate. I bought some stock and stuff, and then two years ago, three cottages on the property next door to the bar went up for sale, so I bought them as rentals. Tourist season goes just about year-round here, so they do well."

"I can't believe it." She looked at him as if he'd sprouted two heads. "This is so not you, C.D. It's all far too tame."

"After losing you, I needed tame."

They'd been so close. Not romantically, but soul to soul. The best of friends. Finishing each other's thoughts, knowing each other's minds and hearts and hopes and dreams and desires. She'd felt that acute sense of unbearable loss, too. "I still hate you." She held his hand and squeezed. "But I'm glad you're back in my life, C.D."

He smiled. "Me, too."

Tears gathered on her lashes, blurring her vision. "Sam's remarried. I just can't wrap my mind around that."

C.D. sighed. "Well, Angel, he might have gotten remarried, but technically speaking he's still married to you."

"That's right." Katie sucked in a sharp breath. "So what does that mean? Do you know?"

"According to the Paxton legal beagles, it means his marriage to Blair will be set aside. Beyond that, only he and you women can sort it all out." C.D. leaned closer and pressed a kiss to her temple. "But that's nothing for you to worry about tonight. You can't fix it alone."

She turned her face to his chest and inhaled his scent, drawing it deep inside her. "I might hate you, but I still adore you, too."

He stood and took her into his arms, hugged her tightly. "I adore you, too, Angel."

They talked nonstop about anything and everything, and stood, arms linked, at the window and watched the sun rise. Katie hadn't seen the sun rise in years.

"As beautiful as you remembered?" C.D. asked, his throat thick, his voice husky.

"Even prettier," she managed to admit, though it was hard to remember that she could voice an opinion without fear of repercussion. She didn't have to be on guard and strong and avoid giving anyone any information they could later use against her. A prisoner quickly learned that in enemy hands anything could be a weapon. Anything liked or disliked or even merely appreciated. *Only indifference was safe.*

It would take time to adjust to not living that way. Even longer, she feared, to not think that way anymore.

Feeling better about her situation, though only God knew why, Katie whispered, "Thank you for being here for me." She swallowed hard, forced herself to turn and look C.D. in the eyes. The tenderness she saw there had her lifting a hand to caress his face. "Thank you for holding me, C.D." She blinked hard and fast. "I didn't know how badly I needed to be held."

"I'll tell you a secret, Katie." He touched a fingertip to the tip of her nose. "I needed to hold you, too," he confessed. "I needed to know that this is real. You really are here."

A light tap on the door claimed her attention. "Yes?"

It swung open. "Good morning." Ashley walked in smiling. "You two been up talking all night?"

"Some of it," Katie said. "I slept a lot, too, though I doubt C.D. did."

Ashley checked him out. "You look good to me."

He gave her his best lady-killer smile.

"Watch him," Katie warned. "He'll sneak in and steal your heart. You won't even know what hit you."

Ashley laughed. "I can see that potential." She turned to Katie. "After…what happened yesterday, Dr. Firestone wants to talk with you."

"Dr. Firestone?"

"The psychiatrist," Ashley reminded her. "Just to make sure you're all right."

"I'm fine." She couldn't do it. She couldn't tell him anything. Not sure what was real or imagined, how could she tell him anything?

"Are you refusing to see him?" Ashley asked, looking worried.

"Yes."

"No." C.D. stepped in. "Katie, just talk to him and let him see that you're fine. This is a military hospital. The man's got squares to fill or someone's going to be crawling up his ass for not doing his job. You know how it works. Say or don't say whatever you want, but go." He shrugged. "Listening to people bitch all day every day makes his life miserable enough without getting his ass crawled, too."

"All right, all right." She frowned at C.D. "I was hoping you'd grown out of your nagging stage, but I guess you're never going to get past it."

"While there's life, there's hope." He pulled his lips back from his teeth in an exaggerated smile. "Keep working on it."

She rolled her gaze. "I'll talk to him." Still, she grumbled and groused. "But just this once—and he's not getting inside my head, C. D. Quade." No one was forcing her to expose her underbelly so they could pity her or judge her or condemn her—or lock her up in some hospital until she knew for sure what happened and what she only thought had happened. No way.

Images of an interrogation room at the prison camp flashed through her mind. The stark emptiness of the room, save one chair. The oppressive heat and lack of circulation pressing down on her. The smell of perspiration, the iron scent of blood and the strong stink of urine. The bastard Lieutenant Ustead, leaning against the stone wall, eating chicken that had her starving stomach growling and her salivating. He took perverse pleasure in pretending to show her compassion, holding a newspaper clipping he wouldn't let her see. *I'm sorry to have to tell you that two men broke into your home, Captain Slater. Your children were there alone. Your son, Jake, was blinded so that he couldn't identify the invaders. Your daughter, Molly, was beaten to death. Your husband later returned from the hospital and found them. The guilt was too great. He committed suicide….*

Ustead had known that her family was Katie's deepest vulnerability, and he'd mercilessly used that knowledge to hurt her. She hadn't known whether or not to believe him, of course, but the haunting images tortured her just the same. Was that exchange a dream? Or had it happened? She didn't know.

The next time she'd been dragged into the interrogation room, she hadn't said a word. Not one. Ustead, frustrated by his inability to break her, had beaten her to within an inch of her life. And—dreams or actual events—the same thing had happened the time after, and the time after that, until a miracle occurred.

Ustead was determined to reduce her to screams, and decided to rape her. She didn't move, didn't utter a sound, and his temper exploded. He threw her against a stone wall, cursing her, telling her all the vile things he was going to do to her, and General Amid heard him.

Like the knight he'd been to her in returning her photo, he'd come in, immediately grasped what was happening and shot Ustead. Her torturer had died at her feet.

That had to have happened. Her flight suit still bore the stains of splattered blood. Yes, yes, it had happened. And then General Amid had put his men on notice. She was a soldier, as they were, and she deserved the respect they would wish if their roles were reversed.

Under his protection, the guards still tormented her,

but she didn't think she had been severely beaten or raped again. Or taken back to the interrogation room. There were no nightmares or flashes of images in her mind that she didn't associate with his murder. None like those.

That was fourteen months and three days after she'd been taken captive, or so General Amid had told her.

And that was the last time anyone other than General Amid had spoken a civil word to her.

"Katie?" C.D. touched her arm. "Are you okay?"

She shook off the memories of the past and looked over at him. "I'm fine."

He didn't believe her; she saw it in his eyes. But to his credit, he didn't push.

"Thanks for agreeing to see Dr. Firestone, Katie." Ashley smiled in thanks to C.D. "Being the sweetheart he is, he made getting you to him my primary duty."

"He's not getting inside my head," she warned them again.

"I'm sure he'll be relieved to hear it," C.D. said. "He has to be tired of getting into people's heads."

Katie frowned at C.D., but caught the twinkle in his eye. Endearing, the lengths he went to, trying to make her feel normal.

"Do you need a wheelchair?" Ashley asked, holding out a robe. "Or are you up to walking?"

"I'll walk." Too grateful she still had legs, she crawled out of bed. "C.D., for the record, I let you win this one. But you put everyone short of God around here on notice. Either I see my kids today, or I'm going to take this place apart and walk out." She shrugged into the robe, cinched it at her waist, then pointed a finger at him. "I swear it on my wings, C.D. I'm done waiting."

He winked. "I'm all over it, Angel."

Grumbling, she walked out of her room and down the hall.

"He's crazy about you," Ashley said.

"He's crazy. Period," Katie retorted. "But I adore him. I still hate him for leaving me, but I adore him." Her anger at him was subsiding, and frankly, she was grateful for it. She had too much anger and upset at too many people rumbling around inside her, taking up space. If she really wanted to reclaim her life, she had to let it all go and make room for positive stuff. How? She wasn't sure. But maybe it happened with everyone like it was happening with C.D. The bad stuff just dwindled a thimbleful at a time as other feelings came around and pushed in.

And maybe that was a good thing. She'd have to think about that later. Now, Ashley was waiting for Katie to say something about C.D.

"The truth is he's been the best friend I've had in my whole life." The confession spilled out.

"Well, at least you have him to help you get through this." Ashley turned the corner and pressed the button for the elevator.

The light came on. "True, and that's important." After all the years of isolation, Katie Slater knew the value of having someone.

DR. FIRESTONE MET Katie in the hallway and walked her into his office. "I'm glad you decided to come."

She glanced over at him. "C.D. reminded me that you have squares to fill to keep people off your ass." She lifted her chin. "I have nothing against you personally, Dr. Firestone, and I don't want to cause you any trouble."

"I appreciate that." He waved to his tidy office, which held a sofa, two chairs and a desk. "Please, have a seat."

A candy dish full of foil-wrapped Hershey's Kisses sat on the desk edge within easy reach. Her mouth watering, she sat in the nearest chair. "I still don't want to discuss the past."

"No problem." He settled behind his desk, rocked back and forth in his seat. The chair springs squeaked in a familiar way that appealed to her. "Just tell me that you're not pretending nothing happened."

"Even God lacks the imagination to accomplish that." She folded her hands in her lap, swearing she wouldn't reach into that candy dish. "When I was taken prisoner, I knew what to expect. And I knew that to come out on the other side of it, I had to be realistic about it. I don't deny what happened, Doctor. I believe that if I focus on it, then the captors not only stole that time of my life from me, but the time I spend now, focusing on it, too." She swept her hair back with a steady hand. "I'm just not willing to give them any more. For me, it's over. It's that simple." *Simple?*

"But you're coping with what happened."

"Does one have any other choice?" *Cope, or let it drive you insane. Those were the only options. When being held prisoner, insanity appealed, but not now.*

He paused. "Some people in your position go through Stockholm syndrome—"

"I'm familiar with it, and not a chance. These men were bastard enemies through and through. I have not confused the issue." *General Amid might be an exception. I couldn't shoot him. He protected me, treated me with respect, and he put me in that market so the Frenchman would see me. He wanted me rescued before he was transferred. But the rest of them?* "Stockholm syndrome? Not hardly. I could rip out their hearts with my bare hands and not even blink."

Dr. Firestone nodded. "And there are no physical symptoms manifesting as a result of your treatment there, then?"

A very polite way of asking if she'd contracted STDs or symptoms of AIDS. "I'm fine." Deliberately vague, with no intention of admitting she'd been violated, she stared at him until he looked away.

Frowning down at his hands, he hesitated. "Katie, I'm sorry about what happened yesterday with Sam." He looked up at her. "It wasn't the way I would have told you...."

His regret was genuine, and remorse was written all over his face. "It's not your fault. Sam is—" She started to defend him as she always had, but couldn't. Now she saw him and his actions in a different light. Still in a loving light, but one less rosy and more clear. "It wasn't the homecoming dreams are made of, that's for sure." She hiked a shoulder. "But in an odd way, it fits."

"Fits?" Firestone rocked back. "I'm not following you."

The candy dish called her like a siren, and her mouth was watering so much she could barely speak. "I, um, should have been prepared for Sam…for that. His re-marrying, I mean. But I didn't once think about it. I don't know why. I've asked myself that a thousand times since he left here yesterday."

"Perspective, I suppose. He was in his normal world. You were isolated."

"And forgotten, yes." She nodded, shoving back the memory of just how isolated she had been. "I can't change what is, Doctor. But regardless of what Sam has done, my children are still my children. I've been patient, but I want to see them. Today."

"C.D. already called." Dr. Firestone smiled. "He said you'd take the place apart, and he'd help you."

Standing by her. Clearing the path. Ever C.D. A flash of warmth swept through her stomach. "So?"

"So…" Firestone passed the candy dish to her. "Have some candy. All you want."

"Thanks." She held the dish in her lap but didn't touch or eat any candy. "My children?"

"Will be here shortly," he said, his smile broadening.

"Really?" Joy welled up and spilled over inside her. Abundant and flowing, it swelled and filled every inch of her with eager anticipation. "Really?"

He nodded. "But remember not to expect too much. You're a stranger to them, and they need time to adjust to your return as much as you do."

"I know. I know. It'll be hard not to smother them with attention, but I do realize that they remember very little of me."

"They're beautiful children," he said.

"You spoke with them?"

"Yes, I did." He smiled again. "Jake remembers more than Molly. She was awfully little—just three—when you were taken captive, right?"

Katie nodded, too emotional to speak.

Dr. Firestone's face turned red and he couldn't hold her gaze. "I would have preferred Sam be with them during this reunion, but I've been informed that he won't be available."

"Why not?" How could he not be available? *For this?* Sam wouldn't be there? The kids would be afraid….

"He's delivering a baby."

"Delivering a baby?" The son of a bitch. "He couldn't get someone else to do it? This matters, for God's sake. It's supremely significant to the kids. They need his support."

"I can have the children wait to meet with you until Sam is available," Dr. Firestone said. "But you and C.D. have to swear you won't do any damage around here."

She knew the doctor was teasing, trying to ease the tension and lighten her mood, but it couldn't be done. Sam was avoiding her. *Avoiding her?* Same old nonsense. If it's not pleasant, ignore it and it'll go away, or Katie will handle it and make it disappear. Even now, he thought *she'd* go away?

Oh, God. He *wanted* her to go away.

Don't feel it, Katie. Don't feel it. Just put it behind the shutters and forget about it for now. The children...

She locked down her emotions. "If Sam's not bringing the kids over, then how are they getting here?"

"Blair brought them, Katie. They're in the waiting room."

"Blair?"

"Sam's, er... Um..."

"New wife?"

Dr. Firestone nodded.

"He sent his *wife?*" Katie couldn't believe it. Couldn't freaking believe it! "How could he do that to us?" To her? To the kids? To his new wife? "She's got to hate getting stuck with his dirty work."

"Actually, Katie, she said you had to be eager to see the children, and she didn't want you to be disappointed. She thinks you've had too many disappointments to deal with already."

Katie remained outraged at Sam—and irritated at

this Blair woman. Katie had been determined to hate her on sight. But it just wasn't working out that way. How can you justify hating someone when that person brings you your babies so you won't be disappointed, and brings them to your parents so they will know them?

"She's right," Katie sighed. And, though it still galled her to say what she felt, she made herself do it. "That was very thoughtful and considerate of her."

Katie wanted to hate her. Had sworn to herself she would hate her. But all Blair had done forced Katie to look at things a little differently. In her absence, Blair had cared for Katie's children and parents, and now she'd shown remarkable compassion for Katie, too. And she done it after no doubt swearing to herself she'd hate Katie, too, for messing up her orderly life.

So Kate reconciled all the good and bad and decided she'd meet Blair first and see how the kids were with her. Then she would decide how much to hate her.

Until then, she was curious. What kind of woman had Sam married?

Dr. Firestone's intercom buzzed. He lifted the receiver. "Yes, Janeen?"

A pause, a smile, a thank-you, then he hung up the phone. "C.D. was successfully persuasive."

"That doesn't surprise me," Katie said. "He can be sinfully charming." She tilted her head. "So who's his victim?"

"Dr. Muldoon." Dr. Firestone stood up. "He's agreed to the reunion."

"Was he opposed?"

"He felt it was in your best interest to wait for Sam."

"But C.D. changed his mind."

Dr. Firestone nodded and snagged a piece of chocolate, unwrapped it and popped it into his mouth. "You two have a very unique relationship."

"We do," Katie said. "It's hard to describe. The closest I can come is it's like a marriage without the bad parts—and of course, without the sex."

"Of course." His head bobbed up and down as he assimilated that information. "Interesting."

"And complex." Katie admitted. "It's always been complex."

"Isn't every relationship?"

"No," she said, speaking frankly. "Just the important ones."

A smile tugged at Dr. Firestone's lips and he stood up. "Bring the candy and let's go see your kids."

CHAPTER FIVE

"IT'S COLD IN HERE. I don't want them to be cold." Katie sat in her lilac dress and heels in the chair beside her bed.

"It's eighty degrees, Katie," C.D. said. "If anything, they'll be hot."

"Right." Dr. Muldoon had said that acclimating to a new environment could take her up to a year. But who could stand this for a year? She was freezing, and she was so nervous she doubted she could stand up. *Oh, God. It's happening. They're really here. They're really here!* Her mouth went as dry as a stone.

C.D. stood behind her, and when the door opened, he gave her shoulder a reassuring squeeze. "It'll be okay."

Don't let me cry. Please, don't let me cry and scare them.

The door opened and a woman about forty walked in. She was tall, lithe and graceful, with a sweet face, enormous eyes and short black hair that brushed her forehead and cheeks. She held hands with the kids.

Katie feasted on the sight of them, hardly able to believe her eyes. Molly was tall and a little gangly like Sam, and her hair was long, pulled back in a ponytail at her nape with a green ribbon that matched her dress. Jake was so big, at least five foot six, with swimmer's shoulders and a strong jaw that reminded her of her father's. He wore a navy suit with a red tie, and he—they both—looked all grown up.

Oh God, they'd grown up without her.

Stop it! Stop it! Be grateful, fool. Would you rather they hadn't? That they didn't look fresh-faced and healthy and well-fed and loved?

Blair let go of their hands. Jake let her, but Molly refused and hid halfway behind her. "Hi, Katie. I'm Blair," the woman said, her gentle voice soft and melodious. She licked her lips, clearly as nervous as Katie, and nodded to the children. "This is Molly and Jake." She then urged the children, "Say hello to your mother now. She's waited a very long time to see you."

Katie looked at Blair, let her see her gratitude. "Hi, Molly. Jake." She paused to grab a deep breath. "I'm so glad to see you." Tears welled in her eyes. She blinked furiously to hold them back. It was hard—so hard, because the kids clung to Blair as if they were afraid of Katie. Her heart felt like a boulder. She didn't know what to do.

Blair nudged the boy. "Go say hello, Jake."

He walked over, nodded. "Hi, C.D."

"Champ. Good to see you."

"You know C.D.?" she asked, surprised with familiarity warranting a nickname.

"Sure. He was at your funeral—and other stuff." Jake didn't elaborate or flinch about mentioning her funeral, just stood before her with mistrust in his eyes.

She lifted her hands to him and he stepped closer, gave her a hug reserved for distant old aunts you don't really want to touch, and then quickly backed away. "Hi."

She gave him a watery smile. "Thank you, Jake." She swallowed hard. "I can barely believe you're you."

She sniffed. "You look very different than the last time I saw you."

He glanced back at Blair, shuffled his feet and stared at the floor. "Yeah. It's, uh, been a long time."

Far longer than you'll ever know. "Yes, it has." Kate paused, then felt overwhelming guilt about that, and went on. "I'm very sorry about that, Jake. That it's been so long, I mean. I—"

"It wasn't your fault." He shrugged. "Mom explained it to us."

Mom. Meaning Blair, not Katie. She tried not to let that hurt, but it did. It stabbed her heart like a sharp knife and twisted. "That was very kind of her."

"Did they make you say and do stuff like on TV?" he asked.

"Jake," Blair interjected. "That was a hard time for your mom, honey. Today, she needs to talk about happy things." Blair gave him a reassuring smile, then suggested, "Tell her about your swim meet last Saturday."

"Sorry," he said to Katie. "I—I didn't know what to say."

God, he reminded her of her father and herself. Same expressions, same phrases, same body language. It had to be in the genes. "Me, either," she confessed, then smiled again. "So what happened at the swim meet?"

He launched into telling her, and as she listened, she saw him relax a little, though he was treating her with kid gloves and it was clear from the way he kept looking back at Blair for approval that he was not at ease. Molly wouldn't budge. Wouldn't speak, wouldn't move from Blair's side. She held her hand in a death grip, and though Blair tried several times to encourage her, Molly wouldn't give an inch.

Katie was grateful, but she was envious of Blair, too. As hard as it was to admit, she was envious *and* jealous. The woman was living Katie's life, with her husband and her children, and they all loved her.

And the truth Katie hadn't dared consider stared her straight in the face.

Things would never be as they had been before she'd been taken as a POW. Her children would never really be her children again. She'd missed too much during their formative years, and there was no way to get that time with them back.

"Molly, do you remember your mother's garden?" Blair asked.

"At our old house?" the girl asked.

"Yes." Blair smiled. "You and your mother used to plant flowers there. Irises and roses."

"I kind of remember that." She looked up at Blair. "Did I have a green thing?"

Blair looked at Katie, who smiled. "You did, Molly," Katie said. "A green pad for you to sit on and a green pail to carry the bulbs we planted." Katie smiled broadly. "Do you remember that?"

"No." She denied it and hid behind Blair.

They talked for a few more minutes, but it was difficult, and exhausting. Dr. Firestone watched Katie carefully, and it was he who said that time was up for now.

Molly and Jake looked so relieved Katie wanted to weep. And the tension that had held Blair's back ramrod straight released. "Katie," she said. "Would you like for us to visit you again tomorrow?"

A tear rolled down her cheek. "Yes, please."

Jake waved and the kids went into the hall. Blair stopped at the door. "I can't imagine all you've—" She stopped, then tried again. "I know this is difficult—" Again she stopped, and shook her head. Her shoulders lifted and fell. "Tomorrow will be better for all of us, Katie."

She nodded. "I hope so."

Blair walked out and Dr. Firestone winked, then left behind her. The door closed and Katie slumped in her chair.

C.D. walked around and hugged her hard. "Aren't they beautiful, Katie?"

"Yes." Her chin quivered. "But Blair is their mother, C.D. They love her."

"Yes, they do. And she loves them." He looked into Katie's eyes. "But isn't that a good thing?"

"Of course it is. But I want them to love me, too. I'm their mother."

"They will, given time. They don't know you right now, honey." He sat on the edge of the bed and held her hand. "You know, you have to give Blair credit. She's one class act."

The last thing Katie wanted to hear were compliments for Blair. "Go to hell, C.D."

"Sorry." He frowned. "You're hating her, right?"

"What do you think?" She slung him an exasperated look. "She's got my life."

"I see your point."

Katie rubbed her arms. "No, I don't hate her."

"Okay."

"She loves my kids. She's been good to my parents. And now to me. What kind of idiot would I be if I hated her?"

"A good one?"

Katie glared at him. "Stop it."

"Okay." He lay back on her bed and ate a Hershey's

Kiss, then wadded the silver wrapper between his fingertips. "I'm getting a little confused here. Do we like her or not?"

"We're grateful to her, okay?" Katie snagged a piece of candy. "She could have been a bitch. She could have resented my kids and ignored my folks. But she wasn't and she didn't. And she didn't have to bring them to see me, or to try to help Molly remember me, either. She didn't have to do any of that. She could have resisted me coming back into their lives and done things to make sure they stayed distant. She could have deliberately turned them against me. Instead, she's breaking her ass—and I suspect, her heart—to make it easy for them and me."

C.D. ate another piece of candy, and tossed Katie one. "Which explains, of course, why you're pissed to the gills right now."

"I'm pissed, you moron, because I might just have witnessed the greatest personal sacrifice I've ever seen in my life, and the woman who made it did it for me and my kids." Irritated to the point of distraction, Katie tore the wrapper off the candy.

"Ah, it's clear to me now." C.D. sat up. "You like her. You wanted to hate her, but you like her."

"No, I don't like her." Katie tossed her rolled wrapper at him. "But I owe her."

"Liar. You do like her." C.D. stilled. "But while you're pissed because you can't hate her and you owe her, here's a thought, Angel—for what it's worth."

"What?"

"Blair owes you, too. She's gotten to be a mother. And from the looks of things, she's worked hard to be a good one." C.D. rocked back on the pillows and closed his eyes. "Guess that makes you two about even."

Katie thought a second, then slapped him on the thigh. "I hate it when you do that."

"What? Make sense?"

"You've got to be joking," she said, meaning exactly that—and that it irritated the hell out of her that he'd thought through something significant faster than she had. He'd always done that, and it had always rankled. "I meant, you eat the candy, then stuff the damn paper back into the candy dish."

He cut her a slow sexy smile that had gotten him laid regularly. "Sure you did, Angel."

She eased off her shoes. "Why was I glad you were here?"

"Finally. A question I can answer with a hundred percent certainty." He sat up and hugged her hard, growling into her neck. "Because you adore me." He nudged her. "Say it!"

"Okay." She laughed deeply. "I adore you. I adore you." She giggled. "Jerk."

Dr. Muldoon walked in, saw them and smiled. "Well, I see we're doing just fine after that visit."

Katie smiled back. "Other than this cannibal trying to snort the skin right off me, we're doing fine."

Muldoon laughed. "Keep this up, and you'll be out of here in no time."

Katie sobered and stilled, watched him walk out the door. *Out of here.* Where would she go?

She had...nowhere to go....

"DO YOU NEED TO REST?" C.D. asked. "Are you tired?"

"No. I'm rested out. I need to get out of here for a while, I can't think. Claustrophobia is setting in." If she didn't get out soon, she was going to start crying again about Sam and the kids and being homeless, and that wouldn't do her a bit of good or change a thing.

Katie adjusted the thermostat. "It's impossible to get warm in this place."

"Yeah." C.D. walked up behind her, looked at the gauge over her shoulder. "It's a frigid eighty-five."

"Sorry." She stilled. "Are you too hot?"

"I'm fine. For you, I gladly swelter." He grinned. "Big difference, huh?" His voice turned gentle. "The desert is a bitch this time of year."

She turned to face him. With her back to the wall, she looked up into his eyes. "September was bad, but July was worse." She blinked, feeling lost, out of step and sync with everything around her. "How long is it going to take, C.D.?"

He stroked her hair, tilted his head. "Awhile."

She sought the truth in his eyes. "I'm looking at my life, and I can't see what's ahead of me now. I can't see anything ever feeling normal again." She leaned her forehead against his chest. "I don't fit here anymore, C.D. I don't fit...anywhere."

"You will." He closed his arms around her. "Things change, Katie. Day to day, we don't notice it much. But you've walked into six years' worth of changes, and when you do that all at once, you get body-slammed. Put in that position, nobody fits."

Afraid and too anguished to speak her feelings out loud, she whispered, "I don't know what to do."

"Just be, Angel." He held her close. "Just be. Water finds its level all on its own, and things here will, too."

"They'll never be as they were, C.D. The kids... Sam... Nothing will be as it was for them or me. My life will never be the same."

"No, it won't." C.D. reared back and cupped her face in his hands. "It can't. So things will be different, but that doesn't mean they won't be good." He touched his forehead to hers. "You have a second chance here, honey. Many would kill for that. You can make your life exactly what you want. You just have to accept the changes in your old life and believe that the life you choose to create for yourself will be better."

"That requires a lot of faith." She thought about it a long minute, then sighed. "After everything else, you're asking me to have a lot of faith."

"I guess I am," he admitted. "But it's faith in yourself, Katie." He stroked her cheek, softened his voice. "I believe in you. You have to believe in you, too."

"I don't know if I can."

"You can try," he said. "And until you do, I'll believe enough for us both."

She looked up at him, saw a tear trickle down his cheek. "Oh, C.D." Her chest went tight, her heart squeezed and her voice faded to a bare echo of sound. "I would be so lost without you."

He smiled. "Then we'd better stick together, eh?"

She smiled, her hand on his chest over his heart. "Yeah."

"Let's blow this joint, grab a burger and hit the mall."

"Food? Yes, absolutely. But shopping?" She wrinkled her nose. "You hate the mall."

"True, it's not my favorite place." He backed up a bit. "But the kids will be here tomorrow again, and you need some different clothes to wear and some shoes you can stand up in without wobbling."

"Great idea, but my pay hasn't come through yet."

"Money is no object, Angel." He grunted. "Didn't Sam tell you?"

"Tell me what?"

"I'm financially independent." C.D. exaggerated a toothy smile.

"You own a bar, hotshot, not a string of—"

"Okay. Okay. I own a couple of things," he interrupted, waggling his eyebrows. "Remember I mentioned owning a little stock? Well, it actually pays dividends."

"No way." She couldn't believe it. "How the hell did that happen?"

He laughed.

"No offense." She had the grace to sound contrite and repentant. "But a financial whiz you're not." Had that changed, too? "Or at least you never were."

"I'm still not," he said. "But do you remember that little blond bombshell, Samantha?"

Her image formed in Katie's mind. "Your Barbie doll." She lifted a hand. "Yeah, I remember her." When she was around, every man in a five-mile radius had to pick his tongue up off the floor to keep from stepping on it—every man except C.D., which was why Barbie latched on to him.

"Remember you telling me to listen to her, that she was smart on money?"

Katie nodded. C.D. had told her he'd lost his ass twice, trying to invest, and this specific Barbie doll, Samantha, was also a gifted financial analyst. "Don't tell me," Katie said. "You actually listened to her?"

"Technically, I listened to you, and paid attention to her. I still am. She's made me…" He hesitated, then continued. "Comfortable."

"Wow." Katie smiled. "I'm surprised you didn't marry her."

"Not a chance." He swung over to the bedside table and chugged down half her glass of water. "We were great in bed, but outside it, she bored the hell out of me. All she's interested in are mergers, stocks and business news. The woman doesn't know a weed from a fern."

Katie was a master gardener, and when she'd been planning her garden, she'd driven him nuts regularly with talk of plants. C.D. had indulged her, pretended to be interested and even stated his preferences, which had to be as exciting for him as viewing a thousand green color swatches to choose one. So why hadn't he indulged Barbie?

"She has no knowledge of plants?" Katie feigned shock.

"None." He grunted again, hamming it up.

"How sad for her."

"It was pitiful," he said. "She still manages my finances, but we haven't slept together in a couple years."

"How *really* sad for her." Katie grinned.

Her teasing made him smile. "Come on, you heartless minx. Let's see how many clerks we can drive crazy by buying more than they can ring up."

Katie grimaced. "I don't feel right about spending your money, C.D."

"Consider it a welcome home gift," he said. "Or consider it a partial payment toward buying you off so you don't hate me anymore. Bribery works. I'll sleep fine with it." He grinned. "Or you could consider it restitution, or even a commission, for all the advice on women and finances you've given me over the years. Actually, since you're the reason I'm financially stable, it's only fair you get a cut."

"That I can accept, until they get my pay straightened out." She frowned. "Will the powers that be let me leave here?"

"I'm sneaking you out," he confessed in a conspiratorial whisper. "With the help of my trusty accomplice."

"Ashley?"

He nodded.

Katie smiled. "Let's go."

THE MALL WAS LARGE, loud and freezing cold.

"First stop, we get you a sweater before your chattering cracks your teeth or your jaw." C.D. led her into a boutique and spotted some on a round rack. "Here you go."

Katie pulled a white one in her usual size from its hanger and put it on. It hung everywhere, reminding her yet again that things were not as they had been.

C.D. smoothly dropped down two sizes. "Try this one, Angel."

And so it went. From store to store, with C.D. snagging clothes left and right, then resting his knee by sitting on a chair outside the dressing room while she tried them on. Funny, but she couldn't remember Sam once going shopping with her like this. Had he? Or was that just one more thing where her mind was playing tricks on her, leaving her to guess whether what she thought was real actually was, or just imagined?

In the dressing room, she eased a pink sundress on over her head. Surely at some time he had been shopping with her and she'd just forgotten it. In her old life, that wouldn't have been significant to her. Now, everything was significant. The little things should have been important then, too.

In her mind, she heard her father's voice. *Live and learn, Katie girl.*

"Hard lessons, Daddy, but I've learned them now." She connected the top around her neck, searching her memory, but no images of her and Sam ever shopping together came to her. She met her eyes in the mirror. Sam had never gone shopping with her—or with her and the kids; she was certain of it. He'd always begged off, needing to go to the hospital or to the office or something.

How odd. Such a simple thing. She counted in her head. Thirteen years of marriage, and they had loved each other, but facts were facts, and they hadn't had much in common except love and their home and children.

He'd hated her job. Resented her having to go TDY for temporary duty on short notice, though he'd loved being able to tell people his wife was a pilot.

She'd hated his job. Resented him having to interrupt plans with her or the kids to go to the hospital to deliver a baby, or do this or that surgery, or whatever else he actually did with his time. He was rarely with them. That's how she'd gotten interested in gardening to start with; it was something to do while waiting for Sam.

She'd spent a lot of time waiting for Sam.

Funny. None of that had ever bothered her before.

You have a second chance.... Remembering C.D.'s words, she looked into her own eyes in the mirror. *You can make your life exactly what you want.*

"Okay, great," she told herself. "But what in hell do I want?"

That, too, was going to take some time to figure out.

She stepped back into her shoes, then went out to where C.D. sat waiting, surrounded by stuffed shopping bags. "What do you think?"

He took his time, his eyes warm and appreciative. "It needs sandals."

Because it did and he knew it, she laughed hard and deep. "You've got way too much experience shopping with women, C. D. Quade."

"I've put in a lot of hours on these chairs." He stood up. "Wear it, Angel," he suggested. "It looks great."

"Thanks. I will." She smiled and grabbed the clothes she'd worn in: jeans and a T-shirt borrowed from Ashley, C.D.'s coconspirator.

He pecked a kiss on her nose and then gathered the packages. "On to shoes!"

CHAPTER SIX

THE SECOND VISIT with Molly and Jake didn't go much better than the first. Molly still hid behind Blair, Jake acted as if he'd had to be roped into being there and, while Blair continued to encourage the kids to open up to Katie, she looked even more nervous than she had yesterday, when they had first met.

After thirty very tense minutes, everyone's nerves were wired tight. The time came for them to go, and Blair told Jake, "Honey, take your sister out in the hallway and wait there. I'll be out in just a second."

He and Molly left.

Neither of them told Katie goodbye.

Blair walked closer, midway between the bedside chair in which Katie sat and the door. Tension lined her face and she frowned. "I'm sorry, Katie."

"For what?" She kept her hands in her lap and her expression neutral, though she sensed that whatever Blair was about to say would be critically important.

"That this is…hard." She took in a breath that lifted her shoulders. "The kids are confused and scared right now, but given a little time, they'll come around."

"You've been a good mother to them."

"I've tried to be." Blair looked terrified. She was shaking.

"They love you." Katie couldn't deny it; it was evident in the kids. They looked to her for protection and direction.

"They'll love you, too, once they get used to…whatever comes after this."

Blair *was* terrified. As terrified as Katie of what would come next. "I talked with my father," Katie said. "He thinks the world of you. Your bringing the children to see them has meant everything to him and my mother."

She looked down and then forced herself to meet Katie's eyes. "When I came into the picture, your things were still where you'd left them in the house. It was like you'd left for work that morning and not yet returned home. You'd been 'buried' for over a year then." A wistful smile tugged at the corners of Blair's mouth. "And of course, you were everywhere in the garden. It was so beautiful, and I thought, how can I compete with all this? There's no room for me here."

Surprised, Katie didn't know what to say.

"So I decided I wouldn't," Blair stated. "Compete with you or your memory, I mean. I decided to create my own space." She shrugged. "I never knew my grandparents, and, well, who wants to know Sam's parents?" She made a goofy face.

Katie understood perfectly. They were anal retentive and drove everyone nuts within two minutes of contact. "Believe me, I understand."

"I was grateful for what you'd done for America, Katie. What you'd done for me. I know that sounds corny, but it's true." She fought to verbalize her feelings, and the struggle showed clearly in her face. "I wanted the kids to know that you were fighting for them over there, for their freedom, and that they should be proud of you. I wanted them to know your parents, and I knew your parents needed to know your children because they were all they had left of you. As a woman who lacked one, I know that last connection is a sacred thing, you know?" Blair tilted her head. "Anyway, all of that was very important to me."

Blair had put a lot of thought and heart into her actions. "Thank you," Katie said, acknowledging that. She strongly suspected the reason Sam had been missing-in-action around her was because he was manipulating things behind the scenes. And she hoped Blair was honest enough to admit it. At the moment, based on how she'd handled everything else, Katie bet on Blair. "Does the sorting out you mentioned include Sam?"

Blair nodded.

"He isn't delivering another baby, is he?" He'd left the difficult work of dealing with Katie to Blair. Again.

"No." She couldn't meet Katie's eyes. "He's not."

"From his absence here, I'd say that he's decided to stay with you—even though your marriage has been set aside, or soon will be," Katie said. "Am I right about that?"

"That was what he said before he left to meet with the attorney to find out what we should all do," Blair admitted. "But who knows? Things are changing far too quickly and too often for me to predict what Sam will actually do on anything." Her eyes held the tiniest bit of hurt. "That's as honest as I can be at the moment, Katie. You know what I know."

Well, one husband gone. Katie tried not to feel cheated, but she did. Still, she couldn't be devastated. But oddly it wasn't because of Sam. It was because of Blair. Katie respected her. Enormously. And this return of the dead wife had to be sheer hell for her. After all, it was undeniably hell for Katie, and Blair had an equal amount to lose.

"Katie." Blair blinked hard. "This is delicate, and I don't want to offend you in any way. Understand that, okay?" She waited for Katie's nod and then went on. "I hope you won't demand custody of the kids—not that I don't think you're a good mother, but because…" She paused and swallowed hard, shuffled and blew out a shaky breath. "The change would be so traumatic for them."

Oh, God. Katie had thought about this a lot, too, and she'd thought she was safe—that it would be a discussion between her and Sam—but clearly it wouldn't. Clearly the time had come now, between her and Blair, to openly discuss it. "I've considered this, of course. Deeply," she added, wanting Blair to know that it wasn't an off-the-cuff response, but one given the thought and care and concern warranted. "I don't want to cause anyone trauma, Blair, especially the kids. But I do love them and I want to be a part of their lives."

"Of course." Blair looked genuinely stunned. "Of course, Katie. I didn't—I would never suggest that you not be." A tear leaked from her eye and she shook herself. "Damn. I swore I wouldn't do this."

Katie understood, had made the same vow to herself. "I understand."

"If anyone does, it'd be you." Blair sniffed and snagged a tissue from the nearby box. "God, Katie. Beyond what's happening with both of us, I can only imagine what you're feeling. After all you've already been through, I—I hate it that you're having to deal with even more. I swear, I do. I wish—" Her voice broke. She paused to collect herself, then added, "I wish it could be easier for you."

All the anger and disappointment and resentment inside Katie churned, but it had no place to go. Losing her husband and kids would be so much easier if Blair were a bitch she could hate with passion and conviction.

But Blair wasn't a bitch.

She was a good woman, who'd been good to Katie's kids and her parents, and under difficult circumstances had treated Katie with respect—both in her absence and in her presence. Blair had acted with dignity and grace, and with more compassion for Katie and the kids than Sam. Katie couldn't hate her at all, damn it.

Resigned to it, Katie opened up to acceptance and let it settle in. "Thank you for telling me the truth," she said. "About Sam and, well, about everything."

"Regarding custody…"

"I don't know what to do, Blair. I really don't." Katie swiped her hair back from her face. "But I promise you this—you and I will talk about what is to be done, and we'll work it out together."

Her mouth rounded. "But Sam is their father, Katie. He—"

"Isn't here," Katie said, letting the raw edges of her anger seep through. "He hasn't been here. He hasn't expressed his concerns about the children. You have."

"But, Katie, he's—"

She held up a finger. "Let me ask you one question that will resolve this."

Blair nodded.

"You've brought the children to see my parents every three months for five years."

Again she nodded.

"Did Sam go with you on any of those trips? Even once?"

Blair didn't move.

"Exactly my point." Katie stood up. "We'll work together, Blair. We have the children's best interests at heart."

"Yes, we do." Blair offered a trembling smile, clearly relieved she didn't intend to shut her out of the kids' lives. "Don't be discouraged, okay? Last night at dinner, Molly told her dad all about you two planting iris bulbs. And Jake is fascinated by a mom who can fly planes."

Katie looked at Blair, long and deep. "And you're okay with that?"

She nodded. "I told you, Katie. I decided a long time ago not to try to compete with you. Their hearts are plenty big enough to love us both."

Jake stuck his head in the room. "Mom, I'm going to be late for swim practice."

Blair nodded. "I'm coming." She turned to Katie. "We'll be back tomorrow."

Katie nodded and watched her go. "And she's worried about competing with me?" she asked herself, then harrumphed. Katie didn't stand a chance against the woman. Blair was in a different league.

C.D. SPENT AS MUCH TIME as possible with Katie, trying to help her ease back into a life outside a prison camp. But the one thing she needed and wanted most was her family, and that he couldn't give her.

For the next three days, he was there when they visited. So was a sullen Sam, and a much more relaxed Blair. Katie had told C.D. about the agreement she'd struck with Blair, and that Blair's selflessness awed her. While C.D. admired Blair and agreed she'd handled this like a class act, he wasn't so altruistic as to think she hadn't been acting in a manner consistent with achieving her goals. And she had.

Fortunately, Katie understood that, too.

It was on day three that the kids finally relaxed. And it brought C.D. an enormous amount of satisfaction to know that he was the catalyst.

C.D. had asked Jake if he enjoyed watching the surfers at the beach. To his surprise, Jake and Molly had reacted with unabashed enthusiasm. Katie talked about her love for the sport, and the rest was history. The kids were enchanted.

"I can't believe that you like to surf." Jake laughed aloud.

"Your mother is an excellent surfer. She rides a mean Boogie board, too." Sam smiled. "Remember our trip to Hawaii?"

"I remember." Katie laughed and looked at Jake. "Your father got sunburned on the first day, and had to watch me have fun from the balcony in our room for the rest of the week."

Even Blair smiled. "I hate to break this up, but Molly has piano lessons in thirty minutes."

"You guys go ahead," Sam said. "C.D., will you give us a few minutes?"

"Sure." C.D. sent Katie a reassuring smile, wishing he felt a little more comfortable about leaving her. There was something in Sam's tone that warned C.D. this wouldn't be an easy conversation for Katie.

Katie felt C.D.'s concern, and shared it, though a secret part of her hoped that this was no more than Sam remembering that today was a special day—at least to her. Her birthday, the first since coming home. But that he'd have mentioned in front of the kids and C.D., so the hope that he'd remembered quickly fell, and apprehension replaced it.

She watched Blair and the kids leave her hospital room, and then looked at Sam. Deeper disappointment settled in. It was clear from his expression he was about to level her with legalese.

His hands in his pockets, Sam walked closer to her chair. The skin between his brows knitted, and tension lined his face. "Katie, I wish this could wait until you're released from the hospital. I know that this is a difficult time for you. But Dr. Muldoon feels it's best for me to address these things now, while you're here and he can help you in every way possible."

"If you're going to tell me that you've decided to stay married to Blair, I already know it."

Surprise floated across his face. "Have you and Blair discussed this?"

Katie groaned. "Give me some credit, Sam. You show up once in the first three days I'm here, and then never again by yourself. It doesn't take a genius to figure it out."

He didn't acknowledge or confirm her suspicions. He did sigh. "The truth is, as fabulous as your return is, it's put the family in a precarious financial position." He sat down on the edge of the bed, the only other available seat in the room. "When Blair and I got married, I used your life insurance benefits to supplement funds, and bought the new house." He lifted a hand. "Now, I'm going to have to sell it to pay back the insurance company and give you your half of our joint assets."

She couldn't believe it. Just couldn't freaking believe it. How could this really be happening? She'd been married to this man for thirteen years—*thirteen years*—and the best she deserved from him was a backdoor notice that he was going to divorce her? For him to talk about how her not being dead had put him in a financial bind? All he could talk to her about were material things?

Irritated and annoyed, hurt and disillusioned, Katie confronted him. "What exactly did the lawyer tell you, Sam? Or do I need to hire one of my own to make sure that I hear the truth?"

"I have to repay the insurance company, give you your half of our joint assets and reasonable visitation rights. As soon as our divorce is final, I'm going to re-marry Blair. For the children's sake, I would like for you to be there, so that they know you approve and I'm not abandoning you."

Katie stared at him a long moment. "Isn't that exactly what you're doing?" Shaking inside, she stood up and moved to the window to look outside, her heart so heavy she could barely breathe. "I don't blame you. Blair is a wonderful woman. She's been a good mother to the children, and I'm sure she's a good wife to you. But truth is truth, and you are walking out on me, Sam. I don't want to make things difficult for the children, but I won't lie to them to make things easier for you, either. They deserve more from their parents than that, and they'll be getting more from me."

Discarded. Thrown away. Unworthy.

Katie felt it all, and her heart rebelled. What had she done to deserve this?

Nothing. Sam was being Sam. Rebuilding his life, re-arranging their situation into one that was acceptable to him. Making all orderly in his world. It wasn't selfish-ness—it genuinely and truly wasn't, and no one under-stood that better than Katie except maybe Blair. It was his nature. His insatiable need for order.

It was raining outside. Huge drops pelted the glass in front of Katie. "I know you don't mean to come across like an unfeeling son of a bitch. It's just that you have your priorities, and I'm not one of them." She turned from the window to face him. "But you have to understand, Sam. While you were busy building a new life, I clung tenaciously to the old one to survive. So this is hard for me." Grief stuck in her throat.

"I know it is." He closed his eyes for a brief second and then went on. "It's hard for me, too. I love you. I love the children. I love Blair. I don't want to hurt anyone, and I don't want to be hurt. But no matter what I do, people are hurt, Katie." He slid a hand into his pocket, chose his words carefully. "This is going to sound hard, and I don't mean for it to, but it is the truth and it must be said."

"Just do it." She folded her arms over her chest and braced for the assault and the pain sure to come.

"We're different now, and the life we had no longer exists. I know you think I'm only worried about myself, but that isn't true. I swear, I'm thinking about the children, and Blair and you, too."

His mind was made up. And even if it wasn't, hers was. Her womanly pride was wounded by his preference for Blair, but not to the extent of "divorce." Yet that was the path ahead of her; no way around it. And that, too, must be accepted. "What about my back pay?" she asked. "Do I have to split that with you as joint assets, too?"

Sam frowned. "Technically, yes. But I can't do that to you, Katie. You have to build a new life. You need a home. You need a new career. I just can't do that, and Blair agrees it wouldn't be right."

Maybe he wasn't being such a bastard, after all.

They talked specific figures, and Katie did the math in her head. Half of their joint assets and six years' of her pay came to a whole lot more than the insurance repayment. He had to sell the house to buy her out. The kids would have to move, and then that, too, would be her fault. Leaving friends, changing schools, different neighborhoods—more major upset. No way. Not on her behalf. "Don't sell the house, Sam."

"There's no way I can afford to keep it and do all this."

"Yes, there is," she assured him. "You can pay me back over the next twenty years. Or we can consider the insurance payment child support and my contribution to the children's college funds."

"You would do that?" Jaw dropping, he looked at her, clearly shocked.

"A move now, when so much else is changing, would be really difficult for the children. I think they're facing enough challenges without adding that one. They need stability to feel safe and secure, and home is where they'll most feel it."

"You're sure?" Sam's eyes shone overly bright.

"Positive." She lifted her chin. "It's best for the kids."

Tears ran down his face, and the emotion that she had not seen in him since returning became apparent now. "I'm sorry for the way things have worked out. I know you have to be disappointed."

Disappointed? Try devastated. Try desolate and lost and empty and abandoned and alone. Damn it, Sam. Disappointed is not being able to get a flight reservation when you want one or an appointment with your hairdresser.

"I loved you, Katie." He paused, cleared his throat. "After you died, I just drifted, trying to get from one day

to the next. The kids needed someone, I needed someone, and then Blair came into our world and brought us
all back to life." He paused. "I know you don't want to
hear this, but the truth is she's a remarkable woman and
I owe her so much. I love her, Katie. I—I can't give her
up."

But you can give me up.

Inside, Katie wept. This other woman, this good
woman who loved and was loved by her husband and
children, had been living Katie's life, and she would
continue to. And there was nothing Katie could do but
accept that, too.

Resentment burned in her stomach. What did she
lack? Was it the idea of what had happened to her while
she had been held prisoner? Did Sam consider her dam-
aged goods? Did the sight of her repulse him? She
wanted to know, ached to know and maybe even needed
to know, but she couldn't bring herself to ask him. She
didn't have that much courage.

The expression on Sam's face turned tense, wary and
weary. "I know you think I'm a bastard because of what
I'm doing. But I hope that in time you'll come to agree
that it's the right thing for us all."

"I hope you're right." It would take time to deci-
pher how she really felt about that comment. Time and
perspective.

Katie sat back down in her chair, folded her hands
in her lap and looked up at Sam. Her heart felt hollow,
as if all the love that had at once been at home there
had been carved out. All that was left was a huge
gaping hole.

That was ridiculous, of course. She still loved her
children and Sam and C.D., but for so long loving had

brought her nothing but pain. Painful memories. Painful abstinence. And now painful loss.

She looked Sam right in the eye. "I loved you, too. But that was in another place and time." Stretching, she managed a weak grin. "Actually, in another lifetime."

Sam looked away. "Truthfully, I'm going to have to learn how to not love you, Katie." He shrugged. "Blair says that's impossible, and even if it weren't, it'd be a disgrace for a man not to love the mother of his children. I think I agree with that, but I also know I can't love two women." He let out a laugh that held no humor, and self-depreciating wasn't his style, which proved exactly how upset he was about all of this.

"Oh, I don't know about that, Sam. One thing I learned in the prison camp was to accept the inevitable. The heart is resilient, and it makes up its own mind. It has abilities to forgive, heal and recover—amazing abilities that exceed anything you could possibly imagine without being under extreme duress."

She paused, gauging his reaction. "I'd say that a man can love many women at one time, but no sane man would welcome being in love with two women at once. The women wouldn't much like it, either."

"I'm sure they wouldn't."

She tilted her head. "Yet we both know that isn't the case here, so let's don't insult each other by pretending that it is." In a petty moment, she bet herself he never forgot Blair's birthday.

Sam nodded. "I don't have the wisdom that comes with your experience. I suspect you paid a steep price for it."

She nodded. "Indeed, I did." *Everything. She'd paid everything.*

"I'm adjusting, Katie. There is no perfect solution,

but I'm doing the best I can, and I'm trying to do right by you. I can't say that I know for a fact what right is, but I am trying."

"I know you are," she said, and believed it. Standing up, she faced him. "This will all be easier for everyone if you remember two things, Sam. Are you willing to hear them?"

He hesitated only a second. "Yes."

Satisfied, she went on. "One, be honest with me at all times, even if you think it's being brutal. And two, accept that while we aren't the people we were back then, we are the people we've become, and those people are and always will be the parents of two very beautiful children. First and foremost, we are parents and we do what is best for them."

Sam stood silently. For a long moment, they just stared into each other's eyes. In his, Katie saw her past and her present—her life as it had been. She loved Sam. She wasn't in love with Sam. Had she been? Ever? Or had she been a young woman structuring her vision of love and perfection from a list she'd created as a child?

She'd been proud of Sam, respected him for being a doctor dedicated to healing. She'd loved the looks of him, the smiles and feel of him. But the woman she was now recognized what the young woman she had been hadn't seen or grasped. Weighing all she had felt and all she felt now, none of it rose to the level of being in love with him.

The shock of it thundered through her body, crashed through the chambers of her heart, sizzled along her skin and stung her fingers and toes. She wanted—tried—to deny it, but it was true. A look from Sam didn't make her heart race, or her mouth go dry. The thought of him didn't ignite a fire in her blood, or make her eager just for the sight of him.

Oh, yes. The people they had become were different—with different lives now, and definitely with different, separate futures. Neither had asked for any of this, and if it hadn't happened, they might have stayed married forever. But this *had* happened, and here they were.

Like her, Sam was a casualty of war.

So was their marriage. And what they made of their lives now was up to each of them. They had to look ahead and move forward, not from where they had been, but from where they each stood now. "This is for the best, Sam."

"Yes." Another tear rolled down his cheek and he reached for her hand. "You're a remarkable woman, Katie. Never doubt that." Lifting it to his lips, he kissed her knuckles. "Thank you for everything."

Pretending not to see his tears, she nodded. There was nothing more to say.

Sam turned and left her room.

When the door closed behind him, Katie grieved. She mourned what had ended, and what had never been.

She mourned that she had lived so much of her life unaware of all that had been missing.

KATIE FACED THE WINDOW and watched it rain.

The door behind her opened, and Ashley came in, tucking an envelope into her jacket pocket and carrying a fast-food sack. Smiling, she walked over. "I wanted to slip in to bring you some fuel before C.D. returns." She passed the bag.

"Thanks." Katie smiled. "You're something else."

"Yeah." Ashley grinned. "With women, it's best to check. Do you love or hate birthdays?"

Katie stilled. She used to love them, then was ambivalent about them—Sam never was good with dates—and today she was too upset to really give a damn. "Hell, I don't know. I'm going to have to think about it."

"Well, don't strain yourself," Ashley said wryly. "So long as you don't hate them, happy birthday, Katie." She smiled and passed her the card.

Her gaze locked with Ashley's. Katie's throat thickened. A lavender envelope. Her first card in six years. "Thank you, Ashley." A woman she'd known a little over a week had treated her with more compassion and kindness and thoughtfulness than the man she'd been married to for thirteen years.

Tears blurred her vision and Katie blinked hard, tucked the card into her nightstand, wanting to savor it when alone.

Ashley's beeper went off, and with an eye roll, she said, "Duty calls! I wanted to tell you I've got a schedule break. I'll see you in three days, but if you need me, you've got my cell number. Just call." And then she rushed out.

Katie crossed her arms and held them tightly against her chest, then leaned her forehead against the spotted glass. The window was cold against her forehead, and she silently wondered if she could freeze her thoughts to get a minute or two of reprieve from her life. So many crowded her mind. She just needed...

Someone tapped on the door.

"Yes?" Katie responded, lost in the gloominess of the slate sky and heavy weeping clouds. Feeling battered and weary, she turned to see who had come into the room. "C.D." Eagerly, she rushed to him, locked him in a hug and held on tight.

He closed his arms around her, pulled her to him. "Hey, there. You're shaking, Angel. What did His Majesty do now?"

She thought she had cried herself out, but apparently she hadn't. Hot tears choked her, flowed down her face. "Sam's divorcing me. He—he's staying with Blair." She let out a broken sob. "If you say the best woman won, I'm going to slug you, C.D."

"She did—in getting rid of him." C.D. stroked her hair. "Sorry, I'm pissed off at the man right now."

"Be pissed off later. It's my turn, and I need sympathy."

"Okay. Okay." He smiled against her hair. "I'm sorry, honey."

"You're not, you liar, but I adore you for saying you are, anyway." She sniffled against his shirt. He smelled so good. Warm and damp from being outside, and some faint, subtle cologne she didn't recognize. "I expected it, but still…"

"I know." C.D. sighed. "It's a pretty sucky homecoming gift. If I could change it, I would." He passed her his handkerchief.

She swiped at her eyes and sniffed. Bereft and abandoned, hollow and on her own, she ached from the heart out, and she dared to whisper her deepest fear. "Sam and the kids… I—I think they would have been better off if I had never been rescued." A deep sob tore loose and ripped at her throat.

"No. No, Katie, that's not true." C.D. pulled her closer, rubbed soothing circles on her back. "That could never be true." He shook his head. "You've had way too much thrown at you too fast. I could beat the hell out of Sam for that. But what's done is done, and it can't be changed now." C.D. tugged her closer still. "I know this with Sam is hard. Hell, it's all hard, honey. But you said it yourself last night. You're different now." He took the handkerchief from her and gently dabbed at her eyes. "The thing is, you and Sam have always been different. You just didn't see it then."

"But I do now?" She pulled back to look at him. "Is that what you're saying?"

"Yes, I am." C.D. nodded. "You used to tell me that you were living your perfect life. But the truth is, Angel, your perfect life isn't behind you, it's ahead of you. You were wearing rose-colored glasses then, and you've ditched them. Now you get to choose your *real* perfect life." He paused to look at her a second, then said, "Just do me one favor, okay?"

Only God knew what would come next. "What?"

"Don't make any snap decisions," he said. "Give yourself some time to figure out exactly what you want your real perfect life to be."

"I will."

"That's not all," he said.

"What else?"

"Aim high."

She looked up at him, seeing that he wanted so much good for her, as he always had. "I will," she promised, then kissed his neck—the place her lips happened to land. "God, C.D., I'd be crazy without you."

"Finally, she admits it." He smiled. "I've always told you that."

She swatted him. "Stop."

"I *always* listen to you. Finally, for once, you listen to me, and I'm supposed to stop? I don't think so."

Katie couldn't help it; she chuckled. "What am I going to do with you?"

"Adore me." He batted his eyelashes at her. "I need it bad. You know I do."

"I have to," she said, putting a snide edge in her tone. "No one else can handle your goofy backside."

"True. All true."

He had been fabulous about spending a lot of time with her. How he was keeping the bar going and taking care of his other business interests, she had no idea. He didn't look overly tired. Actually, he looked energized.

Still, because of their mutual adoration, it was time she let him off the hook. "You can stop feeling guilty because you made it out and I got stuck. Seriously, C.D."

That had to be why he was sticking so close to her. "I know you have a life and a business to run, and probably fifteen women waiting to hear from you." He always had. Women flocked to C.D., and no one knew it better than Katie. He understood them. He liked them. He respected them. And they adored him. "You've got to be sick of playing nurse to me."

He released her and sat down in the chair, then leaned his cane against the bed. "I'm beyond feeling guilty. What happened happened and is now history. Can't rewrite it. My businesses are low-maintenance and doing just fine. And the women—all fifteen of them—will wait." He waggled his eyebrows. "I am exactly where I want to be, doing exactly what I want to be doing."

"Seriously?" He'd never lied to her, but he had to be lying now.

"I swear it on my wings," he said, lifting his right hand. "Don't look so shocked—it offends me. I've always enjoyed your company, and you know it." He stopped, turned somber, then took a different tack. "Wait a second. Are you discreetly saying you're tired of me? If so, just say the word and I'll give you a little space."

"Me, discreet? Ms. Blunt? Not hardly," she admitted. "I'd be a nutcase without you, C.D., and that's humbling, I don't mind telling you." It was true. So true it scared her.

She needed to look at that. There was something squirrelly in it. Sam not being here with her hurt her pride. But the idea of C.D. not being here just plain hurt, and the pain would be tenfold worse. The pain would hurt…her heart.

Uneasy, she shifted to change positions. C.D. understood her better than anyone else alive. And he knew more about the real her than anyone else, too, so all of that made sense. Some, she supposed, would think she should have that kind of relationship with her husband, but too many couples she'd known didn't for those opinions to matter. And she would feel vulnerable with C.D. but she knew him just as well as he knew her, so détente had become the norm between them a long time ago.

But because she knew him equally well, she also knew he was blowing smoke her way about letting go of the guilt. He was protecting her, and though she should call him on it, at the moment, her pride was too tattered to feel anything but grateful. "I thought you had better things to do. That's all."

He propped his elbow on the chair arm, rested his chin in his upturned hand and sent her a level look. "You might be able to lie to Sam and get away with it, but don't even try it with me, Angel. I think I'm offended that you did try it."

"I didn't lie to you," she said, and meant it. "What are you talking about?"

"I know you, and I know that right now you feel more fragile and more vulnerable than you've ever felt in your life. So don't pretend you don't need me. You do." He paused, then added, "You need me every bit as much as I need you."

Her heartbeat rocketed and every nerve in her body woke up and tingled. *He needed her?* She stared at him, perplexed and unsure exactly what was happening here. "I'm not sure what to say to that."

"It wasn't a question, Katie. It was a statement of fact."

Tense, she pushed her hair back from her face. "Define need."

"No." He didn't blink, didn't try to shun the baldness in his refusal.

"Why not?" This wasn't making any sense. But then why should it be any different from everything else? Nothing made sense anymore.

"Because it's not the right time."

A light rap sounded on the door.

Dr. Muldoon stuck in his head. "Am I interrupting anything?"

"Not at all." Katie smiled.

"Katie, America wants to welcome you home. Are you up for a press conference? I've also been asked to tell you that you have several book and film offers waiting, and a couple agents offering to represent you with them."

"Why?"

"People want to hear your story." He held up a finger. "If you're not ready to mess with any of this, just say so. I'll hold them all off as long as you like."

Katie stared at C.D., thought about it for a long moment, and then decided. "Hold them off forever, then," she said. "I'm not interested in any of it."

Muldoon cast her a blank look. "Excuse me?"

"I'm not interested in any of it," she repeated. "The press conference or the offers."

"Why not?" he asked, clearly surprised.

While she wasn't eager to say it out loud, she'd be nagged on this until she did, so she might as well do it, and have it done. "America loves fairy tales, Dr. Muldoon. In my story, there is no Cinderella. There is no Prince Charming. And there certainly is no happy ending. I'm assuming Sam told you that he is divorcing me." She waited for his nod. When it came, she continued. "Who wants to hear a story where a woman returns home and her husband's remarried, her children have another mother, so she has no family, no home, no career—nothing?" She let out a little groan. "As home-comings go, it falls pretty short of the joyful mark. See what I mean?"

"I wish I didn't, Katie." Dr. Muldoon's face flushed. "I'm sorry."

She'd made him uncomfortable. He'd been nothing but kind, and she'd made him uncomfortable. "No, I'm sorry. I haven't yet readjusted to social subtleties, and I was far too blunt." She tried a smile, but it was weak at best. "It's difficult to remember. I'm going to have to work at it."

"I like blunt," C.D. said. "There's nothing wrong with blunt."

"C.D.'s right about that, though I understand what you mean, Katie. It's not a problem for now, but the media is going to insist on speaking to you at some time. If not now and here, then they'll dog you to death later."

"No one is going to dog me to death, Dr. Muldoon." She'd been dogged to her limit and then some in the prison camp. Those days were over.

"Okay." He didn't argue. "Would you rather talk to them now, or after you leave the hospital?"

"I'd rather not talk to them at all." Especially considering her challenge on discerning what happened from her nightmares. Katie sighed. No way was she admitting that, though. She'd be stuck in some institution under some stupid mental health study for the rest of her days. "But if I must talk to them to get them off my back, then later is better."

"Very well. I'll handle it, then." He sounded confident, but something in his tone warned her the press wouldn't be put off easily.

"Has the media been camped out here?"

He didn't answer.

"Yes," C.D. said. "Every entrance. The base commander authorized it under pressure and, I suspect for PR purposes, in case you agreed to talk to them, or Drs. Muldoon and Firestone cut you loose."

"I'm sorry," she said to Muldoon. "I guess they've been driving you and your staff nuts."

"We're dealing with it, Katie. It's nothing for you to worry about. You have enough—"

C.D. stepped in. "Ashley's taken her phone off the hook at home. They found out she'd been shopping for you, and they've been all over her."

Katie looked at C.D. "She didn't mention a word to me."

He lifted a hand toward Dr. Muldoon. "As he said, you've got enough on your plate."

She had been avoiding asking Dr. Muldoon about her leaving the hospital, though it hadn't been far from her mind since Ashley had first mentioned it. Now that she knew the media was camping out at the hospital and driving Ashley to disconnect her phone at home, it wasn't practical to ignore the inevitable any longer. "It's time for me to leave."

"There's no rush, Katie. We can deal with this. We *want* to deal with it to give you what you need." Dr. Muldoon watched her carefully. "I don't want you leaving here until we're sure you're ready. Frankly, Dr. Firestone would feel better if you were talking about your time in captivity."

He really was a good man. "I'm not going to talk about that, and I've already explained why."

She couldn't risk it for a multitude of reasons, not the least of which was Molly and Jake. *Your mother is dead. Oops, she's alive. Oops, she's alive, but messed up in the head. She can't tell what's real and what's imagined.*

No way. It was the stress of it all, and the truth would become clear to her with time. And, by God, she was going to have that time and not have to fight being tagged as a mental case for the rest of her life.

"As for being ready," she continued, "hell, Dr. Muldoon, I don't think I can get ready. Honestly, I think I'm going to have to just dive in and deal with whatever comes."

Fingering the stethoscope dangling around his neck, he thought about all she'd said. "Did Sam talk to you today?"

"He's divorcing me and staying with Blair," she said without emotion. "It's okay. I'm not in love with him. I thought I was, but I'm not. I never have been."

His eyes widened in shock. He opened his mouth, but she lifted a hand to stay him. "I know. It surprised me, too. But there it was, staring me in the face."

"You're okay with it, then?" he asked.

"I will be, once the shock wears off." She nodded.

"Blair and I have an agreement on the kids. It'll all work out."

He looked taken aback, but recovered quickly. "Quite a revealing time for you, then."

"Yes, it has been," Katie agreed. "Not without pain, but endurable."

He nodded. "Sam aside, you've been pretty insulated here, Katie. Are you sure you're ready to leave?"

Hadn't he heard her? Who could be ready? Ever? "Some things you just have to do, and find your way as you go. Sign the papers. I'm leaving."

"All right." He stepped to the wall. "Your pay is settled. They opened an account for you at the credit union and direct deposited it for you."

She nodded. "A lady from social services brought me the cards to sign, but I didn't know the money was in. That's terrific news." Katie would pay back Ashley right away, hopefully before her credit card bill had come in. "I'm not a pauper anymore." *Happy birthday to me.*

Dr. Muldoon smiled. "You've also officially been granted thirty days' leave of absence to decide whether or not you want to return to active duty."

"I'm not returning to active duty. I don't know what I'm going to do yet, but it won't be that."

"I can't say I blame you, but give it thirty days before you make a formal decision. Consider it a well-earned vacation." He paused. "This is a difficult question to ask." His face flushed. "Where will you go?"

That, she'd thought about a great deal. So while it was hard for him to ask, because it reminded her she had come for a reunion with her family and was leaving alone, it wasn't a difficult question to answer. "First to see my parents. I'll stay there a few days, and then I'll decide what to do. I'll have to live here in Willow Creek, of course, because the children are here. I won't be far away from my kids again."

C.D. intervened. "If you're interested, I have a vacant cottage. On the off chance that you broke out of here, I had it cleaned. It's ready and waiting when you are."

Katie should have known he would be looking out for her, thinking ahead. She'd been worried about where to go, but once again C.D. had come through for her— just as he always had in the old days. "Awesome." He was. He truly was.

Dr. Muldoon smiled. "I take it this is settled, then?"

"Absolutely." Katie sent C.D. a grateful smile. "I really would be lost without you—temporarily homeless, too."

"When you're ready, I'll sign you out," Muldoon said. "But only under the provision that when you return from visiting your parents, you come in daily for me to do a quick check on you."

"I don't need that. I'm fine."

"They're not for you," he confessed. "They're for me. I respect your right not to discuss what happened to you during captivity, but I need reassurance that you're okay."

She appreciated his concern, but she wasn't sure she wanted it. "For how long?"

"Let's play that by ear."

He wouldn't sign her out without her agreement. *Accept the inevitable.* "Okay, then. Sign me out." She had a home to go to now, and glanced at C.D. "I was wrong, Dr. Muldoon."

"About what?"

She smiled. "It appears there's a Prince Charming around, after all."

CHAPTER SEVEN

THE COTTAGE WAS LOVELY. Two bedrooms, a kitchen, living room and bath, all decorated in soft, soothing shades of green and blue. But the best feature was outside the back door: a large porch and a small garden. Katie turned to C.D. and smiled. "It's perfect."

He leaned against the porch railing. "I'm glad you like it. I bought the essentials, but I thought you'd like to decorate yourself."

She nodded. "Feed that nesting urge, eh?"

"Exactly." He hitched a hip on the railing. "You women don't have the corner on that. We men need roots, too."

"So we nest and you root. Got it." She bit back a smile. "Are you going to show me your bar?"

"Sure." He looked a little surprised. "If you're interested in seeing it."

She nudged his shoulder. "I'm interested in everything that has to do with you, C.D."

He seemed pleasantly surprised. "You used to be. But I didn't know if you would still feel that way." He made the little noise he'd always made when he was moved and embarrassed by it—a sweet sound that teased the fringes of a grunt, groan and sigh. "Why is that?"

"Excuse me?"

"Why are you interested?"

"Because I adore you," she said plainly. "I've always adored you, C.D."

"I've always adored you, too." He frowned, dragged a fingertip down a bit of white column that ran from roof to porch floor. "Exactly what kind of adoration is this? It feels different."

It did. But great. Comfortable. Real. "Significant."

"Definitely significant."

She shrugged. "You okay with that?"

"Yeah, I am." He nodded. "It feels…right."

Amazingly right.

She smiled, hugged him and rested her head on his chest. "Unconditional."

"Ah. The heavy stuff." He planted a kiss on the top of her head. "How's it feel to be out of the hospital?"

"Pretty good." Sunlight streamed across the edge of the porch, and she winced to block the glare. "I see you got me a phone."

He nodded. "The basics. Do whatever you like to the place."

This was temporary. He had plans for the cottage— or did he? "For how long?"

"As long as you want it." His arms looped around her shoulders, and he tugged at a lock of her hair.

"Thanks." She squeezed his sides. "I'm going to buy a car, then go see my folks. I'll get beyond the basics here when I get back."

"How long are you staying in New Orleans?"

"A day," she said. "Maybe two." She shrugged. "I need to see them, but I don't want to be away from the kids for long."

"Why not take them with you?"

She pulled away, looked up at him. "Sam would never agree to that."

"Why not?" C.D. looked genuinely surprised. "They are your kids."

"But they don't know me." It was a ridiculous idea—wasn't it?

"Well, they're not going to get to know you unless you spend some time together." C.D. lifted a hand. "They're used to visiting your folks. A trip there wouldn't be strange to them. Sounds like an opportunity to me."

She was tempted. So tempted. But things were still tense and trying for all of them. Would a trip home with her be a good thing for the kids?

"Tell me."

She looked over at C.D. and sighed. "You know—" she tilted her head "—it's really hard to be with someone who reads your every thought without you telling them."

"It's a good thing. We decided that on the mission over the Devil's Triangle when our instruments went nuts, remember?"

They had, and she did remember. "I remember that we were both pretty rattled."

"At least we didn't have heavy cloud cover, too."

"True." She sat down on the top step, facing the yard, and propped her arms on her knees. "I think we'd have both fainted."

"Probably." He laughed and sat down beside her.

Staring at the flower beds, she felt her smile fade. "It's hard being with the kids. They don't remember, but I do. Every scrape and spat and new word and…all of it." She paused and let the knots in her stomach relax. "I guess I'm weaker than I thought, C.D."

Coward. Coward. Coward.

"You're not weak, Katie."

"I feel weak," she confessed. "I just don't know if I can take a day or two of being that tense without a break." Sunlight sparkled on the grass, and just being outside in the humidity raised a sweat. "The exhaustion…"

"You're scared."

Leave it to C.D. to not even give her graceful wiggle room. "Yes, I am."

"Would it help if I went, too?"

She studied his face, but couldn't tell what he was thinking. Pure neutrality was all she could read in his expression, in the set of his jaw or in his eyes. "It would," she admitted. "They like you."

"Then let's do it." He stood up and extended a hand to her. "Go call Blair and set it up."

He made it sound so easy. *Reach up and pluck a star, Katie.* "It's not that simple, C.D."

"Why not?"

"What if I establish a pattern of asking Sam and Blair for permission about the kids, and Blair refuses?"

"Ah, succession of power. I get it." He frowned. "In that case, you change the rules and assert your own power. At the end of the day, you share equal risks, Angel. Go for it."

"True."

"I can't see Blair refusing," C.D. said. "Sam? Yes. He'll try anything to retain control of everyone and everything around him. But not Blair."

Katie happened to agree with that, so with heavy steps, she walked into the cottage and snagged the phone. She summoned the courage to dial and then paced between the sink and back door, too nervous to be still.

Blair answered on the third ring. "Hello."

"Blair, it's Katie."

"Hi. How are you?"

"I'm okay. I'm, um, out of the hospital."

"That's good news," she said, sounding as if she meant it. "Where are you?"

"I've rented a cottage from C.D."

"Oh, good. You're not too far away, then." She paused to tell Molly to drink her milk. "Sorry. Afternoon snack," she explained, then went on. "Why don't you and C.D. come over for dinner, Katie?"

Flabbergasted, Katie didn't trust her ears. "Excuse me?"

"Come for dinner and bring C.D.," she said again.

Maybe Sam had remembered her birthday, after all, and he wanted her to celebrate it with the kids. That was a big assumption to make with Sam. He wasn't cruel, just unconscious about those kinds of things. "Why?"

"I don't know if you're interested in them, but when I boxed up all your things at the old house, I couldn't make myself get rid of them. I thought the kids might want them later. But now that you're back… Well, if you want them, they're here."

"You kept my things for the kids?" A bubble of excitement burst in Katie. Her things. Her stuff. Proof of her former life she could have with her now. Sainthood? The woman was pushing for something like it, doing that.

"I told you. I decided not to compete. I wanted them to know you, and you can learn a lot about a woman from her things."

Which meant Blair had learned a lot about Katie, too. Apparently she hadn't hated what she'd learned or she'd have burned the stuff. "That's very good of you." Actually, it was amazing. A little hard to believe, but definitely amazing.

"When you come to dinner, you can pick it all up. It'll give you a chance to see the kids in their natural environment, too."

Ah, see the kids in their home. Accept that they were at home there, and not with Katie. Now that made sense. She looked at C.D., whispered the invitation and then lifted a questioning shoulder. When he nodded, she said, "That'd be great. What time?"

"Seven?"

"Okay," Katie said. "Can I bring anything?"

"Just yourself."

"See you then." Katie hung up the phone, shaking all over. Shaking in ways even the tormentor, Lieutenant Ustead, had never been able to make her shake.

"What's wrong?" C.D. swallowed a drink of ice water, then set his glass down on the counter.

"She's not normal." Katie snitched his glass, took a sip. "No one is that good."

He laughed. "She's trying to stay on the right side of you so she doesn't lose the kids. That's all."

"Considering the circumstances, sharing is best. But even if it weren't, it'd probably be working. I'd feel as if I were snatching the heart out of the Easter bunny or something."

"Which proves she's an excellent strategist."

Katie considered that for a second. "I think that's just a perk. She's confident, secure in who she is and with the life she's built. I really think she's just doing what comes natural to her."

C.D. frowned. "Now that's scary."

Katie rolled her eyes heavenward. "Only if you're trying to match her."

"Which of course you'd never try to do."

"No, I wouldn't." Katie didn't have to think about that. "I want to live my life my way. I paid for the privilege."

And she had. Dearly.

C.D. WENT TO TAKE CARE of some business at the bar, and Katie stood in the backyard and checked out the little garden. It needed work, but the beds were in decent shape. It had potential.

There was a little potting shed at the back lot line, and it wasn't locked. She opened the door, and smiled when she saw new gardening tools, gloves and knee pads. "C.D.," she said to herself, "you awe me, baby."

Though tempted to pull out a spade and get busy, she fought the urge to get her hands in the dirt, and went back inside to look around. After hanging some of her clothes in the closet and stuffing some in drawers, she went to the kitchen for something to drink. There were fresh lemons in the fridge, and tea in the pantry—he'd remembered that, too—and so she put the kettle on the stove. A pitcher of iced tea would hit the spot.

The bare white front of the fridge mocked her. There were no kids' colored pictures hanging there. No magnets in funny shapes or with cute or profound quotes on them. No notes scribbled in a hurry. No pending appointment reminders. It was bare. Barren. Empty.

Like me.

"Don't go there," she warned herself. "Do something. Even if it's wrong, do something to fill the space."

Scrounging in a kitchen drawer, she found a notepad

and two pens. One was a clear-barrel Bic, and a long-ago memory flashed through her mind.

Katie Cole and Her Perfect Life.

Her list. She smiled, brushed her hair back from her face and mixed the tea in a pot, since she didn't have a pitcher. What had she been—seven? No, she'd just turned eight. Eight years old, and she'd known exactly what she'd wanted for the rest of her life. Wow, what she'd give to be that sure of anything now. Anything at all.

With a half grin, she pulled a glass from the cabinet near the window over the sink, then went to the fridge for ice. The motor clicked on, humming, sounding almost friendly.

One thing about that kid and her list…she'd gotten every single thing on it. Reaching into the bin, Katie pulled out a couple cubes of ice, plunked them into the glass. A husband, a son and a daughter. She became a pilot and had a house with a big front porch.

Pouring hot sweetened tea over the ice, she recalled how she'd felt when writing that list. Empowered. Strong. In control of her destiny.

The ice crackled, melting fast in the heated tea, and she added more cubes. She'd known what she'd wanted, gotten it and lost it.

So what do you want now?

Good question. Of course she wanted her children with her, at least part of the time. She had to be realistic about that. And she didn't want to be in the military anymore and risk being called away from them. She'd done her part; it was time for others to carry the torch. So what else did she want?

She sat down at the kitchen table and stared at the notepad, but she couldn't make herself pick up the pen.

Maybe she was being a coward. Maybe she didn't want
to put in writing that, unlike when she was eight, now
she didn't have a clue what she wanted. And maybe she
was most afraid to commit to ink that she wasn't
through with her old life yet.

*You need time. That's all. Then you'll be able to write
your new list.*

Grateful for the self-imposed reprieve, she grabbed
her glass of tea, hit the back door in a full run and
headed for the potter's shed. She wasn't running away
from anything, she told herself, reaching for the shovel,
then stepping back outside into the sun. She was just
taking everything to a place where she didn't feel so
pressured to solve all her problems at once. She needed
to think. And she'd always been better at thinking in
the garden. She'd always been better at everything in the
garden. It was her sanctuary, her sacred space, and she'd
mourned it as she had mourned the loss of everything
else important to her.

This wasn't the same garden, but she'd work it and
claim it and make it hers. For now, that would do....

Hours later, she heard C.D. call out to her. "Katie?"

Hot and sweaty, she stopped shoveling and looked
around, but didn't see him. "Where are you?"

"Up here."

She looked toward the bar, up to a little balcony on
its second-story rear wall, spotted him and smiled. "Ah.
I didn't notice that. Nice little retreat."

"It's almost six. If we're going to make His Majesty's
by seven, you might want to hose off the dirt pretty quick."

Almost six? Good grief, she'd no idea. "Thanks. I
guess I lost track of time."

He smiled, clearly happy to hear that. "I figured

you would. I turn you loose to play in the mud, and you're happy."

She was happy. It startled her. For the first time since she could remember, she felt peaceful and calm and not at all anxious. "You're not fooling me. You bought these tools so I would make you a beautiful garden, not so I'd get busy playing and lose myself. Then you can up my rent."

"Did I say buying the tools wasn't mutually beneficial?"

"No. But you would have, if you could've gotten away with it."

He harrumphed loudly enough to make sure she heard it, then turned to go inside. Stopping suddenly, he looked over at her.

"What?" She shielded her eyes from the sun with her hand.

"You didn't take exception to my calling Sam His Majesty."

She hadn't noticed. Odd. Why hadn't she noticed? She'd always given C.D. hell for that. "Defending him is Blair's job now. I've been…" She hesitated, not sure what to say. Put out to pasture? Retired? Tossed out with the garbage? Replaced by a new, improved model?

"Liberated," C.D. said. "We should celebrate."

Maybe they would. She tried to tamp down any expectations about this dinner, but she couldn't squelch a tiny sliver of hope that her babies would tell her happy birthday. That would really make the day special. Proof she was home.

Don't, Katie. You know Sam. You know the odds of that are slim to none. Why put yourself through the disappointment? Do you really need more disappointment?

"When it's time." She put her tools in the shed, slapped the dirt from her gloves, hung them on a peg and then shut the door.

They should wait to celebrate until she could celebrate without having to fight the urge to cry her heart out.

SAM AND BLAIR'S HOUSE was a cozy thirty-five hundred square foot redbrick mansion in a gated community on the bay. The landscaping was photo perfect, and inside, everything was photo perfect, too. Decorated mostly in gray and various shades of red, it was formal but not cold. Family photos littered the walls, and thick rugs with geometric designs were scattered on gleaming hardwood floors. A winding oak staircase led up to the second floor, and Katie quickly averted her eyes. She didn't want to think about what happened in that part of the house.

The first fifteen minutes were sheer hell. Everyone was uncomfortable and the tension was too thick to cut with a knife; you needed a machete. But once they sat down at the dining room table and started eating, everyone relaxed. Katie couldn't say exactly why. Maybe it was the simple smells of hot bread and zesty spaghetti sauce. Or the refreshing sips of iced tea and sweet wine. Or maybe everyone just got tired of being tense and said to hell with it.

For Katie, it was the latter, and before she realized it, they were halfway through a simple and surprisingly pleasant, casual dinner. Jake talked about a science test, and admitted that he'd gotten velocity confused with momentum again. Molly told Blair that her friend Jessica had gotten detention for passing notes in Mrs. Holloway's class for the third time, and if it happened again she'd be suspended. And Sam announced that the Jeffersons' cat was expecting kittens again, and they all knew what that meant. Simultaneously, all four said Mrs. Jefferson would be having another baby.

Laughing, Sam explained to Katie and C.D. that whenever the cat had kittens, Mrs. Jefferson soon had a baby. The vet had confirmed Daisy's pregnancy that morning, so a resigned Mrs. Jefferson, who was already the mother of four, called in for her appointment with Sam.

Katie laughed until her side ached.

Jake swallowed a bite of crunchy hot bread. "So what have you been doing since you got out of the hospital?"

Katie appreciated his asking. "Settling into the cottage," she said. "It has a little garden, and I spent the afternoon working in it."

"We have a yard man. He likes to do everything by himself." Molly's eyes gleamed. "Maybe I could help you plant some flowers in your garden sometime."

A knot lodged in Katie's throat. "I would love that." She glanced at C.D. Now was as good a time as any. "Actually, I have something I want to ask all of you. I'm going to buy a car in the morning, and tomorrow afternoon, I'm going to drive to New Orleans to see my parents. I was hoping that you guys—" she looked from Molly to Jake "—would like to come along." She glanced from Sam to Blair. "If that's okay."

Sam's lips flattened into a straight line. Obviously he wasn't too happy about her suggestion, but Blair smiled openly, far more receptive. "I think it's a great idea. It's about time for the regular visit to see your grandparents, and I'm sure they'd be thrilled to have you guys there with your mom."

Molly sent Blair an uneasy look. "Will you come, too?"

OFFICIAL OPINION POLL

Dear Reader,

Since you are a book enthusiast, we would like to know what you think.

Inside you will find a short Opinion Poll. Please participate in our poll by sharing your opinion on 3 subjects that are very important to all of us.

To thank you for your participation, we would like to send you your choice of **2 FREE BOOKS** and a **FREE GIFT!**

Please enjoy them with our compliments.

Sincerely,

Pam Powers

Editor

P.S. Don't forget to indicate which books you prefer so we can send your FREE gifts today!

What's your pleasure...

Romance?

Enjoy **2 FREE BOOKS** that will fuel your imagination with intensely moving stories about life, love and relationships.

OR

Suspense?

Enjoy **2 FREE BOOKS** that will thrill you with a spine-tingling blend of suspense and mystery.

Whichever category you select, your **2 FREE BOOKS** have a combined cover price of $11.98 or more in the U.S. and $13.98 or more in Canada.

Simply place the sticker next to your preferred choice of books, complete the poll on the right page and you'll automatically receive **2 FREE BOOKS** and a **FREE GIFT** with no obligation to purchase anything!

We'll send you a wonderful surprise gift, *ABSOLUTELY FREE*, just for trying our books! Don't miss out — **MAIL THE REPLY CARD TODAY!**

Order online at
www.FreeBooksandGift.com

"Not this time." Blair didn't miss a beat. "I think it'd be good for you to spend some time with your mother. Remember? We talked about this."

Molly nodded, then shot an even more wary look at Jake.

Sam started to voice his objection. "Don't you think it's a little too soon?"

"Too soon?" Blair looked at him as if he'd lost his mind. "It's the perfect time, Sam. Katie's waited an awfully long time already, don't you think?"

Resigned, he nodded. "Yes, I guess she has."

"What time would you like them to be ready, Katie?" Blair asked.

Katie paused, studied Molly and then Jake. They looked caught and cornered. If she took them on this trip, they'd go, but only because she'd be dragging them. It'd probably work out okay in the end, but shoving this down their throats wasn't an option. She couldn't do it. Wouldn't do it. "Would you guys rather not go this time? Maybe wait a bit and do that later?"

Molly looked her in the eye. "I don't want to go."

"Okay," Katie said, swallowing her hurt. The child didn't know her yet, and forcing the issue wasn't something Katie was willing to do. "Jake, what about you?"

He looked at her through compassionate eyes. "It's not that I don't want to be with you, but I had plans with Trevor and Greg. I was kind of looking forward to that, you know?"

C.D. watched with open curiosity. Would he be disappointed that Katie wouldn't push the point? Or would he grasp her rationale?

Either way, she was going to do what she felt was right. "No problem, Jake. I understand." Katie smiled

at them. "Let's go to Gran and Grandpa's together another time, then."

"You're not gonna make us go?" Molly sounded
stunned.

"No, honey, I'm not." She let her eyes hold her promise. "I am going to have to go without you, though. I
haven't seen your grandparents in a very long time, and
I know they need to see me, just like I need to see you
guys."

"But you're coming back, right?" Jake sounded as if
it was important to him. "Right?"

That tone did Katie more good than anything else in
the world. She nodded. "I'll be back on Sunday. Molly,
maybe we can plant some flowers then. Would you like
to do that?"

Blair and Sam exchanged a private glance, like all
couples do, and Katie picked up on it. "Or is that going
to mess up plans you already have made?"

"Honestly, it will," Sam said. "My parents are having
a small gathering to celebrate their anniversary."

"Oh, well, that's important." Katie wiped her mouth
and put her napkin on the table. "Of course Molly has
to be there for that."

"No, I don't." Molly looked at Blair. "I want to go
plant flowers and make a garden like at our old house."

"Then that's what you'll do." Blair smiled at Molly
and winked. "Right, Sam?"

"Actually, I think the adults need to discuss this
privately." He dabbed his mouth with his napkin.
"Kids, homework."

The kids went upstairs.

"Sam," Katie said after they'd gone. "This time it's
right because it's about them. But please don't protect

them from all disagreements. They'll get on their own and not realize it's normal."

"Katie's right, Sam." Blair nodded. "It's important for children to live in a realistic environment so they develop strong conflict resolutions skills. If you prevent them from learning, then they won't know how to deal with challenges constructively, though not when they're being discussed, of course."

Sam frowned, but didn't oppose. "Wanting to protect them is normal, but I'll keep what you said in mind."

Blair returned to the original topic. "Molly would like to be with her mother, and that's a good thing."

"I guess so." Sam said it, but he looked miffed and close to sulking.

He'd often done that, and Katie had always hated it. To get his way, he'd verbally agree, but then silently show disapproval to induce guilt. It was a sucky way to treat people. Katie had ignored it before. She wasn't ignoring it now.

"Sam," Katie said. "We're all adjusting and we need to make a special effort to understand that the kids have full lives. I'm grateful for that, and I expect you are, too. We all want to be with them, but they only have so much free time. We have to share. And all of us—the kids included—need to have an attitude of gratitude that there are so many of us to love them. That's a wonderful thing. If we all remember that, then we'll have a little grace about sharing. Otherwise, we're going to be spending a lot of time unhappy, and that's just not necessary."

She stood up. "Life doesn't fit neatly into little boxes. It's messy. Sometimes really messy, you know?"

"Not my life," Sam retorted. "My life was organized and orderly and just as I wanted it—" He caught himself.

"Until I came back." She sighed. "I know. I interrupted your life. Well, that's unfortunate, but I am back
now, and I am going to be here and a part of the kids'
lives." That notice was clear enough. "We will always
be their parents, and that makes us a part of each other's
lives, too. You're going to have to make room for me,
Sam. Because I've already forfeited a lot, and I might
forfeit even more from here on out, but I will never forfeit my children."

Blair came around the table and stood beside her.
"No one expects you to, Katie."

"Thank you." Katie clasped Blair's hand, grateful
for the show of unity. Sam wasn't pleased, and standing
with Katie had to be hard for Blair, but she knew this
was right, and thankfully, she had the backbone to stand
up for it. "I'm going to say goodnight to the kids. I'll
tell Molly to talk with you two," Katie said, "and if she
wants to come over Sunday, to phone me."

Katie called and Molly came down the stairs. Katie
spoke to them and said it was time for her and C.D. to go.

"Not yet," Jake protested. "I want to show you my
room—so you can see me there."

At the hospital, she had said she'd sleep better if she
could see them in her mind—where they were. Jake
remembered.

"Go ahead, Jake," Blair said. "Take your mom up."

Blair hadn't faltered, calling Katie *mom,* she noticed.
That had to be a good sign.

Smiling, Blair turned to C.D. "Can I recruit you
and Sam to put some boxes in your truck? Some of
Katie's things?"

"Sure." C.D. stood up.

"Thanks. They're in the entryway. Sam will show

He remembered! Overwhelmed, Katie couldn't speak, and settled for a nod.

They talked quietly for a few minutes, and then Katie stood up. "Well, I'd better go. From the looks of that stack of books, you've got tons of homework."

"Yeah." He stood up, too, threw his arms around her neck and hugged her hard. "I'm sorry they hurt you, Mom."

Mom. Dear God, had any word ever sounded so sweet, been cherished so deeply? Katie's nose, the back of her eyes, burned and her control frayed. "It's over now." She held him tightly, closed her eyes and savored the feel and scent of him. "And we're together again now. That's all that matters."

"I'm glad you're home."

Tears blurred her eyes and she blinked hard. "Thank you, Jake." Overwhelmed, she confided, "I have to tell you, what you just said to me is the best birthday present anyone has ever given me in my whole life."

"It's your birthday? Today?" His face flushed and his jaw dropped. "But I didn't get you a card, and you didn't have a cake or real presents or anything." He seemed horrified.

"Those things aren't important, honey. You just gave me something worth a lot more." She hugged him again. "And I really needed it."

He looked embarrassed and pulled away. "Want me to walk down with you?"

"No, you go on and get to your homework."

"Okay." He plopped down at his desk and reached for his headphones. "Have a great birthday, okay?"

"Thanks." Katie walked to the door.

"Hey, Mom?"

It hadn't been a slip of tongue. He'd said it twice. *Mom.* Smiling inside, she stopped and looked back.

"If Molly comes over on Sunday, I might come, too—if that's all right."

All right? It'd be fantastic. "Of course. Jake, you can come see me anytime." Smiling, she walked out into the hallway and shut her eyes as she passed Sam and Blair's room, then took the stairs two at a time, her step a lot lighter than when she'd been going up.

When she got into the car, C.D. said, "Well, you're looking awfully pleased with yourself."

"Jake hugged me. He said he was glad I was home *and* he called me Mom. Not once, but twice, C.D. It wasn't an accident or a mistake." She grinned. "He also asked if he could come over with Molly on Sunday."

"Now, that's great news." C.D. smiled. "I had my doubts about you not just making them go with us to your folks anyway—they'd get used to you during the visit—but it seems you know best. Your way is working out better."

"I can't force them, C.D. I've been forced and I hated it. I won't do that to them or anyone else ever again in any way."

He reached over and squeezed her hand.

"I was a maniac going over there," she admitted. "But it really did work out fine. And with Jake—well," she adopted a singsongy voice, "color me happy."

C.D. passed her a brown envelope. "After we put the boxes in the car, Sam gave me this. He said to give it to you after we left."

She took the envelope and the joy she'd been feeling dissipated.

"What is it?"

"Divorce papers." She opened it up to verify that. "Yep."

"The sorry son of a bitch had me hand you his divorce papers?" Muttering, C.D. hit the brakes. His tires screeched and lifted a cloud of dust on the soft shoulder. Whipping the car around, he stomped on the gas, heading back the way they'd just come.

Even though Katie was buckled in, her shoulder slammed against the side door. "Where are you going? And why are you driving like an idiot?"

"I'm going to do what I should have done a long time ago."

"What?" she asked as he slammed on the brakes at a stop sign and barely managed to keep from sliding through the intersection.

"Kick his lousy, sorry, selfish ass." C.D. glowered, radiated barely leashed outrage. "I can't believe any one man is that damn cold and unfeeling. To have *me* give you *his* divorce papers."

"You're not kicking his anything, C. D. Quade." Katie tossed the papers down on the seat. "Turn around and let's go home. I'm not in the mood for this."

C.D. pulled into a Winn-Dixie parking lot, stopped the car and took a moment to cage his temper and calm down. When he had, he looked over at her. "Tell me what you need."

She took a sip of water from the bottle in the cup holder. "A burger, a couple margaritas and a new attitude."

"The burger is easy, though I expect anytime now you're going to start to moo."

"Moo." She wrinkled her nose at him. "I'm making up for lost time."

"With a vengeance," he agreed.

"Moo and double moo." She wrinkled her nose again and added a goofy grin.

"Okay. You win." He feigned a frown. "What else was on your list?"

"Margaritas and attitude."

"Well, the bar's closed tonight, but I think I can throw together a couple margaritas. But, Angel, I'm afraid the new attitude is another story. That one is up to you."

"I know that," she said, leaning toward him, then picking up her singsong tone again. "Which is why I want the margaritas."

"Got it."

"No, you don't, C.D.," she said. "You think I'm going to get drunk to forget my problems."

He looked at her but wisely kept his mouth closed.

"Alcohol's a depressant. I'm not drinking to get depressed or to forget."

"Okay."

"I'm not letting Sam wreck my night. We're going to celebrate my success with Jake, and I am going to be in a good mood."

"And that's final," C.D. said with passion.

"Exactly." She smiled. "I choose."

CHAPTER EIGHT

TOP FLIGHT LOOKED LIKE many of the bars Katie and C.D.
had been in on trips to various bases around the world.

The walls were decorated with emblem and unit
patches from the military members who hung out there.
The requisite dartboard and pool table were in place, as
was a small dance floor that likely saw dancers only on
the rare occasion. People came here to talk about work,
about flying and missions and planes.

The bar itself intrigued Katie. It wasn't just the stan-
dard wooden bar. It was massive, hand-carved from oak
and embellished with eagles and elaborate leaves, and it
stretched from one end of the place to the other. Behind
it, the wall was divided into mirrored sections and separated by large wooden columns. It was a masterpiece,
and its cost probably rivaled that of the building.

She smoothed her hand across the bar top. "This is
beautiful, C.D."

"Thanks." He smiled. "You're sort of responsible for
it."

"What?" She set her purse on a bar stool, turned and
looked back at him.

"Remember when we were stationed at Scott," he
said, referencing the Air Force base near Belleville, Illi-
nois, "and we went to that financial seminar?"

She did, but she still wasn't making the connection between that seminar and this bar. "Yeah?"

"We took out insurance policies on each other."

"Oh, hell." She had forgotten about that. Unable to stop herself, she sighed. "So now you're going to have to pay that back, too."

"No. I put that money in a long-term college fund for Molly and Jake. But it's still there."

She was touched. Deeply. "You started a college fund for my kids?"

"Um, not exactly," he hedged.

"Get exact, C.D., so I know exactly how to react. And be accurate."

He sighed. "Accurately, I've had the fund going for them for a long time. Specifically, I put the insurance money in the existing fund. I didn't start a new one."

"I didn't know that."

"I know, Katie," he said in a flat tone. "I never told you."

"Why?"

"Because you'd have gotten all sappy on me, and Sam might have taken it the wrong way." C.D. sent her a telling look. "I know he put you on the spot about me more than once. I didn't want to give him any fuel."

She'd never told C.D. about that, but it was true. "Okay, color me sappy," she said with far more nonchalance than she felt, "and tell me why you set up a fund for them at all."

He shoved a hand through his hair. "Because I'm it. There aren't any other relatives, and there's no one to come after me. Your kids are as close to having my own as I'll ever get."

Jake had known C.D. Molly had known him, too. "You've gone to Jake's swim meets, and Molly's—"

"Piano recitals and ball games and dance recitals and to open house at their schools—all of which pissed off Sam, but so what? He was always pissed off at me for just existing."

"He was pissed off at you because I adored you," Katie corrected. "Why did you do all that, C.D.?"

"Because I love them," he said simply. "I was there when they were born, went through every new tooth, first step, first word, potty training—you name it and I was there."

"And?" She pushed, because they both needed to know exactly why he'd done those things. Their relationship was different now than it had been before, too, and they both needed to get a grip on the change.

His eyes filled and he blinked hard. "Because they were my last connection to you."

Like her kids to her parents. She'd always known their connection was important to him, but she hadn't realized how important until now. Until coming back and seeing his reaction and feeling the full weight of how much he cared. Her chest went tight, and her heart filled. "In case I've forgotten to mention it lately, C.D., I really do adore you." She swallowed hard. "I am…so lucky to have you in my life."

Tenderness filled his eyes. "Me, too, Angel." He hesitated, then spoke in earnest, as if he wasn't quite sure what he should say and what should be left unspoken. "I knew it before, but after I'd lost you…" The weight of that loss to him grew clear to her. "Well, now I really know." He walked around the bar, started pouring tequila, needing a break from the emotional intensity charging the air between them.

Katie took the hint. "So how can Barbie return that

investment and it still be there? You're getting fuzzy on money again, hotshot."

"Samantha," he said, calling Barbie by her real name, "invested the fund money and added the insurance money to it. She's invested well. When they told me you'd been rescued, I had her pay back the insurance company from the fund, and left the rest invested."

"Oh, I see now," Katie said. "Actually, I only partly see now. The college funds part is clear, but you digressed from my responsibility for Top Flight."

"Sorry." He grinned, not sorry at all. "I wanted to do something special to keep you with me all the time. Barbie suggested ditching the old bar and putting in a new one in your honor." He pointed to the center of the oak bar, near the cash register. "There's a plaque and everything."

Katie moved over to read it. "In loving memory of Katie Cole Slater. She walks forever in my soul."

Her heart beat hard and fast and filled—overflowed—with tenderness. "It's beautiful." She looked to him. "That's…an amazing tribute, C.D."

"It's a Cherokee term," he confessed, stepping behind the bar and mixing the margaritas. "The Lakotas—and maybe other tribes—use it, too. I heard it once and thought it was beautiful…. Special." He smiled. "Like you."

He thought it was the most accurate expression of love he'd ever heard—but being a man, of course, he couldn't just say that.

"It really is beautiful and special," she agreed, then asked, "So that's how I am responsible for this work of art. Lovely."

"You're responsible for other things, too."

"Really?"

He nodded. "I told you, you advised me to listen to Samantha. Hell, you know how I am with money, Angel."

"A walking disaster."

"Exactly," he agreed, rubbing the rims of glasses with a wedge of lime. "If you hadn't told me to listen to her, I wouldn't have done it, and—"

"Because you did, I'm responsible for all kinds of other things like…"

"The cottages, for one, and other stuff here and there." He ground the glass rims in salt.

Katie smiled. "You're giving me a lot of credit."

"That's okay. I give you hell, too, so it evens out." C.D. blended the slushy drinks, then poured them into the glasses. "Because of that tribute I also lost Barbie— as the woman in my life, I mean. She still handles my investments, of course."

"Why did you lose her over the tribute?" Katie didn't get it. Barbie, aka Samantha, had known them both.

C.D. came around the bar and passed Katie a chilled glass. "She said no woman could compete with that."

She walks forever in my soul. "It does sound pretty daunting. Didn't you explain that between us it's different?"

He sipped from his glass. "Her bottom line was that if a woman's in a man's soul, she's in his soul. He has no heart left to lose to anyone else." He set his glass on the bar and looked at Katie. "She had a point."

"Did she?" Not sure what to make of that, Katie denied a little flutter of pleasure in her own heart, slid onto the bar stool and began to drink. The tangy salt felt great going down her throat.

He nodded, tapped the stem of his glass with his thumb. "I've always compared other women to you,

Katie. Barbie knew it. She said that when you were alive, any woman measuring up was difficult. But after you were immortalized in death, no other woman could ever rise high enough to meet the mark."

Nearly breathless, Katie set her glass down. "You know, C.D., when I walked in here, I intended to do some serious drinking and have myself a hell of a pity party."

"I know."

"But I have to tell you, I'm not feeling so pitiful at the moment." Actually, she was feeling pretty damn special.

"Good. Then you must be doing something right."

"It's not me," she admitted, studying his face, the line of his jaw, the curl of hair against the collar of his shirt. "I think I'm seeing myself through your eyes."

The tenderness in his eyes turned smoky and warm. "Then a pity party is way out of line."

"I know." She frowned, feeling a little confusion. "But divorce, kids with Sam—I should be wallowing in one, shouldn't I?"

"I don't know," C.D. said, then sipped from his glass. "Should you?"

"I think I should." While she decided, she took another drink. "I think I must be really screwed up because I'm not."

He shifted on the stool beside her. "Do you want to have your debate to music?"

She wanted to, wanted to be held by him, but he had to know as well as Sam all she'd been through in the tribal prison. How did he feel about that? "I, um, haven't danced in a long time, C.D. Since before the crash."

He searched her face. "What are you telling me, Angel?" he asked. "That you don't want to dance, or that you want to but you're afraid to because…?"

"Things happened there." She lowered her gaze to his chest. "I, um… I…" Her breathing didn't want to work. Suddenly, it was if as her lungs had deflated and couldn't expand.

"I don't remember a lot of it. I'm not sure why. But I know I can't let anyone know. They'll shove doctors in my face for the duration and it could cause so many complications with the children."

C.D. cupped her face in his hands. "Katie, you're safe with me. You don't have anything to fear from me, ever. Not about anything. I don't give a damn what it is." He stroked her cheek, her chin. "Do you understand what I'm saying?"

About dancing, about the growing physical awareness between them that had them both as tense as teens and thinking about making love, about anything that happened in the tribal prison. "You can do that, C.D.? You can accept me—not as a friend you adore but as a woman—unconditionally?"

"I always have." He gave her that slow, sexy smile that kept women up nights and waiting by the phone.

Her heart beat hard and fast. "Really?"

He nodded, his expression tense, as if nervously awaiting her reaction. "Really."

She put her hands over his on her face. "You know, as I recall, you were a pretty good dancer."

"As I recall, you danced about as well as you walk in heels."

She rolled her eyes. "I'll give you that one, but we always did pretty good together."

"A perfect team." He slid her a suggestive grin. "So do you want to dance?"

To dance and more. She walked in his soul. Did that

mean he loved her? What she felt for him she felt in the marrow of her bones, in every chamber of her heart. It was complex. The same as before, only different. Bigger, deeper, more. Very complex. Too complex for tonight. "Why not?"

He picked out some tunes on the jukebox, then returned to his seat and hung his cane on the ledge of the bar beside him.

Nervous, she switched topics. "For the record, I definitely think I'm entitled to a pity party." She took a drink from her glass, letting the shift in her feelings settle.

"Whatever you want, sweetheart." He lifted his own glass.

"I did my duty to country and family, and now I'm forty and I have everything I never wanted, C.D. Sam's divorcing me because he loves his wife in ways he never loved me."

"I wouldn't use Sam as a measuring stick on anything, Angel," C.D. said. "Just my personal opinion, of course."

"Why not?"

"Because he's a selfish moron. I've never figured out why you loved him. And now I can't figure out why you want him to love you."

She frowned up at him. "Because he said he would, damn it."

"He did," C.D. countered. "Then you died, and he fell in love with someone else."

"I did *not* die."

"You were dead to Sam."

"Whatever!" She huffed. "Don't you get it?" she asked, guessing she wanted a little bit of that pity party, after all. "He loves her more than me. My kids don't look at me or think of me as their mother. I have no career anymore. I wanted to be a pilot my whole life. Now that's gone, too. I have *no* life, C.D."

"Not exactly." He grunted. "Jake called you 'Mom.' He and Molly want to come over to play in the garden. You can choose any career you want from this minute on, and you're already building a new life."

"But, damn it, C.D. The point is I wasn't through with the old life yet." She downed a healthy swig of margarita. "Everything's pretty much shot, and I wasn't done. Nobody asked me if I was done. I didn't get to choose. I just get to live with everyone else's choices." Her head was a little fuzzy. How could that be on half a drink? Well, half a drink and two glasses of wine? "You know…" She settled a hand on her hip. "I think I'm pretty ticked off about that."

"I can see that you are."

"Well, wouldn't you be? I gave everything, C.D." She turned to him, knee to knee on the bar stools. "I have nothing left, and I can't even hate the woman my husband loves more than me, because I actually like her."

"And considering she's living your life, and she's not yet close to forty, that might just suck most of all, right?"

"Oh, yeah," she said with gusto and conviction. "Now you're getting it."

C.D. chuckled, pulled Katie off the stool and into his arms, between his thighs. "You said you've got nothing," he whispered, his voice a husky rasp. "That's not true, Angel." He looked deeply into her eyes. "You've got me."

"Because you feel guilty," she countered. "No matter what you say, I know you feel guilty, honey. You can't hide it from me. I feel it in you."

"I *am* guilty, but that's just a fact. It's not the only

reason you've got me." He stood up and led her to the dance floor. Willie Nelson was singing "You Were Always on My Mind."

"Doesn't it hurt your knee to dance?"

"Not when, it's slow and easy like this."

She moved with him as one, their bodies fitting together, their steps in tandem. "I'd forgotten how well we danced together." She smiled against his shoulder.

"I hadn't." He pulled her closer, twirled.

"You thought about me a lot, didn't you, C.D.?" She looked up but only saw the underside of his chin.

"Every day of my life, Angel." He looked down at her. "You walk in my soul, remember?"

Love burned intensely in his eyes. Love for her. It spoke to her mind and heart and soul, and she lifted her mouth to his.

They kissed, but this was not a kiss between partners or friends; it carried too much fire and passion, too much desire too long denied, and even more gratitude and love. So much love.

C.D. pulled back. "Katie, are you sure you want this for us?"

"Do you?" She rested her hands on his chest. "You and the kids are all I've got, C.D. I want you. I won't lie and say I don't. I do. But I know you go through women like water and I can't lose what we have." She let him see her vulnerability. Her fear. "I can't lose you, C.D."

"You won't," he promised. "Not ever. Not for any reason."

She looked into his eyes, saw truth and let out a little mewl. "Promise me. Swear it."

"I swear," he said, then kissed her again. Longer, deeper, hotter, letting her feel the fury of his passion.

One minute they were dancing, the next they were prone on the floor making love, and all the feelings of isolation and abandonment, of betrayal and loss and devastation, faded and fell to a stronger, more potent and powerful certainty that she was cherished and desired, beloved and loved.

And somewhere during the night, long after they'd left the bar and crawled into her bed in the cottage and she'd snuggled deep in his arms, she realized and accepted the truth. While she and C.D. never before had made love, and neither of them had ever violated her marriage vows, they had always lived love, sharing a special bond that was undeniably intimate. They had shared a life where he had welcomed her to walk in his soul, and she had welcomed him to walk in her heart.

And only now was Katie Cole Slater grasping the true meaning of what their hearts and souls had known all along.

They belonged together.

SOMETIME BEFORE DAWN, Katie turned over and looked at C.D. The bathroom light was on and the door was cracked open, letting enough light into her bedroom to see the outline of his face, but little more. His eyes were closed, but she couldn't tell from his breathing if he was asleep, awake or languishing in that netherworld somewhere in between. She touched his shoulder gently, and he turned to look at her. "I think I owe you an apology, C.D."

"For what?" he whispered back.

"I imposed on our friendship a little too much." Inside, she was shaking, afraid of losing that special bond between them in spite of assurances he'd made under the influence of margaritas and raging hormones. "I didn't mean to make you feel you had to do…this."

His response was immediate and blunt. "I didn't."

"I know you just felt sorry for me because of the way things have gone for me since I got back, and then Sam giving me the divorce papers through you…well, that just added to it." The truth in that hurt, and made her sick. She'd never in her life been to bed with a man because he'd pitied her. That it had now happened with C.D. made her want to throw up.

"Is that what you think this is about, Katie?" He shoved up on one elbow to look into her face. "You think I made love with you because I felt sorry for you?"

He was angry. He shook with it, and that confused her. "I understand it, C.D., and I'm apologizing for putting you in that position. Don't come unglued on me for it."

"I'm not coming unglued."

"You're damn close," she insisted. "Don't you think I recognize when you're angry? Honey, I know you better than—"

"No, you don't." He cut her off, pushed her shoulder so that she lay flat on her back. "If you think I'm in bed with you out of pity, you don't know me at all."

The truth was written all over him. She touched his face, smoothed the anger from it with trembling fingertips, and reassessed, doing what she should have done the first time. "Why are you here with me, C.D.?"

"Why are you here with me?" he challenged.

She moved the covers, rolled to face him, then nudged his knees open and sandwiched hers between them. "That's a fair question."

"Do you have a fair answer?"

She thought for a long minute. "When I was a

young girl, I created a list of what would make mine a perfect life."

"I remember all about your list, Angel."

She had first told him about it in a drunken stupor one night in a bar after she and Sam had argued on the phone about her return home from a mission being delayed for three more days. She didn't remember what mission, or even where they were at the time. Italy, maybe. Or Guam. It didn't matter. She and C.D. faced whatever came whenever and wherever it came. They had stood together from their very first meeting, shortly after she'd married Sam. "There wasn't anything elaborate on it. It was a simple life."

"Home, husband, kids, front porch," he recalled. "Wait. There was something about the husband…." He let out a groan.

He remembered it; Katie could feel the tension winding up in him. "That's right," she said. "A husband who wouldn't leave me for a younger woman—"

"When you turned forty, which you just did." C.D. hugged her to him. "Oh, hell. I'm sorry, honey."

That's exactly what Sam had done to her. "Me, too." Her grandmother had been forty when her grandfather had walked out to live with his twenty-two-year-old assistant. Her grandmother had been devastated and never had recovered. "I got my perfect life," Katie told C.D. "But at forty, poof! It's gone." Just like her grandmother's.

"That was your old perfect life, for the woman you used to be, and it wasn't so perfect, Katie, as you've already discovered."

"But I didn't know that then."

"You're digressing," he said, tossing her words back

at her. "What I want to know is who are you now. And why are you in bed with me?"

Nothing less than the truth would be honest, and she couldn't be anything but honest with C.D. "Because you love me." She said it simply, but no words ever spoken carried more feeling. "I see it in your eyes, C.D. I felt it in your tribute on the plaque. In the way you look out for me and cherish me and care for me. You always want the best for me, even if it isn't best for you. You say *and* live it. You love me."

"I've always loved you, Angel." His eyes shone, they were so earnest. "But I've never before been to bed with you."

"I know." She stroked his chest, his neck and arm. "That's why I apologized."

"That's why you shouldn't apologize," he said. "I can't decide if you're refusing to see the truth because, despite what you say, you can't forgive me for costing you six years of your life and your marriage, or if it's just too soon."

"See the truth?" Perplexed, she frowned. "What truth?"

"That I love you, Katie," he said sharply. "That's the only reason I'm in bed with you. Because I love you."

Her heart raced and her blood thrummed through her veins, pounded in her temples. She didn't dare believe it. Didn't dare dream of it. The letdown would be… She'd never recover. Never. That could *not* be endured nor conquered.

He stared at her a long time, either unsure of what to say or unwilling to say it. Finally, he answered with a question. "You asked me why I never married, remember?"

She nodded.

"I told you I always measure other women against you, remember?"

Her heart raced faster still, and she nodded again.

"What would you say if I told you that I didn't just fall in love with you, I really have always been in love with you?"

"I'd say for a man in love, you sure worked your way through a wide swath of women."

"What if that was because you were married, and I was looking for a woman who made me feel everything I feel for you and I couldn't find one?"

He wasn't kidding. He wasn't committing—he was sticking to hypotheticals—but he definitely wasn't kidding. "I—I don't know what I'd say," she answered honestly. "I'd have a hard time wrapping my mind around that."

"Then let's forget it for now," he whispered against her lips, and slid atop her, "and communicate in a way we clearly understand."

Reeling, Katie welcomed him and lost herself in sensation.

BY NOON, Katie and C.D. had made love four times, showered and dressed, eaten and bought Katie a new loaded silver Highlander with gray leather interior and a sound system powerful enough to blast her out of her seat.

By one o'clock, there was a yellow magnetic ribbon above the rear bumper that read Support Our Troops, and Katie and C.D. were on I-10 midway between Pensacola and Mobile.

It was just after four when they pulled into the wooded driveway that led to the secluded twenty acres north of Lake Pontchartrain outside New Orleans that her parents called home. By the time she stopped the car in front of the farmhouse and opened the door, her dad was down the porch steps, heading to her with his arms open and his jaw trembling.

"Katie girl." Emotion made ripples in his voice that washed over her. He closed his arms around her and sobbed. "My baby. My baby." He clutched her to him and she felt his shoulders shudder, the sobs wrack his frail arthritic body.

"Hi, Daddy." Hot tears slid down her face and soaked his blue work shirt. She hugged him hard, letting him know she was strong and well and really here.

C.D. got their bags from the car and went on to the house, not wanting to intrude on this moment. It belonged to Katie and her dad, and that was as it should be.

When he walked inside, Grace, Katie's mom, was sitting on the sofa. C.D. set their bags down next to the staircase, walked over and kissed her. "Hi, Grace. It's good to see you again."

She didn't respond, and hope fell in C.D. It was a bad day. Katie just couldn't seem to catch a break with both hands. He sat down by the door, willing Grace to come around, so at least this reunion would be a happy one for Katie.

Minutes later, she and her dad walked in, laughing. Grace didn't acknowledge hearing them.

Frank walked over to her. "Grace, Katie's home."

Katie moved closer, dropped to her knees on the carpet at her mother's feet, "Hi, Mom." She looked so much older. Frail and thin-skinned, and her eyes were not glistening with recognition. "Mom, it's me, Katie."

"Of course it is, dear." She patted Katie's arm,

looked at C.D. and frowned. "I thought you divorced Wonder Dick."

C.D. smiled.

"I did." Katie flushed. "That's C.D., Mom."

"C.D." She winked. "I always liked you best. You love my Katie. Wonder Dick and Sam never did."

Frank cleared his throat. "Mmm, Katie, why don't you get you and C.D. something cold to drink. That's a long ride." He patted Grace's hand and whispered something to her—no doubt asking her to be quiet or at least a little more discreet.

"I have always liked him best and I won't lie about it, Frank. She's my daughter. I get an opinion."

C.D. walked back over, bent down and planted a tender kiss on Grace's cheek. "You're right, Grace. I've always loved her."

She beamed. "See, Frank." She swatted at his arm the same way Katie did C.D.'s. "You think I'm not all here—" she tapped her head "—but truth is truth, and I know what I know."

"Of course, Grace."

Looking over at C.D., she whispered, "He never believed I was psychic."

"Katie told me." Grace had, too, when he'd visited to check on her and Frank. Then her mind had started going, but she never failed to mention Wonder Dick, which he was sure mortified Katie, or her dislike for Sam, or that she liked C.D. best because he loved Katie. Why those things stood out in her mind when so much else failed, C.D. had no idea. Neither did Frank or Grace's doctors, and they were the best. C.D. had seen to that.

Katie returned with lemonade for everyone, and soon they were lost in conversation, and only twice did Katie have to tell her beloved father that she didn't want to talk about her time in captivity.

He still asked questions in roundabout ways, but her mother, being as protective as she always had been, caught him every time and intervened with a sharp, "She doesn't want to discuss it, Frank," which put to rest Katie's greatest fear that her mother wouldn't recognize her.

And every time her mom reprimanded him, her dad would groan and say, "I know, Grace."

To which she'd reply, "Well, if you know, then why are you nagging the girl? Stop nagging the girl, Frank."

And every time, C.D. and Katie would exchange a private glance, as couples do, and try their best not to laugh out loud.

It was a very good day.

CHAPTER NINE

IT WAS A VERY BAD NIGHT.

The sand had blown nonstop for three days, choking man and beast and whipping into Katie's cell through every crevice, stinging her skin, keeping her constantly on her toes, trying to protect her eyes. Her eyelids were bruised, her face tender, and the backs of her knees hurt so much she could barely bend them. There was no escape from it.

Sand got into her food, her water, her bed. Though covered with her tattered flight suit, her arms and legs, neck and throat, were raw from the constant pelting, and her nose had been bleeding for the last two days from filtering out the coarse grains inhaled in breathing.

All up and down the row of cells, men complained and cursed, facing her same challenges. Tempers were short, the guards were mean and Lieutenant Ustead was meanest of them all.

Darkness fell, whether due to the storm or because it was night, she had no way of knowing. Three guards appeared at her cell and dragged Katie to the interrogation room.

"Sit down," Ustead ordered, then for the next two hours taunted her with the deaths of her family.

But he'd done that before, and while she cringed and cried inside, she showed no emotion outwardly.

Angered more because she didn't, he beat her and literally threw her to the guards, screaming at them, "Take her back to her cell! Get her out of my sight—now!"

His punching her in the face drove the flesh of her inner cheek into her teeth, and it split and bled. Before she stopped spitting blood, the guards returned for her, pushed and shoved her back to the interrogation room.

Ustead slammed her against the wall, then stripped her down to her skin and stood her in front of a window where the winddriven sand drove into her back like nails. He asked her questions, demanded she not move or he'd lash her to within an inch of her life, and she feared the pain of the sand firing into her back would drive her to her knees. She locked them, retreated in her mind to a place he couldn't reach, and by some miracle stayed upright.

His anger deepened, as if her lack of response was a personal slight against him in front of his men, and he beat her again, then ordered them to take her back to her cell.

Oh, God. The humiliation of being shoved naked down that row of cells. Jeering. Ribald, lurid comments from the men locked in them, hanging on the bars, watching her. Like her, those men were tortured, but unlike her, they saw humor in her degradation. The guards tossed her into her cell, then threw her flight suit in after her. It fell to the floor in a crumpled heap, and Katie's gaze lit on the patch of the American flag sewn to its sleeve. *Freedom.* And she prayed, "Please, God. Please, help me."

Her back, shoulders to heels, stung like fire—so strong it had her stomach threatening to revolt—and it took all she had to pull herself to her feet. She bent to pick up her flight suit. A wave of pain crashed through her, so intense she broke into a sweat and saw spots before her eyes.

It took forever to pull on the suit. Rough and abrasive, sand-ridden, it scratched her raw skin and brought tears to her eyes. By the time she had it on, she shook so hard she could barely zip it. When she had, she huddled against the wall in the corner to keep the sand from hurting her any more. She closed her eyes and prayed for mercy, and then she prayed for death.

But neither came.

The guards did, and they took her back to the interrogation room for the third time that endless night.

And this time, Ustead stripped her while his men watched, and then he raped her.

Inside she screamed and rebelled and then she retreated, and somehow she was no longer a victim inside her body, but a distant observer standing outside herself, across the room. He was beyond furious, he was a raging madman, trying everything humanly possible to hurt her, to make her scream and cry and resist him so that he could degrade her more, violate her more. But observing from a distance, she felt nothing. In her, he touched nothing. She sensed nothing.

Mercy had come, after all....

Asleep in the bed she'd slept in as a child and knowing exactly where she was—home in New Orleans—she dreamed the dream and heard his every curse, felt his every blow. She suffered every push of his body into hers, every rip and tear of her flesh, every slap and punch and abuse. And she wept. And she screamed....

"Katie." C.D. touched her shoulder.

She came up out of the bed swinging, landed a bitch of a right hook to his jaw that had his head spinning.

"Don't touch me. Don't you dare touch me!"

"Okay. Okay." He held up his hands. "I'm not touching you. I won't touch you." C.D. paused, giving her a second for his words to sink in. "It's me, Katie. It's C.D. You were dreaming." Her eyes were still wild. "You're safe now. You were dreaming."

Her heart knocking against her ribs, Katie dropped her fist and held her hand to her chest. The last haze of sleep left her, though the vivid images in the dream remained. She took in several cleansing breaths, willed the images to fade, and finally saw past them to a worried C.D., standing beside her bed.

"What are you doing in here?" Respecting her parents' sensibilities, he was sleeping in the bedroom next door.

"You were screaming. I came to see if you were okay."

"I'm not okay, C.D." She shuddered at the memory of Ustead's violation. "I don't know if I'll ever be okay again." She crawled out of bed. "I need a shower."

C.D. stepped back. "It wasn't your fault, Katie."

She stopped dead in her tracks, turned and stared at him.

"What they did to you." He blinked hard and fast and held her gaze. "None of it was your fault."

Katie took a deep shuddering breath. "I know that."

"Then why do you need a shower?"

Her throat thickened. "Because I feel him on me and I want him off." She shoved her hair back from her face. "I can still smell him, and it makes me sick."

"I'm so sorry." C.D. stepped toward her. "If I could change—"

It wasn't just a dream. It was real. It had happened… She shuddered. "You can't. No one can. It just has to be endured." She had wrestled with this issue a thousand times and she'd sworn to herself that if the dream proved true, she would not let the people and events in it ruin any more of her life. She was going to be disgustingly healthy or die trying. Now all doubt was gone. She knew she had been raped. That was a fact and it wouldn't change. But the rape had been an act of violence, and it'd had nothing to do with sex and certainly nothing to do with lovemaking. In her eyes, that's the way it was, and that was the end of it.

But how was it for C.D.?

She worried at her lower lip, but couldn't summon the courage to look at him, so she kept her back to him. "I need to know something."

"Anything."

"Does this change the way you feel about me? About your…being with me?"

"Yes," he answered honestly.

His response hung heavily in the air between them. Katie couldn't move. Couldn't make herself not feel the fear of losing him.

"Of course it changes my feelings, Angel. Now I know being with me has to be harder for you, and yet you still want me." He swallowed hard. "I didn't believe it possible, but now, being with you is even more special."

Tears leaked down her cheeks, and she let out a breath she hadn't realized she'd been holding. She turned and rushed to him, hugged him tightly. "Don't change, C.D." She sniffed. "Everything else has changed and that's okay. I can deal with it. Just as long as you don't change, I can deal with anything."

"I won't." He kissed her hair and held her tight. "I swear on my wings, I won't."

BY ONE O'CLOCK on Sunday afternoon, Katie and C.D. had returned to Florida. They'd teased and flirted so intensely during the last thirty miles, C.D. had threatened that if she didn't tone it down a notch, he was going to just pull off the road and get down to business.

She laughed and teased and toned it down—just enough to make it back to the cottage and into bed.

When they were satiated, she went to the kitchen to refill her glass of water and noticed the red light blinking on the answering machine. On her way to the fridge for ice, she tapped it.

"Hi," a girl said, then hesitated, seemingly unsure what to call Katie. "Um, this is Molly. Jake and I would like to come plant in the garden. Call us if that's okay."

A second message played. "Mom, it's Jake. I guess you're not back from Gran and Grandpa's yet, but when you get back, me and Molly are waiting to come over. Call us, okay?"

Eager. They were eager. Excited, Katie called out to C.D., "Hey, boy toy, get your clothes on and get out here."

"Boy toy?" He walked up behind her, naked. "Now that's the first time I've ever had a woman call me a boy toy *or* tell me to put my clothes on. Usually they're wanting me to get them—"

She elbowed him in the ribs. "Then you're long overdue, hotshot." His breath swooshed out, and she laughed. "The kids want to come over, C.D. They *want* to be with me."

A slow smile curled his lips and lit up his eyes. "I have to say, that's worth getting dressed for."

She reached down and cupped him. "That's the only reason I'm willing to sacrifice the scenery."

"Mmm, that's good to know." He dropped a line of kisses along her neck and throat. "Knowledge is power."

"It is, and I know just how to drive you insane." She smiled and rubbed noses. "Better remember that, too."

AN HOUR LATER, armed with iris bulbs, rosebushes, marigolds and peonies, Katie, C.D., Molly and Jake were all down on their knees planting the garden. Like Katie, Molly loved digging in the dirt. Jake gave it a shot, but didn't really care for it. He'd brought his guitar and just wanted to hang out, so he'd found a spot in the shade under a massive old oak and strummed the instrument, playing song after song for them.

He had a great voice, silky smooth and easy on the ear. And watching him, Katie could see that he played from the soul. Neither her side of the family nor Sam's was known for musical talent. Apparently both sides had saved up their share and given it all to Jake.

"That's beautiful, Jake." She swept back her hair and smiled at him.

"Thanks." He tilted his head as she did, and a flash of her own familiar expression reflected in his.

"Last bulb," Molly called out. She moved four inches over and dug four inches down, then seated the bulb and carefully covered it with dirt. "Yes!"

Katie smiled. Molly was so precise, Katie expected any second she'd ask for a ruler to get the bulbs planted at exactly equal distances apart. Instead, she'd used her hand to measure. Katie had seen Sam do that same thing a million times.

It was comforting to see bits of Sam and her in the kids. To know that even during the time she'd been buried, those parts of her had not been forgotten or left behind.

C.D. grilled some burgers to go with the potato salad and ears of sweet corn they'd picked up at the store when getting the kids, and they all settled down on a blanket in the backyard for a picnic supper.

Molly reached for a plate and realized she hadn't washed her hands. "Oh, gee. I'll be back."

Molly, Jake and C.D. were totally at ease with one another, and now Katie was at ease with them, as well. And once again she silently thanked Blair for having her and C.D. over to dinner. That's when she and Jake had turned the corner in their relationship, and Katie suspected that Jake had opened the door for Molly, though she and Katie still had a long way to go.

C.D. buttered another ear of corn. "Molly's taking a long time, Katie. Want me to run see—"

"I'll check on her." Katie stood up and went into the cottage through the back door.

Molly was sitting on the floor in the living room. Spread across her lap was the tattered flight suit Katie had worn at the prison camp. "Molly, what are you doing, honey?"

Serious, sober and unsmiling, she looked up at her mother. "Did you wear this all the time you were gone?"

Katie didn't know what to say. She refused to lie to Molly, but there was something frightening in her tone, in her stillness. Katie didn't want to upset her, or make things harder for her. She didn't know what was best to do. How frank should she be with the kids about these things? How much was too much, especially for a sensitive child? Yet if Jake was right, and Molly was as psychically attuned as Katie's mother, then Molly already knew the truth and this was a test to see if Katie would be honest with her.

"Did they make you wear it all the time?" Molly asked again. "Even when it was really hot?"

"It was really hot most of the time," Katie said softly. "That's why I get cold so easily here." She sat down on the floor beside her daughter. "And I didn't wear that all the time, but some of the time, yes."

Molly stared into her eyes. "You wore it most of the time."

"Yes, most of the time," she confessed. "Why do you have it?" It'd been in the closet inside a box.

"I need to know if what I saw at the hospital—when Jake and I first came to see you—if that was true," she explained. "That's why I hid from you. You were scared and it made me scared."

"Is that what you saw?" Katie asked, struggling to understand.

Molly nodded and slid her fingers through the frayed tears in the back. Slashes where Ustead's whip had sliced through the fabric and into Katie's back. She studied them a long time, then frowned at her. "Jake said they hurt you there."

Katie's vision blurred, and she blinked hard. "But it's over now, Molly. Let's don't talk about it. Let's have a good day."

The girl didn't move, just fingered the fabric. "You don't have to lie to me just because I'm a kid."

"Honey, I haven't lied to you, and I won't. Ever." Katie let her hear the truth in her voice, and took the flight suit from her, then shoved it under the sofa, out of sight. "I just don't want any of that to touch you. I don't want you to think about those things."

"Why?" Molly stared at her. "You think about them, don't you?"

"That's different. I went through it."

"Daddy says they tortured you. Jake said so, too." Molly looked Katie right in the eye. "Is that true?"

Tenacious. But these weren't idle questions, and Molly's expression proved it. Katie's answer would set the tone of their relationship. *Be honest. Just be honest. Not graphic, but honest.* "Yes."

"How did you stand it?"

"It was hard, but I didn't have any choice, Molly. I had to stand it." Katie pulled in a shuddery breath. "Sometimes, I'd just try to get through an hour because a day seemed too long. Sometimes I'd pray to just get through a minute because an hour seemed too long. I guess I got through it a little bit at a time, honey."

"What did you do when a minute seemed too long?"

So insightful, to know that there were many times when a minute had seemed like a dozen lifetimes. Katie let her daughter see the ravages of pain that scarred her soul. "I'd ask for a second. Just for one second."

"I knew they'd tortured you," she said. "The blood on the back is yours. I knew it when I touched it."

Katie's stomach sank and she frowned. "Molly, are you like Grandma Grace?" Her mother had been amazingly psychic. Eerily psychic and consistently tested off the scale, trying to prove to her father her gift was real and verified by science. He'd ignored the evidence because it was easier than accepting what he didn't understand.

Molly shrugged. "I know things. I'm not sure how, I just do."

Was that a blessing or a curse for her? For Katie's mom, seeing her daughter in the tribal prison had pushed her beyond endurance and over the edge into dementia. "Does your dad know that?"

"No, but my mom…does." She sighed. "Dad only likes science you can explain."

Boy, did he. He'd always been wary of Katie's mom because of her gift. "Does knowing things frighten you?"

"No." Molly cocked her head. "It's not weird to me. It's just normal." She rubbed her nose with the heel of her hand. "Until Daddy got upset, I thought everybody knew things."

Katie smiled. "I didn't mean that you know things, honey. I meant the things you know. Do those things scare you?"

"No." Her eyes were far older than her years. "Mostly it's just funny or sad." She stood up and started to walk toward the door, then stopped and turned back to Katie, who was still sitting on the floor. "Is it wrong for me to love you and Blair?"

With a lump in her throat, Katie shook her head no and borrowed a phrase from Blair. "Your heart is big enough to love us both."

Molly walked back and looped her arms around Katie's neck, then bent down and kissed her.

A well of tenderness rose from deep inside Katie, and she squeezed her eyes shut, struggling not to sob.

"I wish you'd killed them."

Her daughter wanted peace for her mother and herself, as well as revenge. Katie understood wanting all of those things. "The man who did that to me is dead."

"Is it his blood on the front?" She nodded to the sofa, indicating the hidden flight suit. "Did you kill him?" She eased around to see Katie's face.

"No, I didn't. Another man did." Katie shuddered. "He was good. He gave me food and made the doctor fix my legs. He gave me back my picture of you, Jake and your dad, and he helped me get rescued." Tears slipped down Katie's cheeks.

Anger gleamed in Molly's eyes. "I wish you could've killed the mean man."

Katie had to admit she wished she'd killed him, too. "Dead is dead, sweetheart." *Acceptance. Peace.* She looked at Molly, took a leap of faith and held out her arms.

Molly stepped into them and Katie drew her daughter in and closed the circle, making it complete.

CHAPTER TEN

SEPTEMBER GAVE WAY to October, with more gardening days and pizza nights and games of goofy golf and trips to Big Kahuna's Water Park. While she'd once loved to surf and ride a Boogie board, since her return, Katie couldn't make herself go to the beach. The beach meant sand—though logically she knew the sugar-white substance wasn't really sand, it just resembled it—and sand reminded her of the prison camp.

Needing more time to work through that, she had kept her appointments with Dr. Muldoon, and to his credit he'd probed but not attempted to force her talk about her time in captivity. The nightmares were down to three or four a week, and other than the rape, she couldn't tell if any of them were real memories—not that she'd been so foolish as to mention her not knowing to a soul, not even to C.D. With the divorce from Sam pending, she couldn't risk a mental label interfering with her and her rights with her kids.

C.D. had suggested that maybe by talking through everything that had happened to her, she would stop having the nightmares. But Katie knew that wouldn't work. Merely thinking about any part of what she'd encountered there seemed to open the shutters in her mind and in her emotions, and every time she did, she consistently dreamed the horrific dreams. Real or imagined, when she dreamed, she lived those moments. Talking about them, focusing on them, would only make them worse.

On a rainy day in mid-October, she sat in Dr. Muldoon's tiny waiting room, weighing her options. It wasn't as if she was playing ostrich, burying her head and pretending everything was rosy and nothing bad had happened in the tribal prison. She acknowledged every single bad thing that she remembered happening there, and every good thing, too—such as General Amid positioning her in that market, likely paying that Frenchman so she'd be seen, recognized and rescued. She didn't deny the bad things. She just refused to accept ones that could be imagined as fact until proven, and to let the ones that proved to be real ruin the rest of her life. She couldn't reclaim the last six years, but she didn't have to give the bastards another day, either.

With time, the sharp edges would soften and dull, and the nightmares would fade. She had no illusions of forgetting them. She'd never forget what had happened there. But as when Ustead had raped her and she had watched it happen from a distance, with time, she would remember it all from a distance.

What was wrong with that? How was that not healthy?

When you go to the beach, Katie. When you can separate real from imagined and step onto the sand and not resent and hate, then you'll know the worst is over and you're okay....

An hour later, she officially separated from the Air Force, then stopped back by Dr. Muldoon's office to officially say goodbye to him and Ashley, though she'd see Ashley socially the rest of her life.

With their good wishes, she left and then drove down to the beach. If walking in the sand was what she needed to do for the worst to be over, so she could reclaim her life, then by God that's what she'd do.

She pulled into the parking lot near the pier and shut off the engine. Her breathing was rapid, her heart rate fast. *Just take your keys and go, Katie.*

Her teeth sank into her lower lip. She pulled the key from the ignition, her hand shaking, her palm sweaty.

Just do it, Katie. It's no big deal. Just walk out to the water's edge and call this done. You'll never have to look back to that time again.

Desire to put the past to rest burned strong inside her. She blew out a steadying breath and reached for the door lock, her heart banging against her ribs, her pulse so strong in her head that the roar in her ears deafened her to everything going on outside. "Just do it, Katie. You can do it."

Lifting her hand, she pressed her fingertip against the lock and tried to push, but it didn't move.

She tried again.

Nothing.

She couldn't make herself depress it and unlock the door.

It's too soon. It's just too soon.

Her mouth dust dry, she jammed the key into the ignition and cranked it. The engine roared to life and she hit the gas, whipped out of the parking lot and headed north, away from the sand.

Away from the demons not yet ready to let go of her mind.

BY THE THIRD WEEK of October, Katie felt more settled. Sam had shed some of his fear of losing the kids, and had come around on sharing them. He, too, wanted what was best for them, and with urging from them and Katie—and no doubt from Blair—he began acting like the man Katie had loved when they'd first met. It was odd, she told C.D. She would always love Sam because he was the father of her kids, but it still boggled her mind to know that if all that had happened never had, she might have lived her entire life and never known she hadn't been in love with him. Wasn't that just nearly impossible to believe?

C.D. thought her realizing the truth was a blessing. He still considered Sam a selfish son of a bitch, but he didn't say it aloud anymore. The kids respected their father, and C.D. wanted them to continue to respect him. Unlike C.D.'s dad, who had departed when C.D. was seven, and hadn't been seen or heard from since, Sam showed up. In C.D.'s book, showing up was half of being a hero. Kids needed heroes, and heroes started at home.

Katie and C.D. were together all the time, as were Sam and Blair, though their long-term plans were clearer than Katie and C.D.'s own. As soon as Sam and Katie's divorce was final, Sam and Blair would remarry. Katie had no idea what, if anything, C.D. saw in their future, and she didn't intend to raise the topic for discussion and risk upsetting the status quo.

Status quo with C.D. was richer and more fun and fulfilling than thirteen years of marriage to Sam. If what she and C.D. had now was all they ever had, for Katie, it was more than enough.

Of course, how C.D. felt about that, she had no idea—and she had to work at not letting not knowing trouble her.

"KATIE?" C.D. came in through the back door. "What do you think of having a costume party at the bar on Halloween?"

She dried her hands on a paper towel and tossed it into the trash. "Sounds like fun."

"Good," he said. "We'll do it then." He filled a glass with water from the fridge. "Still no list, eh?" He ran his fingertips down its bare front, looked to the countertop beside it, where a pencil and pad lay waiting.

"Not yet." She lifted her chin. "I'm thinking about it more, though, now that tensions have eased up with Sam and the kids."

C.D. nodded. "That's good." He drank from the glass, set it on the counter next to the sink, and snagged her, then pulled her close. "You know, Angel, the only time you look truly at peace is when you're in bed with me or outside with your hands in the dirt."

Because he was right, she smiled and looped her arms at his shoulders. "That's an odd way of putting gardening, C.D."

"You connect with the dirt, not with the gardening," he explained. "Willow Creek could use a good garden center. There are garden sections in the supercenter stores, but there isn't a dedicated garden center around."

"Your hints are about as subtle as sledgehammers."

He smiled. "Baby, I never said I was subtle." He kissed her quickly twice, then moved away. "I've got to grab a fresh shirt."

"Hot date?"

"Barbie needs to talk to me about some investment stuff."

Katie nodded. "Tell her I said hi."

"I will." He stopped, walked back and kissed Katie again. "You know I love you, right?"

She nodded.

"You know I'm in love with you, right?"

She nodded again, fought to bite a smile from her lips.

"Katie, do you think you'll ever… I mean, could you ever—"

The phone rang.

Katie was perfectly willing to ignore it, but C.D. looked genuinely relieved, and he stepped away to answer it. "Hello."

A pause, then he said, "She's right here. Just a second, Blair."

Katie wondered what was up. She and Blair had just talked late yesterday, coordinating the kids. "Hello."

"Katie." Blair's voice cracked.

The kids. Something was wrong with the kids. "What's the matter?"

"Sam just called."

Katie gripped her stomach. She couldn't breathe.

"They've postponed the divorce hearing for a month."

Oh, thank you, God! "Is that all?"

"All? Damn it, Katie, we won't be able to get married before Thanksgiving."

Katie mustered some sympathy. "I know. But when you get down to it, what's the difference? I mean, you guys are together and—"

"Sam's parents are going to be here Thanksgiving. They don't know—oh, God, Katie, you know how they are."

"They don't know you and Sam are living together with the kids right now."

"No!"

"Well, you could just tell them," Katie suggested. "These are unusual circumstances, and in the eyes of God you are married because you made vows, you know?"

"Sam won't hear of it or I would. What can I do? They're his parents."

Boy, did this sound familiar. That damn perfect image thing. Again. Still. There was a huge plea for help in Blair's voice. A strong one, and after all she'd done for Katie, Katie couldn't ignore it. Especially knowing how anal Sam's parents could be. "Let me think and call you back in a few minutes, okay?"

"But, Katie—"

"I'm not deserting you," she promised, formulating a plan in her mind. "Just give me a few minutes." Possibilities gelled. "Wait. Is your answering machine working?"

"Of course."

"Great." The plan all came together. "I'm going to call you back in about two minutes. Do *not* answer the phone."

"What?"

"Don't answer the phone."

"But how am I going to talk to you if I don't answer?"

"Trust me," Katie said, not at all sure Blair would agree.

"Of course."

Smiling into the receiver, Katie added, "I'll call again in half an hour. Answer then."

"Katie," she said, sounding pensive and reluctant. "I mean no offense, but are you sure you don't need to see Dr. Muldoon at least one more time?"

"You know, coming from anyone else, I'd resent that. I'm letting it slide because it's you. But don't push it."

"Okay. I'm sure what you're doing makes perfect sense—to you."

"That's what matters." Kate hung up the phone.

"Don't tell me," C.D. said. "She wants you to tell Sam's parents they're living together because Sam won't let her do it."

"She didn't ask. But you know they're the biggest snobs on the planet. If they're not told and they figure it out—which they will because the kids won't think twice about it—they'll treat Sam and Blair like garbage for the duration." Katie grabbed her address book, flipped it open to Sam's office number. He'd be in surgery now. It was safe to call. "Sam is ruled by having the perfect image, and is all about what others think—especially his parents. He always has been."

"He's ruled by his parents' opinions of him?"

"Not literally, but don't look so shocked, C.D. Everyone wants their parents to approve of them and think only the best of them. It's a pride thing."

"I'm short on info in that sector."

"That's right. I forgot for a second about your dad. I'm sorry, honey."

"No problem." C.D. buttoned his shirt. "If this is the kind of crap you have to worry about with them, I think I might have been better off without them."

"Sometimes—especially where Sam's parents are concerned—I'd have to agree with you."

C.D. dropped a quick kiss on her lips. "Well, rescue them, honey. I know I wouldn't want to be away from you, so I guess even His Majesty deserves a little slack. Blair surely does."

"You're the heart of compassion itself," she said, watching C.D. use the tip of his cane to open the back door.

"Dr. Slater's office."

"Miranda?" Katie followed a hunch on who'd answered the phone. "It's Katie Slater. Is Sam in?"

"He's in surgery, Mrs. Slater. Is it an emergency?"

"No, not at all. I'm just trying to make some holiday plans. Would you take a message and have him call me about Thanksgiving when he's done?"

"Yes, I will."

"Thanks." Smiling, Katie hung up the phone, then dialed the house.

Blair didn't answer, though through the rings, Katie could almost hear her questioning Katie's sanity. The machine answered, and she left a brief message. "Blair, it's Katie. I was trying to reach Sam to make Thanksgiving plans, but he's in surgery. I guess you're busy, too. Mmm, I really need to nail down my plans to let my folks know what I'm doing, but I don't want the kids to miss seeing the Slaters. Since I can't get either of you, I'll just give them a call and set it up."

She imagined Blair standing beside the answering machine, listening, and her smile stretching ear to ear.

Katie hung up, flipped the old address book to the Slaters, then dialed the number.

Sam's mother answered. "Hello."

"Elizabeth, this is Katie."

"Katie," she said. "How nice to hear from you."

They hadn't spoken once since she'd been rescued and returned. So much for sincerity. "I'm sorry to bother you, but I can't reach Sam or Blair, and I'm trying to finalize my plans for Thanksgiving."

"Yes?" The woman sounded wary.

"Are you and Jason planning to come to Willow Creek?"

"Yes, we are. We'll arrive the Tuesday before Thanksgiving and leave the day after it."

"All right. I thought Blair had mentioned that you

would be, and she so wanted the children available to spend time with you. If you're leaving on Friday, then I'll plan to take them with me to see my parents on the weekend. We'll have Thanksgiving then."

"That's very good of you, Katie," Elizabeth said. "I realize you haven't had Thanksgiving with the children in a long time."

"No, I haven't." Katie paused. "But the truth is, Elizabeth, Sam and Blair and I are working very hard to keep everything as normal as possible for the children."

"That's as it should be."

Excellent. "My return has required a lot of adjustments, and well, frankly, Elizabeth, I could use your help."

"Whatever for, my dear?"

"It's Blair and Sam."

"Katie, Sam is my son, and of course—"

"No, Elizabeth. There's no problem between me and Blair and Sam, it's between Blair and Sam. It's not good for the children."

"What isn't good for them, my dear?" She sounded as worried as only a doting mother and grandmother can be.

"I'm not dead, and that's set aside their marriage. The court is all tied up and can't grant our divorce hearing for another month. Blair and Sam are insisting on living apart until the divorce is granted and they can remarry."

"Well, that is certainly appropriate…."

"It will be devastating for the children, Elizabeth." Katie let out an anxious sigh. "They've had so many upheavals in their lives lately. They need stability. They feel safe at home with Sam and Blair, and now if they insist on this nonsense of living apart until the paperwork can be done to reunite them, well, the children are just going to be that much more upset."

"I see your point."

"Elizabeth, will you please talk some sense into them? They are married in the eyes of God. Man will catch up as soon as he can, but the children need them together now."

Elizabeth didn't hesitate. "I will, Katie. I'll call Blair this very minute and insist she and Sam put the children first."

"Thank you so much. I knew you'd help me with this." And Elizabeth would now lay down the law to her anal husband, Jason. Sam's dad would go along with whatever Elizabeth wanted, to keep from having to listen to her arguments.

"Of course, my dear. The children must always come first. Take care."

"You, too." Katie hung up the phone and smiled. Elizabeth Slater was now a grandmother on a mission to save her grandchildren. No one could be more formidable.

Except a mom.

"Man, if you ever railroad me like that, I'm going to divorce you."

Katie whirled around and saw C.D. standing in the doorway. "I hate to point out the obvious, boy toy, but we're not married."

He walked over, his eyes twinkling. "Then I'll marry you just so I can divorce you."

Teasing, Katie wrinkled her nose at him. "You'd never divorce me, C. D. Quade."

"No?" He hiked an eyebrow.

"No," she said with total conviction. "I walk forever in your soul." She lifted her chin. "How could you ever divorce that?"

He grunted. "Guess I'm stuck with you, then."

"Yes, you are," she insisted. "And you love being stuck."

"I do," he confessed. "You have no idea how much." He dropped a kiss on her lips. "I got something for you."

A long slender box, black with a red bow. "What? Did I miss an occasion or something?"

"No." He leaned back against the counter. "It's time."

She opened the box. A slender gold Cross pen lay nestled on red velvet. She looked up at C.D.

"When you wrote your first perfect-life list, it was with a brand-new pen, right? That was significant." He nodded to the Cross pen. "Well, I figure you can't write your new one because you need…"

"A new pen," she finished for him, then smiled. "Have I mentioned lately that I adore you?"

"Not lately," he lied. "Actually, it's been a long time. I'm feeling neglected."

"Well, come here and let's fix that."

USTEAD HAD THE GUARDS tie her hands to the bars of her cell.

What was he doing? Oh, God, what was he doing?

Katie didn't dare ask. Didn't dare utter so much as a sound. He was beyond anger and, though she had no idea why, it was clear upon whom he intended to vent.

A short guard walked into view. He didn't glance Katie's way, but averted his eyes to the floor. When she saw what he carried in his hand, she knew why.

A whip.

Her knees threatened to buckle. She leaned her forehead against the cool metal bars, closed her eyes and prayed for death.

Behind her, Ustead cursed her, working himself into a lather. He uncoiled the whip, cracked it on the dusty floor.

Katie tried to slip away in her mind, tried to distance herself from what was happening, but the fear was too great. Too strong. Ustead's voice grew more maniacal, more frenetic, and he cracked the whip again, screaming now, pacing behind her as if he were the animal caged.

He let out a cry that she'd heard the night she'd crashed—a tribal war cry—and then she felt the first bite of the whip into her flesh.

"No!" Heart racing, she sat straight up in bed, gasping for air, still feeling the sting of the whip cutting into her back.

C.D. lay sleeping beside her. She doubled forward and buried her head in her hands. *It was just a dream. Just a dream. I'm home now. I'm safe. Ustead is dead. He can't hurt me anymore.*

Her mouth dry, her throat parched, she downed an entire bottle of water—two rested on her nightstand— then she moved to get out of bed.

"You okay?" C.D. asked in a groggy voice that sounded more asleep than awake.

"I'm fine, honey." She patted him on the hip. "Go back to sleep."

He was snoring again before the last word left her mouth. She got out of bed, used the bathroom and washed her hands, then went to the kitchen and poured herself a small glass of ginger ale. It would help settle her stomach; it always did after one of those dreams. When she reached for the ice, she saw the gold pen beside the pad, still in its box.

Her ice plopped into the glass. The ginger ale fizzed

and hissed. She took a sip, then another, and finally reached for the pen.

"Katie Cole Slater," she wrote. "And her perfect life."

"One," she said, as she wrote. "A warm and loving relationship with Molly and Jake."

The ink flowed smoothly, easily, across the pad. She paused to reflect, take another sip. "Two," she wrote, deciding on her next item. "A business of my own that has nothing to do with flying or airplanes."

She stared at that item, not satisfied. "This isn't about what you don't want, Katie. It's about what you do want."

Putting her mind to it, she still couldn't decide exactly what kind of business she wanted, so she left it as it was, dropped down a line and wrote, "Three."

An image of C.D. flitted through her mind, then stayed.

She wanted him, all right, but she couldn't put that on a list he'd see. Regardless of what he said, she knew the man, and at some level, he still felt guilty. Maybe not responsible for what happened to her, but guilty that he'd escaped and she'd lived through hell for six years. He'd never said it that way, of course, but she'd sensed it often, especially on the nights she dreamed. He hated her nightmares as only a man who loves her could.

"A permanent relationship with the man who loves me," she wrote, then added, "before I turn fifty."

That was enough of a cushion. C.D. would see it and not feel pressured. She wanted him, and she wanted him to want her, but for herself, not because of guilt and misguided obligations. Of course, she asked herself, how much more permanent can you get when you're already in a man's soul?

She ripped the page from the pad and quickly added the last item. "Four. To go to the beach and step in the sand."

There was no need to be more explicit. She knew too well what she needed to do there. But so far, it had proved to be something she could not yet endure nor conquer.

CHAPTER ELEVEN

ON SATURDAY, when Katie and C.D. picked the kids up for a movie, Blair met her at the door and grabbed her in a hug. "Thank you." Her exhaled breath shot across Katie's shoulders.

"What for?"

"Elizabeth called and insisted Sam and I continue our 'living arrangements' uninterrupted for the good of the children. She was emphatic." Blair's eyes glittered with excitement. "I don't know what you said to her, Katie, but it worked!"

"She manipulated her," C.D. said. "I heard the whole thing. It was a work of art."

"Stop it, you." Katie laughed and swatted at C.D. "I'm glad it's worked out, Blair."

"Sam's flabbergasted."

"I'm sure he is." Katie looked up the steps. "Are the kids ready?"

"Yes, they are." Sam came out from the den and shook C.D.'s hand, then turned to Katie. "I understand you offered us a little assistance with my parents."

"I have no idea what you're talking about," Katie hedged with a straight face.

Unsure, he rubbed his neck. "You did talk to my mother."

"Yes, I did. I hope you don't mind, but I couldn't get you or Blair, and I wanted to firm up Thanksgiving plans. Didn't Miranda give you my message?"

"Yes, she did." He seemed more uncertain, confused.

"I left a message on your machine here, too," Katie said.

"It's still there," Blair added. "I haven't gotten around to deleting it yet."

"Right." Sam harrumphed. "More accurately, you preserved the chain of evidence."

"Sam!" Blair frowned at him.

Staying quiet nearly choked C.D. Katie shot him a warning look that he'd better not open his mouth.

"You always were good at bringing them around," Sam said to Katie. "Thanks."

She'd never had a lot of choice. He wouldn't even try. Image, not truth, was everything. But primed for a moment of grace, she left that unsaid. "You're welcome."

"Um, Blair and I were thinking that it's really not right for you to forfeit being with the kids on Thanksgiving, Katie."

Blair nodded. "We can switch off, if you like," she said. "You take them for lunch and bring them home for dinner."

"Or reverse that," Sam suggested. "Or you and C.D. could come here and we could all have dinner together. Solidarity for the kids."

Katie looked at C.D.

"The kids would probably like that best," he said. "Not spending the day being shuffled around, I mean."

Blair took Katie's hand. "We want what you want, Katie. We've had a lot of Thanksgivings, but this one is especially important to you because it's the first since you came home. Whatever you want to do, we'll support."

Katie cut a glance at Sam. When he nodded, she looked at C.D. "It's up to you," he said.

He meant it. They all did. Touched, Katie nodded. "Let's, um, be all together here, then."

"I was hoping you'd say that," Blair said with a delighted little squeal. "Shall we run to New Orleans to get your parents and have them here with us, too?"

"My mother's bad days aren't very flattering," she said. Sam could get an earful. "That might be a little awkward."

"Not at all. Believe me, in the past six years, I've heard everything there is to hear," Blair said, guessing Katie's reluctance. "The kids have, too, and we all know what to hear and what to pretend we're deaf to."

Sam grunted. "She always did like C.D. best."

Blair winked. "You already know the only caveat. Sam's parents will be here."

"Ah, yes." Katie hiked her brows. "But this year, they're your problem, not mine."

Sam frowned, but his heart wasn't in it. C.D. laughed, and so did Blair. "I might call on you for reinforcement," Blair said. "Experience has to pay off." She touched Katie's arm. "But Elizabeth will approve of this. She's positively militant about unity in the family at the moment."

"All right," Katie said. "Let's do it then—provided the kids are okay with it. They might be overwhelmed at having to deal with all of us at once. I want them to enjoy the holiday, too."

"I told you she'd ask us," Jake said from the stairs. "Pay up."

"This is so not fair." Molly shoved two dollar bills at Jake. "Mom?"

"Yes?"

"Yes?"

Katie and Blair answered simultaneously.

Molly smiled and held out her hand. "I told you they'd both answer me."

Jake slapped the two dollars back against Molly's palm. "Shut up."

Amused, Katie said, "I take it you two are okay with the plans to all be together on Thanksgiving here?"

Jake nodded.

"Yes," Molly said. "But do Gran and Grandpa Slater—"

Jake elbowed her in the ribs.

"Never mind." She glared at her brother and rubbed her side.

A bubble of excitement rose inside Katie, and for the first time in a very long time, she really looked forward to Thanksgiving.

BY THANKSGIVING, life had pretty much settled into a routine for Katie. She spent time with C.D., time with the kids, helped C.D. at the bar, prepared her little garden for winter and nested in her cottage. Life was good.

She'd tried no less than three times a week, but still hadn't managed to deal with the beach. She was making progress, though. On Monday, she'd actually gotten out of the car. She hadn't let go of the door, but she'd gotten out and put her feet on the asphalt parking lot.

Why this was such an ordeal in her mind, she had no idea, but it'd been a source of intense speculation among C.D., the kids, and even Sam and Blair. Their suppositions had been all over the place—everything from the ordeal being over to what comes next, and a thousand things in between that were and weren't related. The kicker was, even if they'd been right, Katie wouldn't have known it. And that irritated the hell out of her.

Which was why she was less than enamored when Jake brought the subject up at the table on Thanksgiving.

"Let's not talk about it today," Katie said.

Grace lifted her index finger. "Tell me what's going on with this."

She was having a pretty good day. Not a great day, but so far she'd been doing well, and her eyes were clear. "It's nothing, Mom," Katie said, reassuring her.

"It's a big something, Gran," Molly contradicted without apology. "Mom's scared to go to the beach."

"It's the sand," her mother told Molly. "Damn desert intruding on her life here." She looked over to her daughter. "Katie, I don't see so well anymore," she said, obviously referring to her psychic sight, "and I don't know everything you went through. But I don't need to know. I'm your mother, and I'll tell you this—nothing they did to you can be as bad as what you can do to yourself. Make wise choices."

C.D. watched with interest.

"What exactly does that mean?" Molly asked.

Elizabeth Slater answered. "It means your mother must forgive herself and then she can be content in her life again."

"Forgive myself?" Katie asked.

"Of course, Katie girl," her father said. "You didn't finish the mission. There were consequences. You failed, and you need to forgive yourself."

"I do *not* need to forgive myself for anything they did to me."

"No, Katie." Her mother looked at her, impatient.

"Not for what they did, darling. Because you couldn't stop them."

"Women suffer from this all the time, Katie," Elizabeth said, then took a bite of cranberry. "Though likely not to your degree, due to your unusual circumstances. Not many women are taken POW."

"Can we *not* discuss this now?" Katie asked, growing edgier with each word spoken. "I want to be thankful. I really don't want to discuss this now."

C.D. looked at everyone. "The topic is closed," he said, steel in his voice.

"Sorry, Mom," Molly muttered. "I was trying to help."

"I know you were," she said. "It's okay. I'll figure it out. I just need a little more time."

Grace looked at Sam. "I might have been wrong about you." Her gaze shifted to Blair. "You appeal to his higher angels."

Blair flushed prettily. "Thank you, Grace."

"Frank, isn't it wonderful having both our girls at one table?"

"Yes, Grace, it is."

Elizabeth assumed Grace meant Katie and Molly, but Katie—and obviously Blair, judging by her grin—knew Grace meant Katie and Blair. And Katie was just fine with that. Parched, she searched the table.

"I have news," Sam said.

"Blair, there's no water. I don't have any water." Katie tried to keep panic from her voice, but it snaked through her belly and chest and lodged in her throat.

"I'll get some." She went to the kitchen.

"Katie?"

She heard C.D. but couldn't answer. Her mouth and throat were too dry.

"She went thirsty for a long time, Grandma Grace," Molly whispered across the table.

"Yes, darling, she did."

C.D. reached for Katie's hand. It was as cold as ice.

Blair heard Molly and rushed back, pouring a glassful of water as she moved. "Your water is right here, Katie." She set the pitcher down within reach and lifted her hand, wrapped her fingers around the glass. "Here you go."

Katie emptied the glass. C.D. refilled it from the pitcher, and she drank again, feeling the panic inside her subside. Embarrassed and awkward, she sent Blair a grateful glance.

Smooth as silk, Blair resumed normality. "Sam, what's your news?" she asked, claiming everyone's attention.

Sam let her. "It's about Mrs. Jefferson."

"She's having a baby." Blair, Molly, Jake, C.D. and a recovered Katie all spoke in unison.

Elizabeth nearly jumped out of her skin. Katie's mom and dad chuckled, and Sam's dad, Jason, looked baffled.

"That's right." Sam winked.

"Her cat told us," Molly explained to Elizabeth.

Her grandmother nodded, but now looked as baffled as her husband.

"So, Katie," Jason said. "Have you decided what kind of business you're going to open?"

"Not yet." She had narrowed down her possibilities, but hadn't yet finished her research. She hadn't forgotten C.D.'s suggestion about the garden shop, or his comment about her being at peace with her hands in the dirt. It was on her short list. In ways little else could, peace tempted her.

"What about a doll shop?" Molly said. "You like those old ones with the lacy dresses a lot."

Sam cut into his turkey. "What about a consulting firm for defense contractors?"

Katie grimaced. "No way."

"What's wrong with you guys?" Jake asked. "Mom, you need to sell flowers and yard stuff. You love that. I remember when I was little, you'd let me pick out the seeds from a book, and when they came, we'd put them in those little black cup things. It was cool."

They had done that, and Jake remembered. A lump slid into Katie's throat and she swerved her gaze to C.D., who gave her a superior shrug because he'd predicted more of their memories would return as they did things together to jog them.

"Oh, that's perfect, Katie!" Blair nodded emphatically. "Your garden at the old house was absolutely beautiful. A garden shop is perfect."

"Maybe she doesn't want to take a hobby and make it her life's work," Sam's dad said.

"Jason, if you love what you're doing, it's not work. It's living your passion," Elizabeth said. "Katie, you did have the most gorgeous roses I've ever seen. Blair is right. The entire garden was an artistic delight. You should—"

Katie's mother stood up. "My daughter will do as she damn well pleases, and that's that."

"Thank you, Mom." Katie stood and helped her sit back down. "You're absolutely right." She patted her on the arm. "I probably will open a garden shop. I'm happiest when my hands are in the dirt." She winked at C.D.

Jake held out his hand to Molly. "Pay up."

She frowned and passed two dollars over to him.

Biting back a smile, Katie watched her mom study C.D. "Damn, you're a good-looking man."

"Thank you, Grace." He gave her a killer smile and promptly blushed.

Adorable.

"You always did love her best, C.D." She smiled. "I always loved you for that."

Katie's dad started to push back his chair to rise. "Maybe I'd better take Grace—"

"No, Frank," Blair said. "We're all family here. Family is as it is, and it's all a privilege. Grace is just fine."

Katie admired Blair, and the more she knew of her, the greater that admiration became. What a refreshing thing it was to not hate the other woman. To not stamp her as the wicked stepmother and bitch Katie's husband loved best.

Odd, but refreshing, and Katie added one more thing to her list of things to be grateful for today.

"So when is this divorce business going to be final?" Jason asked Katie.

"December 2nd."

Sam sent her an apologetic look, and she clasped C.D.'s hand under the table and whispered to Sam, "Family's family. It's all a privilege."

He muttered something unintelligible, and Katie gave C.D.'s hand a squeeze.

"So, Katie." Jason sat back in his chair, his gray hair catching in the light. "Sam's told me about the deal you two made on the house. How are you going to open a business?"

She had thought about it, but she wasn't sure she wanted to announce it to everyone at the table. Still, why not? "Just like everyone else does, Jason."

"I'll invest ten thousand," Sam said, assuming they were discussing the financial aspects of it.

"We can do better than that, can't we?" Blair asked. "If I keep the Beemer another year or two?"

Sam nodded. "Twenty, Katie."

"I've got $250 I've been saving for a new bike," Jake told her. "You can have that, Mom."

"I'll add $12.50," Molly added. "Sorry, Mom. I just bought a new iPod, so I'm pretty much broke—except for what I've won from Jake."

"I'll throw in twenty thousand, too," Jason said. "Seems only right, considering."

"We'll match it, Katie," her dad said. "Whatever you need."

Katie was overwhelmed, far too overwhelmed to speak. "I can't tell you how much your offers mean to me...." Her voice cracked, and silent tears streaked down her face. She tried and tried, but she couldn't go on.

"Angel?" C.D. looked to her for permission. Katie nodded, and he finished for her. "That you'd offer to help means a lot to her—especially you, Molly and Jake. But Katie doesn't need your money to open her business."

"Katie," Sam said. "I know what you're getting in the settlement, and it's going to cost a great deal more than that to get a business up and running. There's no reason for you to start out with a huge debt hanging over you."

She dabbed at her eyes, still too moved to speak.

"No, Sam," C.D. said. "Money isn't a problem. Katie has more money than she'll spend in two lifetimes." His voice hitched; he, too, was moved deeply by their willingness to help her. "But I think you just gave her what she did need most."

"What?" Sam looked totally lost.

"Your support," he answered. "You opened your heart to get to your wallet."

They all looked at Katie. She confirmed with a nod what C.D. had said.

"So where the heck did you get all this money, Katie?" Sam asked.

She cleared her throat, let the swell of emotion settle, and then answered him. "C.D. followed my investment advice. I earned a commission."

The color leaked out of Sam's face and C.D. laughed out loud. "I'll bet you're sorry you didn't listen to her now."

"Yes, I am. I really am."

Everyone else laughed and Katie leaned over and kissed C.D. on the cheek. "I adore you."

He put a hand over his heart—his silent signal, reminding her she walked in his soul.

He'd felt that when she'd been dead to him. But was he saying that now because he had then, or did it still apply? Did he even know?

Blair interrupted her thoughts. "Who's ready for pumpkin pie?"

"LOCATION. Location. Location."

Katie surveyed the proposed property—two acres of fertile land two blocks from the busiest shopping center in Willow Creek. "It costs more than the first airplane I flew, C.D."

"You've got the money, Katie."

"I do?" She couldn't make herself ask how much money she had. She wasn't sure yet she wanted to know. Until she was certain, it was best left in Barbie's hands; Katie just didn't need any more pressures right now.

"Yes, you do." He looked at the old house sitting on the far end of the property, facing Cherokee Lane, the side street. "With a little fixing up, that'd make a great office—maybe even a great storefront."

She loved it. She feared loving it. Coming home had been an exercise in discipline. Not caving under all the disappointments had taken more starch in her soul than she'd ever believed she had. But things were sorting out and going well. Maybe too well, and that's why the damn nightmares were back every time she closed her eyes. And why she still couldn't make herself go to the beach and step on that sand. Somewhere deep inside her was the knowledge that she was *too* happy. That things were working out *too* well. And afraid it was true, she kept waiting for the other shoe to fall.

"Honey, it's a great location and a fair price. It's exactly what you need to make a go of the business. All Barbie's research says this is it."

"I know, but—"

"But what?" He stopped and really looked at her. "Are you afraid to be happy, Angel?"

She was. God, but she was. "What if things don't work out?"

"Here?" he asked. "With *your* hands in the dirt?" He smiled. "Of course, things will work out."

She sank her teeth into her lower lip. "How do you do it, C.D.? How you always know what's bothering me, and have that unshakable faith?" She shrugged. "I want that. I used to have it. But now I can't find it."

"You will," he promised, looping an arm around her shoulder. "Until then, borrow mine." He swept her up in his arms. "Say yes, Katie. It's perfect. I just know it."

She giggled and buried her face in his shoulder. "Yes."

KATIE SIGNED THE PAPERS to buy the two acres on Harbinger and Cherokee Lane on the first day of December, and though it was a chilly fifty degrees, she and C.D. and the kids celebrated with a picnic right in the middle of them.

"I can help sometimes after school," Jake said. "And in the summer."

"Me, too," said Molly. "I want to do seeds and bulbs. I don't like roses, they scratch."

Katie looked at C.D. and smiled from her heart. Sometimes life could be so gentle and tender and good.

"Can we come back tomorrow?" Molly asked.

"Not tomorrow," Katie said. "It's divorce day. Your dad and I have to go to court."

Jake's eyes clouded and he looked troubled.

"What's wrong, Jake?"

"My friend Mark's parents got a divorce, and they started acting nuts."

"What do you mean, honey?" He was afraid of something; that was clear. But exactly what, Katie couldn't imagine, considering relations between all of his parents.

"Dating," he said. "Staying out all night. Bringing weird people home and them staying over. We were studying for a science test and Mark had to tell his dad to turn his music down. We couldn't even think."

Katie nodded. "Usually it's the other way around."

"Yeah," Jake said with enthusiasm. "It was awful, Mom."

"Well, I'm sorry that happened to Mark, but I assure you it won't be happening here."

Her son glanced at her doubtfully.

"Jake, your dad and Blair are going to remarry just as soon as the judge says they can," she stated. "Nothing is going to change there."

Jake looked to C.D. but didn't say anything, and Katie didn't know what to add. She wasn't exactly in a position to offer long-term assurances for C.D.

C.D. didn't seem to know what to say, either. "It'll be fine, Jake," he said, keeping his response generic.

The boy didn't look reassured.

"Mom's not going to get goofy, Jake." Molly stood up and dusted the loose grass from her bottom. "Mark's parents were always goofy."

Katie gathered the food and put it back in the picnic basket, and Jake stuffed trash in an empty bag. C.D. got to his feet and struggled a bit to get his cane under him.

"Knee get stiff?" Katie asked.

"A little." He grabbed an armful of their gear and headed for the car.

Jake dumped the trash in a can on the street, then caught up with C.D. "Can I talk with you for a second?"

"Of course." C.D. stowed the gear in the back end of Katie's Highlander. "What's on your mind, champ?"

Jake gazed up at him, as earnest as any man ever looked at another. "My mom loves you, and I think you love her, too."

C.D. nodded, and Jake went on. "She's been through a lot—way more than she's told me, and probably more than she's told you."

"Yes, I know."

"Don't hurt her, okay, C.D.?" Jake's voice trembled. "My dad… He doesn't realize sometimes. Blair reminds him, and that makes him better. But my mom, she needs to be happy, C.D. They hurt her. She told me."

"She did?"

He nodded. "She didn't say how or anything, but I know it had to be bad. I think about it all the time," he confessed. "It gets me that I can't make it not hurt her anymore." He blew out a shuddery breath. "That's why she can't go to the beach. The sand makes her remember." He glanced at Katie, then back at C.D. "That's why no one can hurt her anymore. She can't take it, and she shouldn't have to, you know?"

C.D. nodded. "Because one person can only be hurt so much and stand it?" he asked, just wanting to make sure he was clear about what was going on in Jake's mind.

The youth nodded.

"Don't worry, son." C.D. hugged him. "I'd die before hurting your mother. You have my word on that."

Jake looked up at C.D. "That's a promise, right?"

"Yes, that's a promise."

"C.D.," Katie shouted to him. "There's no water in the cooler." She sounded as anxious as she had at the table on Thanksgiving. "Where's the water?"

They'd emptied the last bottle of water, but Jake held a bottle in his hand. "Take your mother that water, Jake."

"It's empty."

"C.D. I can't find any water." Wild-eyed, pale and panicked, she fell to her knees and rifled through their things, screaming at him. "Oh, God, no. No. There is no water!"

CHAPTER TWELVE

"MOLLY WAS RIGHT. Mom's freaking out," Jake said. "She was thirsty."

Yet Katie didn't seem to understand why she always had to have water with her. Why would that be? "Hurry." He nudged Jake's shoulder. "Take your bottle over to the old house. There's a spigot just outside the back door on the right. Fill the bottle and get it to her."

"It'll be hot."

"Do it now, son," C.D. said, letting Jake hear the urgency in his tone. "Hurry."

Jake saw Katie digging through the cooler, rummaging through everything she could reach, searching for water. "She's totally freaking." He ran.

C.D. rushed to Katie. "Jake is getting your water, honey."

"I need it, C.D. *Right now.*" She looked for Jake over her shoulder. "Too far." She fisted her hands, swerved her gaze to her daughter. "Molly. Molly, I need water. I need water, honey."

Molly picked up her bottle, nicked the edge, and the water spilled out onto the ground.

Katie stared at it, soaking into the earth, and tears filled her eyes. "Oh, God."

"Mom." Jake ran straight to her, his chest heaving,

his face flushed. "Here, Mom." He wrapped her hand around the bottle as Blair had at the table. "Here's your water. It's right here. Drink."

"Oh." She took it with both hands. "Thank you." She drank greedily.

Molly handed Jake her bottle and motioned for him to go refill it, too. He ran all the way there and back.

Katie emptied the first bottle, searched for another, and Jake passed her Molly's full one. "Thank you so much, honey."

Her relief was so raw it had C.D.'s eyes burning. Katie's torture had definitely included withholding water from her for long periods of time. Yet she didn't realize it. Should he mention it to her?

Molly turned and looked right at him. "No. She has to see it for herself."

Surprised, C.D. gazed at her, knowing she was right. Katie didn't talk about captivity, and only now was he beginning to understand why. She had memory gaps. Blackouts. Something. He made a mental note, not that he'd need a reminder. If he lived two lifetimes, he'd never forget that panic on her face and in her voice. He would just put an ice chest filled with bottles of water in her Highlander—in all their cars.

Katie would never be without water again.

KATIE DRESSED in a gray wool suit with a pale pink blouse, gray heels and her favorite eel-skin handbag. She took extra care with her hair and makeup, and was a little surprised by her reflection. She was still too thin, but she had gained a solid ten pounds. At least she didn't look anorexic anymore.

"Katie, we're going to be late," C.D. shouted from the living room.

"I'm coming." She snagged a black coat and joined him. "How do I look?"

"Gorgeous enough for Sam to regret what he's doing—God forbid."

She stopped dead in her tracks and the truth settled over her. "I don't want him to regret it, C.D. He's happy with Blair, and I thought…I believed…damn it, C.D., are you happy with me?"

He pressed a kiss to the tip of her nose. "You know I am."

"I know you love me," she corrected him. "But I've known people who loved people and were totally miserable with them, too."

"Do I look miserable?"

"Not at the moment, no." He didn't. He looked tense, but charming and relatively content.

"Do I act miserable?"

"No." He always seemed content, too. Nearly perfectly content.

"Then I must not be miserable."

Katie grew serious, clasped his face in her hands. "Not being miserable isn't enough, C.D. What I want to know is if you're happy." She searched his eyes. "Are you happy with me?"

"Katie," he said, hesitant but determined. "Where do you see us five years from now? Ten years from now?"

Her throat went dry. "I—I don't know. We've never talked about it…."

"Do you think we should talk about it?"

That depended on what he had to say. If they were together, then yes. If not, then she'd rather not know.

Coward. Coward. Coward.

About this? Damn right she was. Damn right. "I guess so, but not now, C.D. We're due in court."

"When?"

"After court is over?" she suggested, half hoping he'd postpone it until later. Much later.

"Okay." He turned for the door. "Let's go, then."

She didn't move.

"Katie?"

Her heart didn't want to beat. She was too afraid to move. "I don't want to go."

He looked stricken. "Because you don't want to divorce Sam?"

"No. Of course I want to divorce Sam." Her certainty surprised even her, but there it was: truth in its bare bones. "Because I'm afraid of what comes after."

"After?" C.D. frowned, wrinkling the skin under his eyes, between his eyebrows. "You've lost me this time, Angel."

Damn it. This was no time for his internal radar on her to go on the fritz. Why could he read her mind at other times, and not now? She summoned her courage and said what she had to say. "Tell me that I'm not going to have to face the rest of my life without you. Can you tell me that?"

"Sure." He offered the solace she sought. "Katie, you've been a part of my life since the moment I met you, and you'll be a part of my life until I draw my last breath. I swear it on my wings."

A part of his life. Not *what* part, but *a part.* Imperfect, but then they were, too. She could live with *a part.* She could be content with that. And she could breathe again. The air she was taking in really was nourishing her lungs, and she could breathe. "Okay."

"Okay, let's hurry. A ticked-off judge is not a good thing." C.D. held up her coat.

She shrugged it on. "But nothing's in dispute."

"I know that, but still. Why tempt him into a bad mood? Ticking off a judge is never a good idea, you know?"

Katie walked out and saw a black Lotus parked in front of the cottage. "Did you get a new car?"

"No." He thumbed his key ring and the door locks clicked open. "I've had it awhile. I've just been driving the Hummer because I like it."

Liar. For some reason, he hadn't wanted her to see the Lotus. Now, why would that be? Katie slid him a suspicious, sideward glance. "A Lotus is a very expensive car, C.D."

"Yeah, it is. But it was my consolation for losing you, and what else was I to do with my money?"

No family. She slid onto the buttery leather seat and then waited for him to get in. "Barbie must have done a hell of a job with your investments."

C.D. cranked the engine and backed out of the driveway, then shifted and took off. "She's done a good job," he hedged. "I told you that."

"Not 'Lotus' good, you didn't." Katie swatted his arm. "Just how good a job did she do?"

"*Really, really* good." He smiled.

This wasn't making sense. "C.D., you're being deliberately evasive."

"Yeah, I am." He smiled again. "We'll talk more about it after the hearing."

"What difference does the hearing make?"

He braked at a stop sign, then made a left and pulled

into the courthouse parking lot. Sam and Blair were standing beside their Beemer. "Trust me." He turned in and parked. "I adore you, sweetheart, but you're too generous for your own good."

The truth hit Katie. "You were serious. You said I had more money than I could spend in two lifetimes—at Thanksgiving, when the family was going to chip in so I could have my garden center," she reminded him. "You really meant it."

He didn't answer.

"C.D., you gave me a commission. That's the money you were talking about then, wasn't it? You weren't talking about my six years' pay."

He checked his watch, then kissed her quiet. "Later, honey. We'll sort it all out later."

"But, C.D.—" Just how much money had he given her?

"It's not important right now." He nodded out the windshield. "Sam looks like he's about to have a stroke."

He did. He was a total wreck. Katie got out and walked up to him and Blair. "What's wrong?"

"The press has found you, Katie," Sam said anxiously. "We did everything that lieutenant from the base told us to do. But somehow they got wind of the hearing. The judge has closed it to the public, but when we come out—I don't know how we're going to keep them away from you."

Katie had refused to meet with the press, and PR personnel at Paxton had moved heaven and earth to help keep her location a secret. She'd even bought her car in C.D.'s name, and his name was on the utilities for the cottage—she hadn't so much as signed a check at the grocery store. Paxton had set up a post office box for her at the base. She'd returned all the offers for books and films and interviews unopened. How had she goofed? How had they found her?

"Where are they now?" she asked.

"In the main parking lot," Sam told her. "There's about fifty of them." He sounded mortified. "I told C.D. to come in this way. Usually only the judges are allowed to park here, but Judge Haines made an exception for us. Special circumstances."

Blair clasped Katie's arm. "Honey, they've called the house so much, we've had three unlisted numbers since you got home."

Katie couldn't grasp it. "But I'm calling the same number."

"That's a special cell we got in Miranda's name just for you and us," Blair said, speaking of Sam's secretary and office manager. "We're still averaging over a hundred calls a day, Katie."

"Oh, God." She couldn't believe it. "Why didn't you tell me they were making you crazy?"

"You had enough going on," Blair said. "Sam and I, well, we couldn't do much, but we could do that."

C.D. grimaced. "They're camping out at your house, too, right?"

"No," Sam said, red-faced. "Judge Haines issued a restraining order on all the places Katie typically is, and the president appealed to the press. Drs. Muldoon and Firestone said it was essential to your mental health that they leave you alone, and the press respected that."

"I'm sorry." Guilt swamped Katie. "I had no idea. I guess I should have thought about it, but I didn't."

"We didn't want you to know," Sam said. "We were trying to protect you, Katie, so you could reorient on your own terms. But one of the jerks cornered Molly.

Judge Haines issued a second restraining order to keep them away from the kids, notified the president, and he had a chat with the reporter's employer. The others have all been respectful. They get what Drs. Muldoon and Firestone said."

"They all did that?" Katie was shocked.

"They did," Blair said. "It was admirable. You hear so much about the press not being respectful, but they were for you, with that one lapse."

He went after her daughter? Anxiety gripped Katie. "Was Molly upset?"

"No," Blair quickly reassured her. "The little ham loved the attention."

"This has got to stop." Katie was shaking inside.

"There's only one way to stop it, Katie," C.D. said. "Talk to them. After the hearing, just go talk to them."

Sam and Blair looked so hopeful. Their lives had been a wreck and had been made even more of one with all this.

"Okay," Katie said. "I'll talk to them, but I'm not getting specific about what happened there, C.D. That's between me and God, and that's that."

"Whatever you say." C.D. led her to the door. Just inside it, she stopped and turned to Sam. "I want you to know that I believe this is right for all of us. I loved you, Sam. I'll always love you. But you belong with Blair. She makes you stronger and wiser and brings out the best in you. I never did, and I'm okay with that. I won't regret our thirteen years. We grew up together, and we have great kids. Those years were well spent."

"Yes, they were." Sam took her hand and brought it to his lips. "I love you, too, Katie." His eyes shone brightly. "But the truth is you've always been in love with C.D. I don't blame you—he's exactly right for you—and I don't even think you realized you were in love with him. But I saw it every time you looked at him. I felt it every time you mentioned his name. He touched something in you I couldn't touch. I was jealous as hell, but I couldn't compete with it. I didn't want to have to compete with it." He gave her a trembling smile. "I won't ever regret our thirteen years, either. I admire you, Katie. The way you came back, and how you were with me and the kids and Blair. I thought you'd be…" Words failed him. "I don't know what I thought you'd be, but you were good and kind and compassionate." His eyes gleamed with admiration. "And so damn strong. Katie, I was never more proud of you than then."

C.D. and Blair stood back, hearing every word and pretending outwardly to be deaf as stones.

Sam bent down and lightly kissed Katie, and she rose on her tiptoes to receive his kiss.

Blair smiled at C.D. "Bet you don't see that every day in divorce court."

C.D. smiled back. "Bet you don't."

"C.D." Blair looked deeply into his eyes. "Oh, my God. Sam is right. You *have* loved her all along. This isn't new love, just since she came back."

"He was right and wrong," C.D. confessed. "I've always loved her. She loves me, but she wasn't and likely never will be in love with me."

"Mmm…" Blair kept her thoughts on that to herself, and they walked into the courtroom.

Judge Haines was in his fifties, had a broad nose and forehead and wide-set eyes that were sharp and intelligent. He watched with curiosity as all parties sat at one table, rather than two, with the attorney seated between Sam and Katie, and Blair on Sam's left, C.D. on Katie's right. Normally that would have raised concerns, but the attorney—technically Sam's—had taken great pains to inform the judge of the special circumstances in this case. And there was the matter of Katie's notoriety to consider, as well. It wasn't often that a case came before him where nothing was in dispute. That nixed a lot of the usual protocol, and frankly, he was grateful for it. Because of all Katie Slater had endured already, he had no desire to see her upset further.

Small mercies made all the difference to returning POWs. Small mercies, the support of loved ones and the passage of time. Her husband was divorcing her, but truthfully, she didn't seem upset by that; she was facing him smiling.

Judge Haines took off his glasses and glanced under the table where she sat. She and C. D. Quade were holding hands, probably certain their judge couldn't see it. But of course he could see it—a necessity due to security concerns these days. One never knew when a defendant would somehow get in with a gun. All the metal detectors in the world couldn't stop a determined man.

At least the judge now understood her smile. "Mr. and Mrs. Slater, it would trouble me to see you in my courtroom today if I didn't know more about this case than is in these documents. Because I do, I feel confident that granting this divorce is the right thing to do. The couples filing through here don't realize how heavily that decision weighs on their judge, particularly when there are children involved. But it does."

"Yes, your honor," Katie said. How could it not? His decisions irrevocably changed lives. True, the decision to do that came from the couples, but the judge's signature on the dotted line was the knife that severed.

He folded his hands atop the bench. "Most people have no idea what service to this country really costs those who serve. I want you to know," he said, then glanced at Sam, "and you, too, Mr. Slater—that I'm aware of the specific costs to both of you and your children." He lifted his glasses and tapped them on the blotter in front of him, then gave Katie a look laced with misery that only the two of them could fully understand. "I was a POW in Vietnam, Katie. I really do know and I understand…." He choked up, looked down and cleared his throat. "I'm grateful for your service and sacrifices. Your divorce is granted."

Katie smiled at C.D., at Sam and Blair, who kissed, and then at the judge. She walked up to the bench and extended a hand. He clasped it, and she whispered, "Thank you for your service and sacrifices, too." Tears blurred her eyes.

He nodded. "You go on. I'll stay here another ten minutes to give you time to escape the press." He frowned. "I'm sorry to say there are a lot of them out there."

"It's okay, Judge. I'm going to talk to them," she said. "I didn't know they'd been haunting Sam and Blair. They've been protecting me from it. I can't stand by and allow that to continue."

"I understand."

He really did; it showed in his eyes. "Thank you for the restraining order to keep them away from our kids."

"You're welcome." He frowned. "It's a damn shame one was needed, but that's part of the price of freedom."

"It's worth it." She nodded, then pointed to a door on the opposite side of the courtroom from which they'd entered. "That door?"

He nodded. "Katie, have a good life. It's the best revenge."

"I figured that out." She smiled. "But thanks for sharing."

"Do you want us to come with you?" Sam asked.

"No, you've been aggravated enough. Go celebrate." She smiled. "C.D. will be there to hold me up."

C.D. ventured, "More likely, to keep her from punching somebody's lights out."

Sam nodded in agreement. "I'll help, if you want backup."

"I can handle her." C.D. smiled. "I think."

"Oh, hush, you two." Blair swatted at Sam. "She's going to charm them, not beat them up."

Sam grunted skeptically. "I wouldn't bet on it."

"I would." Blair looked Katie in the eyes. "The kids will be watching."

Katie wasn't so sure what she'd do, but that nixed any violence. "I'll do my best to behave."

"Just don't be nervous," Blair said, then smiled. "You'll dazzle them."

"Right." Katie rolled her eyes, but damn it if Blair wasn't making her want to be charming because she believed Katie would be. How did she do that?

"It's hell when she tags those higher angels, isn't it?" C.D. opened the door.

That was it exactly. "Yeah. It's like blackmail—a hotline straight to your conscience."

"That's why it works, Angel."

It did. Katie walked outside and then up to a concrete podium. Thirty or so microphones were attached to its edges. "I'm Katie Slater," she said, looking out on the crowd. "I'll talk to you and you can take pictures, but no flashes. Turn them off now—please." Katie took a shaky breath and repeated a scaled-down version of last night's dream. A dream she knew now, standing before these cameras, to be true. *It was real. It happened.* "They tied me to a chair in a closed room and flashed lights on me nonstop for three days straight. I—I can't see a flash without reliving it."

Should she have said that? Oh, God. She hadn't meant to, but she'd opened her mouth and it'd just poured out. She glanced at C.D., a single step away from her.

When he gave her a reassuring nod, she turned back to the reporters and issued her terms. "Please do not crowd me or push me to answer questions I don't want to answer, or this dialogue will be over before it starts." Inside, she felt like a quivering mass, but her voice sounded strong. Calm and strong and sure. "And no screaming, please. I—I haven't yet adjusted to loud voices not being accompanied by torture."

Where had that come from? She had no idea, but she knew it, too, was true. She stiffened, drew in a low, deep breath and let it out. She could do this. She really could do this. Hiking her chin, she went on. "If you have a question, please just raise your hand."

Hands shot up and a hush fell over the knot of reporters. To Katie's utter amazement, they had heard her and wanted to make talking to them easy for her.

And so, for the next hour, she talked, and took their questions, and no one pushed too hard or too deep or broke her rules. The quivers stopped, the shaking stopped and her fear of them faded. She even smiled once or twice, and when she did, she heard the clicks of their cameras, but not one flashed. The clicks reminded her of the guards circling her, their guns clicking as they cocked their triggers, but she braced for that and endured it, controlling the memory by reminding herself that she wasn't there in the tribal prison. She was here, in Willow Creek, standing in the sunshine and rebuilding her life. Her perfect life.

Then a blond TV reporter about thirty, with a sunny smile, perfect teeth and apparently a lot of ambition, asked a thorny question that went too far. "Were you raped, Katie?"

Katie stared at the woman, outraged and seething. For an instant she held her gaze, giving herself a minute to leash her temper and bury it before answering. Of course they wanted to know. Of course they all speculated that she had been raped. But Katie had no obligation to feed their freaking curiosity. What did she want to tell them? *Yes, repeatedly?* That would just give them their sensationalism, they'd use it, and that would be that. No good would come from it. *It's none of your business?* That would just lead to more speculation and they'd use that speculation to sensationalize. Nothing positive there, either. What could she tell them that would make a difference?

She glanced at C.D. He looked ready to commit murder. She smiled to let him know she was okay, though she wasn't at all sure she was. Fingering the edge of the podium, she decided what she wanted to do and exactly what she wanted to say.

She looked at the woman who'd asked the question, walked out from behind the podium and right up to her. Stopping three feet from her face, Katie looked deeply into her eyes. She saw the woman's fear, smelled it in the light perspiration filming her skin. "That which is endured is conquered."

Perplexed, the woman laughed nervously. "Excuse me?"

"No, I won't excuse you. We're all responsible for

our every action, and that includes you." Katie paused, and then added, "You asked me if I was raped. My answer to you is this—you endure what I've endured. Then you stand behind that podium where I stood. I'll ask you the same question in this same public forum, where your children and America's children are listening and watching and learning. And then you tell me how you feel about answering it. Under those circumstances, would you excuse me?"

The woman paled, stood completely still, as if she feared moving would incite Katie to do her bodily injury.

Katie didn't expect that reaction, but she understood it. Scream and yell and the woman was prepared to cope, but reversing their roles took the starch right out of her journalistic "the people have the right to know."

The hell they did. "Being a journalist gives you great power, but also great responsibility. Judging by your lack of sensitivity toward my family—my children and parents—and me, you have far greater things to fear than me," Katie said softly. "You have yourself."

She turned to C.D. "I'm ready to leave now."

He walked down, and the reporters parted, clearing a path and making no attempt to detain them. Clasping his arm, Katie smiled.

"What's next, Katie?" a man asked as she passed.

"I'm opening a garden center," she said over her shoulder without breaking stride. "Here in Willow Creek—at the corner of Harbinger and Cherokee Lane."

"But you're a pilot," someone said.

"I'm also a master gardener," she retorted. "It gives me something flying planes can't."

"What's that, Katie?" Yet another voice rang out.

She stopped and looked at the man who'd spoken.

At his thin face, the razor burn marring his throat, and then into his eyes, obscured by his thick glasses. Wise eyes. Kind eyes. He wasn't smiling, and neither did she. "Peace."

CHAPTER THIRTEEN

"I'M PROUD OF YOU, Katie."

In the front seat of the Lotus, she slipped on her sunglasses and looked at C.D. "I could have pulverized that bitch for asking about rape. Molly and Jake must have heard that."

"I was afraid for a second you might."

The temptation had been strong. "I wanted her—all of them—to think, C.D. When they ask questions like that, it doesn't do a damn thing for strangers who hear it, but it hurts a victim and those close to her, making them victims again."

"I think you made your point, Angel." He reached over and clasped her hand, brought it to his lips and kissed her knuckles. "But that wasn't what I was talking about."

"Oh?" She saw a McDonald's sign. "Hey, pull in there, will you? I need an iced tea. My throat's as dry as dust."

He veered over and into the drive-through, ordered her tea, ice water and a burger, and then pulled around.

"You're so good to me."

"I hear your stomach growling from over here, and service is slow at the restaurant. We'll likely have to wait."

When he passed her the tea, she asked, "Why are you proud of me?" It wasn't vanity, she told herself. Okay, maybe it was, but she really wanted to know.

"Everything." He gave her that slow, sexy smile that drove her pulse up forty notches and wiped from her mind all thoughts but getting him naked.

"Hmm." What did she say to that?

He chuckled. "I know you're curious. You might as well ask and get it over with."

"Well, it's just that that's not very precise," she said, unwilling to humiliate herself any more than that.

He drove out toward the gulf. "The way you were with Sam this morning. It was beautiful, Katie. And how you are with the kids and Blair and me." He spared her a glance, braked at a red light. "You say Blair has this way of making people want to be better, and you're right, she does do that. But so do you."

She finished off the burger. "I think you're a little less than objective."

"I love you. I'm as opinionated as a heart attack," he admitted. "But that doesn't make me blind or stupid."

"Thank you." Touched, she rubbed his hand with the back of hers, slid over and nuzzled his shoulder. "I adore you, too."

"You do," he said, then pulled into a parking slot at the Summer House, an elegant restaurant on the water with a grassy shore, no sand in sight. "And you love me."

"Of course." She stuffed the burger wrapper back into the bag and smiled at him. "Now feed me. I'm starved."

"Your treat." He reached into his jacket's inner pocket and passed her a small brown book. "This is just the little bank stuff. Barbie has the rest," he said, sticking with their pet term for Samantha. "There's some limit on insurance the banks have, she says. I don't know. I let her mess with anything to do with money."

Katie and C.D.'s names were printed on the outside of

the book. She took it and then cracked it open. Seeing the sum written there, she gasped. "Are you insane?" She stared at C.D. "There are at least a dozen account numbers here, and every damn one of them is FDIC maxed."

"Oh, you know about that, then. Good. You can worry about it."

"C.D., I can't take this." She still couldn't believe her eyes, and there was no way her brain would work enough to calculate the math.

"You're not taking anything. It's yours." He got out of the car, walked around and opened the door. "Damn, Katie, if I'd known all it took to daze you was money, I'd have shown you that a long time ago."

She got out and shoved the book into his chest. "I'm not taking this. It's yours."

He didn't argue, just put the book back inside his jacket pocket. "Whatever. Let's eat. You're starved, remember."

"I mean it, C.D.," she warned him. "I don't want your money."

"I know, Angel." He smiled at her. "You never did."

And others had. Hell, he must have been rich to begin with.

"You've always had money, haven't you?" she asked.

He nodded.

"Why didn't you tell me?"

"I thought you knew." He shrugged. "Everyone else did. Then, when I figured out you didn't know, I saw no reason to tell you. I mean, what's the difference?"

"There isn't any." She had a flash of insight. "But that's not why you didn't tell me. You were scared it would make a difference."

"Okay," he confessed. "At first I was. But then when you and I got close, I knew you cared about me—well,

I'm not sure why, but I knew money had nothing to do with it. So it really didn't matter, then."

She pulled him aside on the porch of the restaurant. "C.D.," she said, deadly serious. "I don't want your money now, but I do want you." She glanced away, then pulled her gaze back to his. "I meant what I said this morning. I can endure anything but a life without you in it."

"I'm here, Angel." He straightened his jacket on his shoulders. "I promised."

"I know you did. But I need to know you're here because you want to be with me, not because you know I'll be nuts without you. There's a difference."

"I'm right where I want to be." He frowned. "I think I told you that, too. Weren't you listening to me?"

"A lot's been happening. You might have changed your mind, or I might have forgotten, okay?"

"Well…" He wrapped an arm around her and led her to the door. "I guess I'll just have to remind you more often."

She sniffed. "That wouldn't hurt."

He snickered. "You're a bigger ham than Molly."

Over lunch, they talked about the garden center. The contractor was neck-deep into the project and the goal was to have everything ready to go by the middle of March. From all signs, they were going to make it.

Barbie had taken care of getting all the permits and licenses, and someone on her staff did the research and set up suppliers and contacts, including the listing of Katie's old favorites. Molly was pushing for Katie to have a proper flower shop, too, and Katie was considering it, but until a few days ago, no one suitable had applied to run it. Then, to Katie's delight, Ashley had come in, résumé in hand. She'd had all the nursing she could handle and was ready for a change.

Katie had hired her on the spot—and enrolled her in a flower-arranging course. Ashley was happy, Katie was thrilled and C.D. watched with shining eyes and a closed mouth. When Katie asked for his advice, he'd refused to give it, telling her, "When women band together, a man saves himself misery by staying out of the way and minding his own business."

Blair had found a great deal of humor in that, and had confided to Katie that Sam had said something similar to her not long ago. "Must be something they teach them at man school," she'd said.

Katie had wistfully sighed. "I wish they'd teach them to put the toilet tissue on the roller and not park it on top of it."

Blair had laughed herself silly. "No school, man or otherwise, seems able to teach them that."

Over dessert—a slice of chocolate fudge cake that was so huge it was probably illegal in thirty states—Katie looked across the table at C.D. "Sam and Blair are going to get married again as soon as the papers are filed."

"In two weeks, according to Jake." C.D. took a sip from his steaming coffee cup. "He wants me to make sure you don't have a meltdown. His friend Mark says that's a very vulnerable time."

"Did you reassure him?"

"I tried," C.D. said. "But Mark's right. It is a vulnerable time."

"I won't be having a meltdown."

"You sure?"

"Positive." She swallowed a bite of cake, letting the chocolate roll around on her tongue. "I guess Sam was right about the kids needing to know his marrying Blair is okay with me."

"Is it?"

"Sure." What was going on with C.D.? He had a weird look on his face, and he was acting even weirder. "They fit, C.D. Like me and you."

The tension slid off his face. "So what do you want to do?"

"I don't know," she said. "Would it be too bizarre if we had a little reception for them or something?"

"Jason would probably have a cow," C.D. said. "Elizabeth would have starched shoulders about it. Could be fun."

"C.D." She swatted him. "If Elizabeth thought it was a show of unity for the kids, she'd be all for it."

"And she'd be all over Jason to keep his mouth shut."

"It'd work, but silent disapproval can be worse than voiced disapproval. I'd hate to screw it up for Blair." Katie reached over and snagged C.D.'s hand. "Maybe we won't push it, giving them a reception. But I do think we should go to the wedding. You agree, right?"

"Angel, I'm with you wherever you go."

Katie smiled, happy from the inside out. Unprepared for it, she stilled.

C.D. noticed. "What's wrong?"

She pressed a hand to her chest, dropped her voice so only he could hear. "It's odd, C.D. All the bad stuff— it's still here." Every memory. Every violation and cruelty. "This morning in court, I closed the door on most of my adult life. But I'm happy. Inside, I'm *really* happy." She looked worried. "Shouldn't I be sad? I mean, after thirteen years, I should be sad, right?"

"Why should you be anything?" C.D. refilled his

coffee cup from the silver pot on the table. "Because someone somewhere decided you should be? Hell, Katie, you and Sam have a much better relationship right now than you ever had when you were together."

"That's true," she said. "But there's more to it than that, C.D. I'm just not sure what it is—yet."

He looked away, out onto the stretch of lawn to the water, and at the waves rolling ashore. "Maybe when you figure it out, you'll be able to walk in the sand." He gave her a bittersweet smile. "I'll rejoice that day."

"Because…"

"Because then the past will be behind you, and we can look ahead to the future."

"Aren't we doing that? The garden center, the—"

"Not you, Angel. *We.*" He signed off on the bill, then wiped his mouth with his white linen napkin. "In the meantime, let's put our heads together with Molly and Jake and think of something nice to do for Sam and Blair."

"After the ordeal they've had with the press, and with me coming back, they deserve it." Katie stood up. "It'll be fun to bring Molly and Jake into it, too."

"There's nothing like a good conspiracy to strengthen the ties that bind." C.D. winked at her.

C.D., KATIE, MOLLY AND Jake sat on the concrete floor inside the new flower shop. The walls were up and the roof was on, but the fixtures weren't yet in place, nor were the floors tiled. The windows were in and still had the stickers on them.

"So you guys really want to send them to Europe for two weeks?"

"Yeah," Jake said. "Blair talks about Sweden all the

time. Dad keeps promising to take her but he never gets around to it."

"Sounds too familiar," Katie said. "Let's help them out getting there, then."

"Whoa," C.D. said. "What about his patients?"

"I'll take care of that," Katie said. "I'll have to let Miranda in on the secret, though." She glanced at Molly. "Can your dad's secretary be trusted?"

The girl nodded. "She's never told on me. Not once."

"That's good enough for me, then." Katie looked at C.D. "She can make arrangements for someone else to cover for him, and handle his appointments."

"What about other appointments?"

"I'll take care of that," Jake said. "Mom keeps everyone's appointments on the fridge. Me and Molly can change any that come during their trip."

Molly bounced in excitement. "They're going to be so happy."

Or kill us, Katie thought, not willing to bet a nickel either way. Especially Sam. He was still a pretty tight control freak. She looked around. "C.D., where's the water?"

She heard rustling and looked back to the circle.

Molly, Jake and C.D. all sat with their arms stretched out, passing her bottles of water.

Katie smiled. "God, but I love you guys." Chuckling, she drank a sip from each of the bottles and passed them back.

"Okay, then," C.D. said. "We're armed and ready to go. Everyone knows their jobs, right?"

"Right." Jake nodded. "This is cool."

"Right," Molly said, then stuck her hand out to Jake. He slapped two dollar bills into it. "Okay, okay. Stop gloating. You said Mom would come to the wedding, and I thought she wouldn't." He glanced at Katie. "No offense, Mom, but I thought it would upset you."

"Not at all, Jake. Your dad and Blair love each other and we all love you and Molly. I'm not sad. I'm very happy for them."

Jake looked totally baffled. "So when are you going to go nuts, tell us all this bad stuff about how rotten Dad is and buy us stuff to bribe us into liking you best?"

"What?" Katie couldn't believe her ears.

"Bribery? Ooo," Molly said. "I want a new TV for my room."

"Then you'll work here at the center when it opens and earn the money to buy one."

Molly looked at Jake as if betrayed. "This isn't how you said it'd work."

"They're weird. Everyone else I know says it works just like I told you."

C.D. couldn't help himself; he laughed, which ticked off Jake, and that pleased Molly. "Sorry, champ. It's just that your mother *never* does things the way other people do."

"That's not true, C.D." She whacked him on the arm. "You're going to have Jake thinking I really am weird."

"He already said you were."

Jake looked worried about that. "But it's a good weird, Mom, like Molly knowing stuff. I hate the way Mark's parents fight all the time. It really sucks."

"I'm sure it does." She looked at her son. He was struggling to make his world make sense. "Honey, our situation is a little different. Your dad and I didn't divorce one another because we didn't love each other anymore. We still love one another, and of course we love you and Molly. Our lives just changed a lot while I was gone. *We* changed a lot." She rubbed Jake's shoulder. "Usually when people divorce, there's anger and bitterness and both people are hurt and the kids are hurt, too. But we're lucky. We don't have any of those things making times rough for us. That's the difference."

He nodded. "It sure is easier on us," he said, motioning between him and Molly. "I'm glad you're not stressed out like Mark's mom. Man, she's a wreck." His eyes were serious, too seeing and too old for his years. "It cuts Mark up, seeing her like that."

"I hate to break this up, but time's running out." C.D. stood up. "Meeting's over, or you're going to miss swim practice, Jake."

"Remember, this is a secret. No slipping," Katie said. "Molly, are Blair's parents coming for the wedding?"

"She doesn't have any."

"I see," Katie said, and thought she might. When Katie was supposedly dead, had Blair adopted Katie's parents, who had no other children, because she had no other mom or dad? And then when Katie had returned, she'd removed herself from them—likely feeling that to continue that relationship would be infringing on Katie.

Considering the odds good that's what had happened, Katie told C.D., "Mom and Dad are going to be at that wedding."

"I think that'll mean a lot to Blair," he admitted. "She got really close to them while you were dead."

"*Gone,* C.D. I wasn't dead," Katie reminded him. "But I know what you mean, and now I know why she did." Why C.D. had, too. "She was alone."

Alone. Isolated. Empty.

No one knew better than Katie how merciless those feelings could be.

TWO WEEKS LATER, Katie's dad gave Blair to Sam in a simple ceremony in Judge Haines's chambers. Jake stood up for his dad, and as Katie stood next to C.D. and watched, she beamed with pride. Jake looked so handsome in his gray suit. So grown up. In her heart, she ached a little because of all she'd missed, but mostly she was just the proud mama of all he'd become. In no small part that was due to the loving care of the woman now marrying his dad.

They exchanged vows, and Katie remembered. The church where she'd stood before the altar next to Sam. The words they'd spoken and the pledges they'd made. They were divorced now and their lives had taken different roads, but in her heart she didn't feel she'd violated those vows, just expanded them and let them come to mean what they should have meant all along.

C.D. curled an arm around her shoulder. She smiled at him, weepy-eyed. He brushed her damp cheek with his thumb and rubbed their noses together. He knew what she was feeling, that she was remembering, and yet there was no jealousy in his eyes. No fear of his place in her life being second or less important. He really did understand her as well as she understood herself.

But he, too, had his secrets.

And she hoped that she lived long enough for him to share them with her.

"You may kiss your bride."

Sam and Blair kissed and she flushed prettily. Jake cast

Katie a worried look—no doubt Mark's warnings were nagging at him again—and she smiled to reassure him.

"Congratulations." Katie hugged Sam and then Blair. "I know you'll be very happy."

C.D. shook Sam's hand. "Nicely done, Sam."

He grunted. "Just wait. Your turn is coming."

Jason was flustered by Katie and C.D. and Katie's parents being there, and made no bones about it. "This is the damnedest bunch of people I've ever seen."

"Jason, not another word." Elizabeth sent him a look that warned if he crossed her there would be hell to pay.

Katie imagined it was odd. But the kids weren't depressed or in trauma, Sam and Blair were happy—she'd cried on seeing Katie's parents there, which was very touching—and Katie and C.D., well, things seemed to be great for everyone. C.D. still hadn't talked to her about a lot of things, including her own net worth, but what difference did it make? They worked together at the bar, worked with the contractor and team setting up the garden center—the flower shop part of it was Ashley's domain and that suited Katie just fine—and Katie and C.D. were together most of the time. They hadn't looked down the road five years or ten yet. But was that bad or good?

Sometimes Katie thought it was great. Other times, she sensed impending doom. Hell, she didn't know. But she was happy. Everyone was happy. Why push it? Happiness was far too elusive to risk losing just to speculate on what might be happening down the road.

The reception was at Sam and Blair's, and Jason finally stopped shaking his head, thinking his family had gone off the deep end. In his esteemed opinion, when you divorced someone, you didn't tell her you loved her, and you damn sure didn't invite her to your next wedding. Sam had finally gotten his priorities on image in order and the balls to tell his dad he didn't care how other families dealt with things, only his, and the way they were dealing with events was working out just fine.

Katie was so proud of him. She and Blair exchanged a high-five in the kitchen to celebrate, gushing in disbelief.

As the festivities were winding down, Katie told Jake, "It's time."

He nodded and pulled an envelope from his jacket pocket, mimicking C.D.'s penchant for tucking things in there. "Mom, Dad?"

Sam and Blair turned to him. "Yes?" Sam asked.

Molly edged up beside Jake. "We have a wedding present for you," she said. "Go ahead, Jake. Give it to them."

He passed them the large envelope. "We're glad you're married again."

"What's this?" Sam took it. "It's too heavy to be a card."

Molly was dancing, too excited to wait another second. "It's plane tickets—to Sweden."

Not to be outdone, Jake added, "And hotel reservations and other tickets to stuff and, well, just look."

Blair's jaw dropped. Her mouth rounded in an O, and she pressed her fingertips against her lips. "Oh, my goodness. You're kidding, aren't you?"

"No way," Jake said. "It's true."

Blair danced with Molly, hugged Jake and her both at once. "Oh, Sam. It's our dream trip!"

He glanced through the contents of the envelope, looked at Katie, then C.D. "Thank you." He shook his head.

"Have a great time." Katie wrinkled her nose, then whispered a taunt to Sam, "And stay out of the sun."

He laughed, clearly remembering his week on the shaded balcony in Hawaii. "Definitely no sun."

"Sam! Sam!" Blair said. "These say we leave tonight."

His face fell. "I—I can't do that."

Blair went still.

"Yes, you can," Molly said. "Mom fixed it. She told Miranda and everything is fixed."

"Katie?" Blair looked at her, eyes shining. "Really?"

She raised her right hand, palm out, and smiled. "Promise."

"That's right." Miranda stepped out of the crowd. "Everything is done. The office is directed to not even take a phone call from you for the next two weeks."

"Oh, Katie." Blair launched herself forward, grabbed her in a hug so tight it nearly cracked Katie's back. They both erupted into giggles.

Katie's mom smiled. "My girls."

"Did you hear that, Elizabeth?" Jason huffed and looked away. "The whole damn bunch of them are crazy."

"Shut up, darling." His wife turned on him. "And loosen your belt a notch. Maybe it'll improve your disposition."

Katie looked at Blair and winked. "A convert."

"Don't you just love it?" Blair asked, then kissed everyone's cheeks—and both of Grace's—all the way back to Sam.

Katie turned to C.D., who was talking to Jake. "They really liked it, didn't they?" Jake was asking. "Or were they faking it, so me and Molly wouldn't be disappointed?"

"Didn't you see Blair dancing around and squealing?" C.D. asked.

"Yeah."

"Women only make that racket when it's real. They can't fake it."

"Really?"

"I swear." C.D. raised his right hand.

Molly walked up and stuck out her own hand, palm up.

Jake groused and grimaced and slapped two dollars into it.

"Lost another one?" Katie asked, feeling sorry for him. Sooner or later, he'd learn not to bet against a sister who knew things.

"I was stupid," he said. "I bet Mom wouldn't cry."

"I can't do it. I can't take your money." Molly passed the two dollars back to Jake. "It was a sucker bet."

"Mom." He looked to Katie. "Did you hear what she said to me?"

"I'm still trying to figure out how you guys can call both me and Blair 'Mom' and yet none of us are ever confused about who you mean. How do we know this stuff?"

Jake shrugged. "Don't ask me. You're the adult."

Molly lifted her hands. "I don't know, either."

C.D. ended the mystery. "It's in the genes."

"Of course." Katie kissed him, then asked the kids, "Are your suitcases in the car?"

"Everything but Molly's iPod," Jake said.

"Good. Kiss your folks bye and let's go home. They need to get ready for their trip."

"Do I have to kiss Grandpa Slater?" Molly asked. "He's still pretty mad."

"Maybe it'll sweeten his mood," Katie said, though she wasn't holding out a lot of hope.

Molly sent her a level look. "That was a joke, right?"

Katie responded with a noncommittal shrug. It was the very best she could do.

CHAPTER FOURTEEN

THE GARDEN CENTER was really coming along.

By agreement, Ashley dealt with a lot of the business, leaving Katie free to "play in the dirt" and spend time with the kids. Those were her priorities, and she was determined to stick to them.

The two weeks Sam and Blair spent in Europe on their honeymoon had been good for them, and an even better time for Katie, C.D. and the kids. A special bond, one developed while Katie was gone, deepened between Jake and C.D., and no one was more glad to see it than she was. They had far more in common than Jake and Sam—not that it was any kind of competition—but Katie worried a lot about the kids. The more she learned about other kids, the more she worried about her own and the world they were growing up in. Life for them was far different than how she'd grown up. Children seemed to be under so much more pressure now. Time after time, kids Jake mentioned were in counseling, on antidepressants or dealing with problems they just shouldn't have to cope with—hell, shouldn't even know existed. Was there innocence in youth anymore?

Initially, C.D. had told Jake his doctor wanted him to start walking and build up to five miles a day, but C.D. was worried about starting off and getting stuck somewhere away from home with his bad knee, not being able to make it back.

Katie would have offered to go with him, or suggested he take the cell phone and call her if he got into trouble, and she'd come and get him, but C.D. hadn't told her his worry. He'd told Jake. And Jake had promptly solved the problem, telling C.D. that he'd walk with him and, if C.D. had to stop, they'd just hang together until they could walk back.

That was the beginning of their special relationship. And in the weeks since, as they walked they'd talked. Now Jake would call and the most Katie heard from him was, "Mom, can I talk to C.D.? Is he too busy?"

C.D. was never too busy—regardless of what he was doing at the time.

This bond between them tickled Katie. A lot. Admittedly, that neither C.D. nor Jake ever mentioned what they talked about had Katie dying of curiosity, but she flatly refused to ask. She and Molly speculated, though. And often, like now, Katie paused and looked across the flower beds to Jake and C.D.

"I'll bet you three dollars it's about girls," Molly said.

She was likely right. Through the years, C.D. had always been charming and women had fawned over him. They still did. If Katie were a guy wanting girl advice, she'd go to C.D. "Sucker bet," she told Molly.

Ever curious, Molly skirted a couple beds and got closer to them.

Jake noticed. "Hey, aren't you supposed to be working over there by Mom?"

"I'm going." Molly marched back toward Katie, wearing a disgusted look.

Katie lifted her eyebrows, amused. Her daughter

clearly didn't much like being caught red-handed at trying to eavesdrop.

C.D. bit back a smile, but amusement still shone in his eyes. And Katie felt that same sense of contentment she always felt when the four of them were together. She took a drink of water from her bottle, then pinched herself.

Molly had dirt smeared on her cheek. "Why do you always do that?"

"Do what, honey?" Katie put down her spade and reached for a handful of mulch.

"Pinch your arm. You just did it again." Molly looked closer. "There's three bruises on it." Suspicion filled her eyes. "Why are you hurting yourself?"

"I'm not," Katie assured her.

"You are, Mom," she insisted. "Why?"

Katie started to evade, but then thought better of it. Kids had a built-in radar on lying, and Molly's was developed more than most because of her gift. Katie wasn't going to damage the good they had going over something that made her just a little uncomfortable to talk about out loud. "When I'm really happy, I pinch myself to make sure I'm awake," she said. "That's all."

"You're making sure you're not really in that prison and this isn't a dream," Molly clarified.

Katie nodded.

"Okay." She accepted that and went back to the greenhouse.

Katie watched her walk away. Sometimes, when her life was going well, it was hard to believe it was real. Oh, there were challenges, sure. Like a shortage of plywood due to the previous summer's hurricane putting pressure on meeting the demand, and one of their key suppliers missing a delivery date. But those things were more a nuisance than a pain. They certainly weren't critical.

The press had made a big deal out of Sam and Blair's wedding—actually, out of Katie attending Sam and Blair's wedding—and it was an odd day at the garden center that at least one reporter didn't show up. But they were largely respectful and some were very kind. Katie hadn't seen the blond TV reporter who'd asked her about rape the day of the divorce hearing. She often wondered if the woman still worked for Channel 3, but didn't care enough to check.

Switching from water, she poured herself a glass of lemonade from the cooler, and sat down under an old oak. Jake and C.D. were still talking. "And men go on about women gabbing?" she muttered, and sipped the tart lemonade.

Life was going well, and it would be even better if the nightmares would stop. But at least once a week, Katie dreamed of Ustead and his cruelties. For the past few weeks, mostly about the night General Amid had shot and killed Ustead, and left Katie crouched on the interrogation room floor, splattered in his blood.

It was late afternoon, hot and humid, but a cold shiver raced up her spine. Maybe the nightmares would never stop. Maybe she'd always wake up in a cold sweat, shaking. Maybe it'd take the rest of her life to keep reminding herself that the ordeal was over.

But she hoped not. God, she hoped not.

Squinting against the sun, she watched Molly working in the greenhouse, singing and planting seeds, and Jake and C.D. still deep in conversation, though they'd now moved over to the compost pile.

That which is endured is conquered.

She hoped the nightmares would stop. But if they didn't, she could endure them. She could follow Judge Haines's advice. *Live well. It's the best revenge.* Because, these days, even when she was asleep and caught up in a nightmare, she was still aware of all the blessings in her life, all the good.

And that held true in spite of her triweekly trips to the pier parking lot—she couldn't call them trips to the beach, since she still hadn't been able to make herself step onto the sand. Yet she had seen progress. This week, she'd let go of the car and made it to the edge of the asphalt. Still, that weathered and worn pier that led to the sand and on to the water's edge…

Well, it reminded her of a bridge to her past, and so far, she just couldn't step onto it.

And that she couldn't figure out exactly why really got on her nerves.

"My God, Katie."

She looked toward the voice and saw Sam.

"Dad's here!" Jake called to Molly. "Get your stuff."

C.D. started walking toward them.

"Hi, Sam." Katie smiled at him. "As you heard, the kids are getting their things."

He didn't say a word, just stared at her, and tears spilled from his eyes and ran down his cheeks.

"What's wrong?" Katie stood up and dusted the grass and dirt from her bottom.

"Nothing." He paused and swiped at his eyes. "Sitting there… You just looked exactly as you did the very first time I saw you." He seemed bemused. "I knew then I would love you forever."

She smiled. "I love you, too, Sam."

C.D. didn't look at Katie. He was transfixed by the raw hunger in Sam's eyes. What the hell was the man doing?

"Katie," Sam said. "Honey, we need to talk."

"About what?"

"About us." He dragged a hand through his hair. "I— I think I made a mistake."

C.D. wasn't sure what to do, but he couldn't stay put and not lay Sam out in the grass. Not just for what he was doing to Katie, but for what he was doing to Blair and the kids. The crazy bastard was flipping women again— or trying to. "Jake, tell Katie I had to go to the bar."

"Okay." Jake frowned. "Are you mad at her?"

"No, champ." C.D. walked away. He wasn't mad at Katie, but he was damn steamed at Sam.

"Two bucks says he's totally pissed," Molly said.

Jake looked at her, then at his mother and his father. His dad looked upset. Really upset. "Uh-oh."

"What?" Molly craned her neck to see what Jake saw.

"Dad's sorry he divorced Mom."

"Don't be stupid."

"I'm not." Jake was not happy. "Look at him."

"Oh, man." Molly groaned. "He's gonna mess everything up."

Sam turned away from the kids, who stood a short distance away, hopefully out of earshot. "Katie, I blew it. Can we go back? Can we just go back and be a family again?"

"What about Blair?" Katie asked. "Sam, I know you love her."

"I do, but she's not…you."

"I'm not her, either," Katie reminded him. "What the hell's gotten into you, Sam?" She didn't know what to think, how to feel. "Listen, I don't know why you're so interested in getting back with me again all of a sudden, but I'm going to put it down to synapse misfires in your brain. Think about it. Remember it as it really was. Hell, Sam, the good times between you and me weren't that good. Actually, I'd venture to say that your most terrible times with Blair are better than your best times with me."

"How can you say that?" He shuffled his feet, stared at her. "Katie, you can't believe that's true."

"I do believe it." She lifted her chin. "Hell, Sam. I *know* it."

"We were happy."

"Yes, at times. But there's one thing we weren't. We've talked about it, Sam, and we both know it's true."

"What?" He frowned. "We can fix it. If we know what's wrong, we can fix it."

"No, honey, we can't." Katie lowered her voice. The last thing she wanted was for the kids to hear any of this. "I'm not in love with you, Sam. I've never been in love with you, and you've never been in love with me." She grunted. "We care more about each other since the divorce than we ever did when we were married." She lifted a hand. "You know it's true."

He stilled. Spent a long, drawn-out minute thinking about it and then looked totally stunned, and ashamed. "You're right," he said, as if the realization had come slowly, then manifested in a crushing blow that hit him blazingly fast. "Of course you're right." He looked stricken. "God, what am I doing? What was I thinking?"

"Hey, you can admit you had a wickedly weak moment where the past snagged your common sense, but let's don't trash the ex in the process of regaining our wits, okay?"

"Okay." He blushed and color flooded his neck and

face. "I'm sorry, Katie," he said shakily, clearly uneasy and embarrassed. "I guess it was just seeing you sitting there like that. It took me right back to the way I felt about you that day, and I didn't stop to think about anything in between. I just reacted to it."

"No problem." It wasn't. She had flashbacks all the time and understood them better than she wished. She cleared her throat. "But I wouldn't mention it to Blair. She might not be quite as understanding."

"No, I'm sure she wouldn't be."

Katie squinted against the sun. "You know, I should thank you."

"For that?"

She nodded. "I think somewhere down deep, I wanted that to happen. I wanted to go back, but we can only go forward. I knew it in my head, but my heart wasn't convinced. Now it is. You're married to the right woman, Sam."

"Are you going to marry C.D.?"

She motioned for the kids to come on over. "I don't know. He's never been married, and I don't think he's much interested in that. But I'll be with him." She smiled. "I walk in his soul."

"Damn." Sam raised his eyebrows. "That's good."

"Yeah. It makes me sappy and my heart flips every time I think it." She sighed contentedly. "I think it a lot."

Molly whispered to Jake, "Two bucks says he tells Mom that as soon as we get home."

"Sucker bet." Jake blew out a slow breath. "Man, I'm glad Mom didn't let Dad screw things up. C.D. would have been nuts."

"Why?"

"I can't tell you."

"Why not?"

"Because it's a secret, and you slip," Jake stated. "But you better not slip at home and tell Mom anything about what Dad said here. She'll leave him."

"I swear I won't tell." Molly crossed her heart. "I don't want her to ever leave."

Their voices carried back to Katie on the breeze as they walked to the car, and she crossed her heart, too. She looked around for C.D. but he was gone. "Jake?" She called to him just as he was getting into the car. "Where's C.D.?"

"He said to tell you he had to go to the bar."

"Is he coming back?"

Jake ran back to her. "I don't think so, Mom. He was pretty ticked off."

"About what?"

"He heard what Dad told you." Jake frowned. "I guess he thought you were going to go back to Dad."

"Oh, no." Katie couldn't believe it. "Jake, don't you dare mention a word of this to Blair. Your dad was just—"

"I know. He just got caught up in the moment. He didn't mean it."

"Exactly." No protecting her pride with this one.

"C.D. was hurt, Mom. I said he was ticked, but he wasn't. He was hurt real bad."

Katie nodded. "I'll talk to him."

Jake shrugged. "Yeah, but will he talk to you?"

"He might not talk, but he will listen." God, she hoped he'd listen. She wouldn't force him. Never again in her life would she force anything on anyone.

"Ask him to marry you," Jake suggested. "That'll shock him into listening, and then you can say anything.

He won't be able to move." Jake gave her a wide, toothy grin, then ran back to the car.

Marry her? Would C.D. marry her?

Katie thought about it all the way over to the bar. Half the time she decided she should ask him. All he could say was no. But if he did say no, then the odds were good it would screw up what they had now, and that was as close to perfection as mortals could get. She didn't want to mess it up or to lose it.

The risks were astronomical.

Oh, man. She didn't know if she could propose to him, anyway. *Marriage?* With nightmares and skeletons in her closet she'd never be willing to drag out and pick bare-bone clean? How could anyone live with all that?

But this wasn't anyone. It was C.D. Her C.D. And he already lived with it, and he seemed to like living with it.

She burst into the bar, short-winded from nerves, not from the run from her cottage.

He stood behind the bar, looked and saw it was her, then turned away.

She forced herself to slow down and walk over to him. "C.D.?"

"Yeah?" He didn't look back.

"Are you upset about something?"

"I don't know, Katie. Should I be upset about something?"

She tried walking around the bar to get close to him, but it was locked. *Well, if you can't go around...* She backed up to the bar, hoisted herself over and dropped down behind it next to him. "I need to talk to you."

"I expected as much." His jaw ticked. "It's okay. I heard enough to figure out what's going on."

"Did you?"

"Yeah." He blinked hard and fast. "You do what you need to do, Katie. I understand."

Jake had been wrong. C.D. wasn't hurt. He was devastated. He thought she was leaving him to go back to Sam, and he was devastated!

"Marry me, C.D."

He went statue still. "What?"

"Marry me," she said again. "You love me, I love you, we're happy. Let's get married."

He glared at her. "Need a buffer between you and Sam, eh?"

"No, I don't." She couldn't blame him for thinking that. But it was really important that she straighten him out fast. "I don't *need* to marry you."

He still didn't turn to face her. "Then why bother?"

She stared at his back. "I *want* to marry you."

"Why?"

"Because we love each other. It's the next natural step."

He turned around and glared at her. "Do not lie to me, Katie. Not now, and never about this."

No grace. No mercy. *Courage, Katie. Courage.* "Okay, you're right. I wasn't being honest."

"Hell of a time to pull that."

"Is there ever a good time?"

"No, but some times are worse than others." He grabbed a beer out of the cooler and popped the top. "This is a very bad time."

She stepped closer, took the bottle of beer from his hand and put it on the bar beside the gold plaque dedicated to her memory. "Marry me because I'm in love with you, C.D. Marry me because the idea of not marrying me makes you miserable. Marry me because you know that you walk forever in my soul, too. Sam was right. I've always been in love with you. Always. I just didn't know it because I've never in my life felt that way about another man—not even the ones I married. I love you, C.D. I want to live with you the rest of my life. Marry me."

"I've already promised to be with you until my last breath," he reminded her.

She looked up at him and searched his eyes. His anger was fading, yet the tension in him still had him coiled. "So it's marriage you're opposing, not marriage to me, right?"

"I haven't opposed anything," he corrected her, then put his hands on her shoulders. "I just don't think you're ready, Angel."

"Because…"

He kissed the worry from her face. "I'll tell you what. The day you walk on the sand, I'll know you're ready, and I swear, Katie, I'll be waiting." He let his thumb slide along her jaw. "For me, that day can't come soon enough."

She thought about what he'd said for a long time. "You know, I hate it when you're right, C.D."

He smiled. "I know."

"You thought I was going to leave you for Sam."

"I thought you might."

"Never happen." She kissed him, then turned to walk away. "I'm going to the cottage."

Wearing his relief, he nodded. "You need to think."

"Quit doing that."

"What?"

"Telling me what I'm getting ready to tell you," she groused. "Between you and Molly, someone's always in my head."

"Sorry." He spun her around and hugged her. "I'll give you some time, then come and answer your questions."

"What questions?" She didn't have any questions.

He winked.

Katie started to complain, but saved her breath. If it turned out he was right, and she did have questions, it'd be that many fewer words she'd have to eat.

KATIE SHOWERED, scrubbing off the grime. Then she shampooed and conditioned her hair, and shaved her legs. "You're dawdling," she told herself. "You could have been finished with all this fifteen minutes ago. You're avoiding thinking, messing around with busy stuff."

She put the razor back in its little holder attached to the marble shower wall. "Either you want to think or you don't. So which is it?"

She squeezed her eyes shut and let the water flowing through the showerhead beat down on her back. "I'm losing it. C.D. must be right, because I'm now not only refusing to think, I'm giving myself hell for it."

She rinsed off the last of the shower gel and grabbed a towel, then dried off. "He thinks you've got questions. You've got no questions."

Why did he pull out the Lotus the day of the divorce hearing?

What difference could that possibly make? She slathered lotion onto her skin. It made no difference to her, but it must have meant something to him. He said he preferred driving the Hummer, so why did he choose to drive the Lotus that particular day? He hadn't driven it once before or since.

To get you to notice that he's loaded?

What difference could that make? So he was wealthy. Apparently, he had always been wealthy. It hadn't ever mattered to her, so why would it matter now?

Apparently, there's a reason. *He did choose that day, that moment to make it evident....*

True. And gauging by the documents Barbie had sent to Katie, he had to be extremely wealthy because, with her commission, Katie was wealthy. His net worth had to be far greater than hers. Odd. He'd never tried to hide the fact that he had gobs of money, but he'd never mentioned it, either. And in all their hours of talking—very intimate talking, and very specific talking about finances, too—he'd never said or done anything to make Katie aware of his financial status. So why had he on that day? Why then?

Maybe he's ashamed of having money? Maybe he needed to know if you'd hold it against him? Maybe he needed to know if it changed the way you felt about him or related to him?

Good grief, didn't he know her too well for that kind of stuff? The man knew her thoughts—half the time before she knew them. Surely he had to know she couldn't care less about his money, one way or the other. Rich or poor, C. D. Quade was and would always be C. D. Quade.

But is Katie Cole Slater still Katie Cole Slater? Some changes in you are apparent to him. But you won't talk about a lot of your experiences. How can he know if you're still you?

She stared in the mirror above the sink. "I am *not* going to trudge through that hell again. Real or imagined—what's the difference? It's all god-awful and best put in the past."

Fine. So tell me. Why does a wealthy man live in a small apartment above a bar?

She stared into her own eyes, wondering. But try as she might, she couldn't think of a single reason that made sense. Why did he? Why didn't he have a lovely home somewhere?

How do you know he doesn't? Have you ever asked him?

She hadn't asked. Water dripped from her hair onto her shoulders. She slung the towel over her head and rubbed. Hell, the truth was she hadn't asked him much of anything about anything. Was that significant?

Cut yourself a little slack on that. You've had your hands full since the rescue. There've been a lot of adjustments. A lot of changes to deal with and a lot of surprises to absorb.

Okay, granted, that was true. She had been totally preoccupied with those things. But she never had given much thought to C.D.'s life other than to solicit his promise to never leave her during it.

She blew her hair dry and waded through all that had happened. And as she did, certainty filled her with guilt and shame. She'd been preoccupied. Self-absorbed. Grateful the team had risked themselves to rescue her, but definitely self-absorbed.

In fairness, shoes reversed, he probably would have been, too. But that wasn't the point. The point was, she hadn't thought to ask. He'd been steadfast and strong for her, giving and giving and then giving her more. And she'd taken and taken and taken more without considering what she could give in return.

Love was like that, of course. Sometimes one person was needier than the other, and then the scale would tip and the other person would be needier. But even during those needy times, the giver had to know that the taker cared. That the taker wanted to know the details, to share....

She tugged on a clean pair of jeans and a soft blue top, took the towel to the laundry room and tossed it on top of the washer. He was right. She snagged a beer from the fridge, opened it and went out to the back porch swing. He was so right. Katie wasn't ready.

The cold beer slid down her throat. She toed the porch floor, making the swing rock back and forth. Until she started looking out, showing at least as much interest in him and his needs as she spent looking in, showing interest in her own, she wouldn't be ready to marry him.

"Damn it." She took another swig of beer.

C.D. must have heard her curse; he walked onto the porch, smiling, went to grab a beer from the fridge and then came back outside.

"Don't you hate it when that happens?" He sat down beside her on the swing.

"What?" She knew what he meant, but clearly he was going to make her admit it, and nail her on it.

"When you've got to admit that I'm right."

She sniffed and took another sip of beer. "Okay. Okay, C.D. You're right. Happy now? Go ahead and gloat."

"I never gloat."

"That's the most ridiculous thing I've heard come out of your mouth in at least…a long time. You *always* gloat, C. D. Quade."

He swung an arm around her shoulder and pulled her to him, laughing hard. "Okay, I gloat. But only when I'm right."

She grunted and shoved at his chest with her hand.

They sat quietly for a few minutes, then C.D. said, "Go ahead, ask me."

She looked at him to see if he had that superior look

in his eyes, but he didn't. He was sufficiently humble. "I'm sorry, C.D."

He raised his eyebrows, clearly not expecting an apology.

"I've been really focused on me and I've neglected talking to you about your life. And it hit me, sitting here, that I've probably really screwed things up for you, and because you're you, you haven't told me."

"Aw, hell."

"What?"

"You're going off in the wrong direction, Katie." He groaned his frustration. "I'm where I want to be, remember? I love you. What could you possibly screw up being with me?"

She knew all that, but still. "Why don't you have a house?" she asked. "Why do you live in a little apartment above the bar?"

His irritation faded and the look in his eyes gentled. "I'm with you more than in the apartment."

"You know what I mean."

He nodded. "Because it's close to you."

"So you don't typically live here?"

"No, I don't." He looked out onto the yard. "I figured when you came home, you needed a small place."

"After being in a cell for so long?" What a beautiful thing to do for her. He'd been so thoughtful about everything.

He nodded. "I was afraid you'd feel lost in a house, but the cottage was bigger, just not too big. It seemed right. The apartment—" he glanced over to its balcony "—was near."

"So you could watch me."

"So I could watch over you and be close if you needed me."

She lifted a hand and stroked his cheek. Let him see in her eyes her love for him. "Why did you drive the Lotus the day of the divorce?"

"I'd rather not say."

Disappointment shafted through her. "I won't force you. I'll never force anything on anyone again. But I would appreciate it if you'd tell me—even if it hurts me."

"It doesn't hurt you or me," he promised. "It's embarrassing."

"You're embarrassed with me? Oh, *puhleeze.*" She grunted, tapped his thigh. "I don't believe it. You and I have always talked about everything—even your women, C.D. What could possibly be embarrassing between us?"

"I was uneasy," he admitted. "I drive the Lotus when I need to feel confident, and that morning… Let me just say I'd rather face an army of terrorists than relive that morning. I was eaten up with doubt."

She'd had no idea, seen no signs of uneasiness in him. And she'd never sensed a lack of confidence. "About what?"

He looked out at the dormant flower beds awaiting the first breath of spring. "I was concerned that you and Sam would get in there and change your minds. I had everything in the world that most matters to me. But it was highly possible that I'd walk through those doors at the courthouse and I'd have to stand there and watch it all slip away." He cocked his head. "You and Sam weren't like most couples. You weren't divorcing because you hated each other. You died." He shrugged, frustrated. "You know what I mean."

She did, and hugged him. "I've told you, honey. I've never been in love with Sam. Never. I am in love with you."

"Are you? You just didn't need love so badly...? Dr. Muldoon said—"

"I needed to feel loved to heal," she recalled. "I remember. You gave me that, but this is different, C.D." Pulling back, she put her hands on his chest and looked him in the eye, then nodded. "I am totally, head over heels, crazy in love with you."

He searched her face. "I've promised you forever. You've promised me nothing. I realize it's too soon, and I don't want to push you. You look at me and touch me with promises, but you still have the nightmares, and you still can't walk on the sand. I figure there's a reason for that, and I'm hoping like hell it isn't because you aren't content with me."

"I'm very content with you," she said. "And I'm committed to you. I don't know why I'm still having the nightmares. I don't know why I can't walk on the sand. But I intend to keep searching for answers, and to keep trying to deal with everything, C.D."

He nodded. "Okay."

She rested her chin on his shoulder. "So tell me about this house of yours. Is it big enough for two?"

"Actually, it's being remodeled."

"Really?"

He nodded. "Jake's been working with me on it."

"So that's what all these secretive conversations have been about."

C.D. smiled. "He's sharp. He has good taste, too."

"Do I get to see?"

"If you want to."

"Sure I want to." She shifted on her seat. "We can grab a burger on the way."

"If I eat one more burger, I'm going to turn into one."

She shrugged. "So have a salad, a chicken sandwich or something else."

He smiled. "Okay."

"So where is this house?"

"I don't think you want to go there yet."

"Sure I do." She fingered the chain running up to the ceiling of the porch from the swing, focused on its little squeak. "Actually, I want to see your home very much."

C.D. frowned. "Katie, the house is on the beach."

Deflated, she blew out a breath, took a sip of beer. "I—I can't—"

"I know." He looped an arm around her shoulder. "Don't worry about it, Angel. It's just a house. When you're ready, it'll be there."

He understood. He hadn't been held captive, but somehow he understood the emotional complexities of being a prisoner. As military pilots, they'd had training, of course, and it did simulate a lot of what she'd experienced. But there was so much more. So many subtleties that had taken her by surprise, and such substantial differences that training didn't really prepare a person for the reality. The degradation, the humiliation, the total dependency for so much as a drink of water, and the futile helplessness felt when that water was denied.

Nothing could prepare a person but the experience itself.

She took a sip of beer, the memories of thirst filling her mind. Memories of Ustead refusing to give her water for two days. Finally, he'd relented, and brought her a metal bowl full. He'd entered her cell, set it on the floor near the door, and then he'd urinated in it.

She'd wanted to kill him. She'd wanted to die. And she'd never forget the gnawing temptation to drink it anyway. God, she'd been tempted, almost driven to obsession. Her mouth was so dry her tongue stuck to the roof of her mouth, her teeth stuck to her inner cheeks. She couldn't swallow; the ridges in her throat stabbed her. So tempted to drink it anyway—and she probably would have, if he hadn't stood there and watched her, wanting to see her do it.

He'd been so frustrated because she didn't drink that he'd tried to taunt her into it. She didn't move, and he'd totally lost it and kicked the metal bowl over. Every drop of water had spilled out onto the sand floor.

Ustead had laughed and left.

Katie had cried, and licked her tears to wet her mouth.

Understanding came to her in a flash. That *had* happened. It wasn't an imagined event. And that incident was why, since coming home, she had to have drinking water with her at all times. Why she panicked when there was none. She probably always would.

The fear following her home wasn't logical—there was no water shortage now—but after what she'd suffered, she feared being thirsty again.

It made perfect sense now. And if it took carrying water with her to cope with what had happened, well, what was wrong with that?

Not a damn thing. She planted a kiss on C.D.'s neck, rested her head on his shoulder and watched the sunset.

If she lived a thousand years, she'd never again take for granted the sun rising and setting, or having the chance to see it.

She'd never again take for granted the privilege of…choice.

CHAPTER FIFTEEN

THE WILLOW CREEK GARDEN Center officially opened on a glorious spring day in an atmosphere Katie could only describe as one fit for a carnival. The local radio station did a live broadcast from there all morning, and C.D. arranged for hot dogs and soft drinks for everyone who came to the grand opening, plus balloons for the kids.

Because of Katie's high profile, a TV crew came to film, too, but the woman who'd asked about rape wasn't there. Before they wound up, a cameraman told C.D. that she'd left the station not long after Katie's press conference at the courthouse. She'd been working on a story involving a child and had crossed the ethical line to get an exclusive. The child had been injured and the woman had been fired. Last he'd heard, she'd told the obits editor she was going in search of herself. The business had sucked her dry. Maybe in seeking compassion, Katie thought, the woman would find her humanity.

Sam and Blair came out with the kids, and Molly made herself right at home in the flower shop with Ashley. She took Blair by the hand and pointed out every single thing to her, which likely drove Blair nuts, but if so, she hid it well. Molly was definitely into flowers. And Blair was definitely into Molly, interested in all that interested her.

The kids had really gotten lucky on the stepmother front, though for Blair to hear anyone refer to her as their stepmother would have broken her heart. Katie never used the word—Blair, too, was Molly and Jake's mother—and neither did anyone else after Jason Slater said it once and Katie set him straight.

A lot of the patrons from the Top Flight came over to wish Katie well and buy a tree. Paxton Air Force Base had a basewide project going on to plant oaks to replace those downed by several hurricanes that had ripped through the area in the past couple years.

Even Judge Haines stopped by. He was a good man, and when he looked into Katie's eyes, she saw that he, too, still carried his POW demons. They shared a glance that no one else around fully understood, and he joined the family under Katie's favorite oak tree while they ate. It was clear from the smile playing on his lips that he was at peace with his decision to grant the Slater divorce. Katie was grateful for that—to give this man, who had shared with her to comfort her, a moment of peace.

By the time the garden center closed for the day, Ashley proclaimed the business off to a fantastic start—an opinion Barbie shared. Sam and Blair left to take the kids to an early movie, and Katie and C.D. headed for his car.

"You knew we'd be successful," Katie said, sliding onto the seat.

"Never any doubt." He cranked the engine. "But how did you know? I deliberately didn't say a word."

She smiled. "You drove the Hummer."

He rolled his eyes. "Dinner out or home?"

It had been a good day. A very good day. She thought of her new list on the fridge at the cottage, its three items that signified her perfect life.

A warm and loving relationship with Molly and Jake. She had that now, and rarely thought of the missing years, unless something came up—and then the kids referred to it as when she was "gone" not "dead." A huge improvement. No one mentioned captivity anymore, and oddly, she didn't always think of those years as "captive time." The edges were dulling.

A business of my own that has nothing to do with flying or airplanes. The Willow Creek Garden Center was a reality now, open for business and off to a good start. Barbie, aka Samantha, predicted success, and who knew money better than she?

A relationship with the man who loves me before I turn fifty. No man could ever love a woman more than C.D. loved Katie. He had for a long time and he would forever. When exactly the certainty of that had seeped inside and whispered itself to her as an indisputable truth, she couldn't say. But it had and she knew it. She felt it and sensed it and believed it with every beat of her heart, down to the marrow of her bones. Ten years ahead of schedule, too.

If not for the nightmares and her still-persistent inability to step in the sand, her life would be fantastic. But those two challenges persisted. Both relentlessly reminded her that the ravages of those six years were a part of her now, and they would not be denied or be eager to relinquish their hold on her.

But Katie wasn't the woman with that wry sense of humor that she had been then. She knew all she had to lose, knew what life with that loss was like. Now she respected all she had, and she had far more than before. Her life itself wasn't the life she'd lived then, either. And what she'd lost, she'd given. Ustead and the guards couldn't take what she'd refused to give then, and they couldn't take it now—unless she permitted it.

She refused.

Taking off her sunglasses, she turned to C.D. "I want to go to your house."

He'd been about to shift the Hummer into reverse, but stopped as if on a dime. "Are you sure?"

She clenched her jaw and nodded, then stared out the windshield. "I'm scared," she said softly. "But I'm tired of being scared, C.D." She looked back at him. "I'm tired of not wanting to go to sleep because I'm afraid I'll dream. I'm tired of the thousand little things that trigger horrible memories of stuff that happened to me there. I'm tired of them playing games with my mind even now." She closed her eyes for a second, steeled her resolve. "I'm reclaiming my life, honey. All of it."

He stroked her face, his eyes glistening. "Okay, Angel. Whatever you want."

It was a short drive, south of the base to Highway 90, which paralleled the Gulf of Mexico. They passed the pier where Katie had parked so many times. The waning sunlight glinting off the cars in the parking lot mocked her, warning her that while she might have made up her mind to reclaim her life, actually doing it wasn't going to be easy. Determined, she didn't look away.

C.D. braked at a red light. "Do you want to grab a burger?"

He was sorely sick of them, but they were her comfort food, and he rightly felt she needed comforting. Yet the truth was if she dared to swallow a bite of anything, she'd be sick as spit all over the Hummer. That would not be a pleasing thing to her or to him. "No, thanks. Is there any food in the house?"

"Always." He reached for her hand.

She clasped it, telling herself not to squeeze too hard, not to hold on too tight. She could do this. She really could.

He drove past little knots of pastel-colored houses, hotels and tourist traps, until he reached the water tower. There, he turned left and drove down three streets to a private road. He turned right onto it. His house was on the gulf. She swallowed hard.

"You okay?"

"I'm fine." She nodded. Her insides were a tangled mass of knots in full spasm. She did some deep breathing, trying to ease the uproar. "There are no houses on this street."

"There's one," he said. "Mine." He turned a curve and the house rose up into view. It was two-story, a soft gray brick trimmed in white, with windows that stretched high into the steep pitch of the roof. The front yard looked like any other, with neat, crisp landscaping and a pretty three-tier fountain in the center of the sidewalk to the front door.

"I like it," she murmured.

He smiled. "I've been doing a little renovating."

"You told me Jake was helping. What have you been doing?"

"Converting it from a single-male household to a family home."

Her heart warmed, and Katie smiled. "That's special, C.D."

"I'm glad you think so." He pushed the opener on the visor and the garage door swung up. "I figured it'd be another year until you were ready to come out here."

"That long?"

He pulled into the garage and cut the engine. "I didn't know," he said. "I wanted it ready when you were."

"So is it?"

"Ready enough." He opened the door.

Getting out of the Hummer inside the garage was just like getting out of any car and walking into any house in any neighborhood she'd ever lived in. Yet knowing that beyond the back door was sand and beach and gulf, she had to force herself to do it. Her knees shook, her palms sweated, but she opened the door, swiveled out of the seat and shut it behind her. *So far, so good.*

C.D. opened the door to the house. "I'll show you around."

She swallowed hard and forced her feet to move, stepped into a little hallway that led to the kitchen.

It was huge, with tons of pale oak cabinets, a gourmet island and every appliance known to God and man. "Wow, C.D. Did you take up cooking?"

"Are you kidding?"

"With this kitchen? No, I'm not."

"Molly likes to cook."

He'd done this for Molly? Moved, Katie looked at the granite countertops, the dual dishwashers and chef's stove and warming drawers. "Wow, this is something."

He smiled, pleased that she liked it. "Come look at this."

Katie followed him through a masculine den done in navy leather, past two rooms with closed doors, a bath that was about the size of the cottage, to the end of a secondary hallway.

He paused outside the door. "I wanted this away from the rest of the house."

"Why?"

"Noise, Katie." He opened the door. "It's a music

studio." Pride filled his voice. "The walls are sound-proof, but I put in an intercom so that if you want Jake, he'll be able to hear you." C.D. grinned. "No playing like he didn't."

"Bet he loved that addition." She grinned.

"He was a good sport about it."

"C.D.," Katie gushed. "Jake must love this."

"Yeah, he's pretty happy with it. He brought Mark over a couple weeks ago. They're going to do band practice here—once you're ready. Until then, they're staying put in Mark's garage."

"You're amazing, honey." She walked up to him, hugged him and then kissed him lovingly. "You really are amazing. I pinch myself all the time wondering how I got so lucky. Out of all the women in the world, you chose to love me. I can't figure out why, but I'm so glad that you do."

"That's part of your charm." He walked back into the hallway. "You have no idea how unique and remark-able you are."

He deliberately stayed away from the rear of the house, steering her from room to room at the front, where she wouldn't see sand or water, only lovely land-scaping. But when they'd seen everything else, he paused. "More? Or have you seen enough for now?"

"I think I need to venture a little on my own."

He looked worried, but he didn't refuse. "I'll be in the kitchen, scrounging up some dinner."

"Okay." She watched him go, sensed his wariness, and with every step he took away from her, her fear in-creased. Drawing in a deep, steadying breath, she headed across the tiled hallway to the back of the house.

She stopped in the middle of the family room. It

stretched nearly the full length of the structure. Cream and green and splashes of yellow; huge rugs on the hardwood floors; enormous canvases with intricate designs stretching fifteen, twenty feet up the inside walls. The outer walls of the house were enormous panels of glass, tinted to protect against the glare of the sun. Beyond the windows, levels of decking went off in different directions. To the left was a pier, where a large boat with a canopy top rocked in the water. To the right another walkway ended in an observation deck. Its floor was brick and on the near end was a huge barbecue pit. The center level dropped down and steps led to a stretch of white sandy beach and the water.

The sun hung low in the sky, a glowing orange orb that streaked the sky pink and lavender and scattered glistening diamonds on the surface of the water. Through the window, she could hear the soft lull of the surf, see the waves curl and creep ashore, then wash out again. Constant. Serene. Soothing. And this window was a perfect place to watch the sunset each night.

Or from outside.

Her insides chilled. Maybe one day, she told herself. But not today. For today, the sunset from this side of the window was enough.

After dinner, C.D. asked, "Do you want to stay here tonight, or go back to the cottage?"

"Let's stay here." He'd worked so hard to make this house a home for them and the kids. She didn't want to disappoint him. "I love this house, C.D."

"I'm glad." He was genuinely pleased. And she was happy that she'd made the decision to stay. He hadn't acted as if it was important, but it clearly mattered a great deal to him.

"Movie or backgammon?"

"Movie," she said. "A sappy chick flick."

"Damn." He grunted. "Okay, but we sit on the sofa and make out."

Katie giggled. "Deal."

THE BEDROOM FACED the water.

Katie loved the huge canopy bed and filmy white sheers looping its shanks; the hand-carved oak furniture with intricate rosettes and leaves, the soothing green walls and warm cream linens. There was a lovely sitting area where she could see herself curling up with a good book, and a luxuriously sinful master bath with a tub that resembled a swimming pool.

In the still night, curled up against C.D., Katie closed her eyes and listened to the soft, steady sounds of his breathing, of the lazy waves kissing the shore.

She willed herself to sleep, vowing she wouldn't dream. In her mind, she imaged Molly planting seeds in the greenhouse, envisioned Jake and Mark in the studio, sitting on stools—Jake strumming his guitar, Mark playing his drums. She imagined C.D. sitting on the porch at the cottage, or sprawled out on the burgundy sofa in the den with a bowl of popcorn in his lap, laughing at her for crying during a movie that touched her heart. She pictured good things. Pleasant things. Happy moments and snapshots of her life with those she loved.

The tension slowly eased from her body, and the grip of fear loosened on her heart. She drifted deeper and deeper into sleep, holding on to good thoughts, to snippets of happy times, to all the good things in her life. The treasures… The treasured…

Katie. Katie.

She closed her mind, ignored his voice.

Katie, come. You cannot hide from me. I control you.

Ustead. She was dreaming; knew she was dreaming. *You're dead. Go away. You don't control me anymore.*

He laughed. Deep and cynical, it grated in her ears. *You cannot hide. I'm a part of you. I will always own you.*

She cringed, whimpered, fearing he was right, praying he was wrong. *No. No, not anymore. Not anymore.*

He whispered with a sigh, *Always.*

She fell to her knees in the dream.

He hovered over her, shoulders back, chest swelled. *Always.*

She stepped outside herself, as she had during the rape, watched him reach down and lift her off her knees.

Even now, you run from me. You say I am dead, but I live in you, Katie. I will always live in you.

As she stood separate and apart, watching him touching her, she shuddered and cringed. He did live in her. Through her. And as long as she ran from him, he would.

Oh, God. I can't endure this, too. I can't endure and conquer this, too.

He flung her from him. Her shoulder banged into the wall. Pain shot through her shoulder and down her arm but, separate as she was, she didn't feel it. Yet even separate, anger exploded inside her. It churned and boiled and erupted, filling all of her—every limb, muscle and nerve, every cell. *No. No, Ustead. No more.*

She stepped into herself, no longer separate or apart.

No longer an untouchable observer.

He slapped her.

She felt the sting, the burn on her face.

He punched her in the ribs.

Pain shot through her side, knocked the wind from

her lungs. She doubled over, felt the throb pulse through her, pounding and pounding. Sweat gathered on her skin, slid down her face, down her chest in rivulets, and the agony finally weakened to a dull ache. She dragged in a shallow breath, stiffened against the next wave of pain that washed through her, and stood upright.

Summoning the courage she had lacked then, she looked directly into his eyes, let him see her outrage and her disgust. "I didn't talk to the doctors or even to C.D. about what you did to me because I didn't want to remember it. I refused to remember it. But bits and pieces came back to me. Horrific bits and pieces now and then, here and there. And every time I remembered, I ran from you. I left myself to you, moved away, where you couldn't reach me. I thought I was a coward, so I didn't want to remember it. Was the dream—the memory—real or imagined? If I didn't know, then I didn't have to be ashamed because I ran, deserting myself. If I didn't feel it, then you never touched me."

Ustead stood facing her, arms folded, chest swelled, but voice silenced.

"But you did touch me, Ustead. You touched my body, mind and soul. I know now what I did. I remember now why I did it. And I'm not running anymore." Tears blurred her eyes, and she cracked open a shutter in her mind. "I remember everything—do you hear me? I feel every damn thing you ever did to me, you sorry bastard, and I'm still not running. Not from you. Not ever again. I'm right here, you sick son of a bitch. I'm standing right here."

Ustead's image faded.

Faded and disappeared right before her eyes.

Katie sat straight up in bed. Her heart raced, her

mind reeled. The dream was still vivid—every image, every sight and smell and sound. She dragged her hands over her face, willed herself to slow her breathing so she wouldn't hyperventilate. Her cheeks were wet with tears, and she was sweat-soaked, hot and clammy.

C.D. snored softly beside her.

She tossed back the covers and eased out of bed. Walked over to the French doors that led out onto a private deck. She opened them, felt the cool breeze blow in off the water.

Breathing deeply, she looked outside. Moonlight, soft and gentle, played on the calm water. The soft lulling sounds of the steady surf coming ashore and washing out again soothed her frayed nerves.

It's over, Katie. He doesn't own you anymore.

She stepped out onto the deck and paused, hesitant, fearful the panic would strike her and she wouldn't be able to move.

It didn't come.

She walked to the railing, looked out and let the flow of the surf, the gentle roar, seep through her. And with it came memories, one by one. Ustead raping her. Ustead torturing her. Ustead urinating in her water. Him giving her to his men. Starving her... Beating her... Tormenting her...

She remembered every gory detail. Every degradation, every humiliation, every lie. So much pain, more pain than she could hold. She'd had to separate to survive. To feel nothing, remember nothing, exist in a place she could hide in her mind.

General Amid. Her captor, her rescuer. Respectful and kind. He had allowed her to reclaim part of herself—enough to hold on to so that she wasn't lost completely to the poor woman who had endured it all. Katie remembered well General Amid killing Ustead, his blood splattering her. He'd protected her as much as he could. He had put her in a position to be rescued. He was the enemy, but a compassionate man.

She walked down the steps leading to the water's edge, one at a time. And as she descended, the images of her in the prison cell grew more and more faint.

Instead, she saw images of C.D., loving and supportive; of Molly and Jake; of Blair, squealing in delight at the wedding gift of their honeymoon trip. Images of Ashley and her kindnesses, and Katie's parents and the Slaters, offering to chip in with the rest of those she loved to help her get her garden center and build a new life. C.D. living in the tiny apartment above the bar because he feared going from a cell to his mansion on the gulf would be too big an adjustment for her. So many thoughtful gestures. So many loving deeds.

It had taken them all to bring her home.

And they had.

C.D. stood on the sand before her. "Angel?"

"How did you get there?" Katie tilted her head. "You were inside asleep."

"It's over, isn't it, Katie?" Hands in his pockets, he stood six feet across the sand from her, the wind blowing his hair. And he was without his cane. "You remember now."

Surprise rippled through her. "How did you know?" She'd told no one. Scarcely dared to think of all she couldn't recall herself.

"That which is endured is conquered," he said softly. "Blocking out what happened was how you endured."

A wind gust blew her hair over her eyes. She swept it back from her face. "You've known this for a long time?"

"Since the picnic," he said.

"The picnic at the garden center," she guessed. "Which is why you put water in all the cars." And he'd never said a word to bring it to her attention, never pushed her to realize what she'd been doing to cope, just waiting until she was ready to face it on her own. "When I overreacted at not having water."

He nodded. "So is it over, Katie?"

"It's over," she told him, knowing it was true. She had endured and conquered. She'd survived and adjusted and now she was healing. The scars would always be with her, but she no longer feared them, no longer felt weak because she had been a victim. The scars were proof of her victory.

They'd done their worst.

She had taken it and survived.

She still stood upright. Was still sane, and still determined to live a full, rich life.

Proof that she had conquered and won.

Proof that this was her perfect life.

C.D. looked up at her, his eyes searching. "Love won."

"Yes, C.D." Battle-worn and scarred, but still capable of loving and being loved, Katie smiled. "Love won." Love for her family, for C.D., and finally, love for herself.

He held out his hand. "Now, Angel, you're ready."

"Yes." Joyful tears brimmed in her eyes.

And she stepped down, into the sand.

EPILOGUE

Ten years later

I WAS WRONG.

It took me five years to admit it to myself, and I didn't confess it to C.D. until the night of our fifth wedding anniversary.

When I began this journey, I believed that life should come with warning labels. That if it did, then I could avoid all the nastiness of failures and hard times in my life. I could steer clear of my mistakes and avoid responsibility for the consequences. So much of what we do affects others, and when we screw up, they pay the price. I really liked the idea of flying in under the radar on that one.

With warning labels, I thought, life would be perfect. My whole family could live and grow and be spared from pain and suffering. There'd be no regrets to keep anyone up nights, and no knots in stomachs from saying and doing the wrong things, and no being torn between sides on making decisions.

But as I sit in the stillness of twilight in our home on the gulf, and I look out beyond the beach to the shimmering horizon, as much as I'd like to, I can't deny the truth.

"Voilà!"

Molly. I smile. Banging pots in the kitchen, cooking something fabulous—it always is—and obviously pleased with her latest creation.

Out beyond the deck and beach Jake and his friend Mark are riding the Jet Skis, white foamy wakes trailing behind them. C.D. stands on the deck and watches over them, just as he has watched over me on my journey back to a normal life. He's quite an amazing man. Really. He must have times when he loses patience or wishes to hell I'd move faster or slower or do something differently, but he never pushes or shoves or urges. He just supports me in whatever path I choose or whatever steps I take at whatever point in time I choose to take them. That respect has made all the difference to me in opening the shutters and reclaiming the part of me that was left in the tribal prison.

Yes, there are still times when I think of Ustead and General Amid. When I relive through nightmares the tortures of hell I suffered there. Not all of them come back to me when I am asleep. And there are times when I catch a whiff of scent that reminds me of the desert or the cell where I spent so much of my time. Or in the strangest places, I'll hear a sound that immediately takes me back to noises made by the other prisoners. These are infrequent moments now, yet I still must steel myself to endure them.

I was wrong. And I know that the woman I was is very different than the woman I've become. I pine for that wry sense of humor I once had, for the certainty I felt that I had all the answers, when clearly life ends long before the questions do. And yet I sit here tonight, a little wiser for the journey.

There was pain and suffering, mistakes and consequences, and many wrong paths and broken dreams. But the difference between me then and now is that now I know it took living through each of those experiences to change me from the woman I was to the woman I am. If even one thing—no matter how small—had not happened or had happened differently, then my life as I know and love it would be different.

I would be different.

I'm often asked if it was worth it—serving in the military, being a POW. I wish I could reply with some witty repartee, but the truth is, things like freedom and liberty and fair treatment and justice mean far more to me than perhaps to one who has not lived for six years as I did.

I think that disappoints some people—my being more serious than most about the value of those things to me. But I don't believe anyone could go through all I have gone through and remain unchanged or frivolous or flighty or even apathetic about those things. If they can, I suggest they be rushed to the nearest psychiatrist, because they are lost in denial and need immediate intervention to find their way home.

So was it worth it? All I sacrificed?

I think of my family—my marriage to C.D.; the children and all of our relatives—and I have to say yes. Yes, it was worth it.

Others think I've had a miserable time readjusting, and at times it has been hell. But there have been other times, too. Ones of tender reawakenings and poignant reminders of the goodness in people, and of the resilience of my own spirit, which at times is so insistent on seeing all the beauty around me, the blessings, that it surprises even me. I'm happy. I'm gardening, and I'm living my life as I choose, with those I love.

The shutters are all open.

I pull everything from the darkness into the light and view the good and the bad and all in between, and I am content.

I am at peace.

I am loved.

A woman can ask for no more in her perfect life.

Everything you love about romance...
and more!

Please turn the page for Signature Select™
Bonus Features.

Her
Perfect Life

BONUS
FEATURES
INSIDE

4   Readers' Discussion Questions:
     Her Perfect Life

8   The Inspiration for *Her Perfect Life*

12   Prisoner of War Information Resources

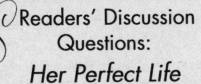

Readers' Discussion Questions:
Her Perfect Life

1. There have been women prisoners of war in every American conflict. However, before the late twentieth century, women were not deliberately put into combat situations. Major Rhonda Cornum's stalwart conduct as a POW in the first Gulf War in 1992 helped reshape the debate on women in the military. The 1994 repeal of the "risk rule" barring women from combat launched a national debate over a woman's fitness to serve and the danger her perceived weaknesses posed to male co-combatants. Presently, one in seven military personnel in Iraq is a female. After reading Captain Katie Cole Slater's story, do you have a stronger position on women in combat? Have your feelings about this issue changed?
For more information visit
www.womensenews.org/article.cfm/dyn/aid/1596.

2. If you had created a list at the age of fifteen, eighteen, twenty-five or thirty-five, what items would you have included to create your "perfect life"?

3. If you should have to suddenly start over and build yourself a new life, what would you change? (Relationships? Money? Prestige? Possessions?)

4. Do you believe that as we accumulate life experience, our priorities broaden and grow more meaningful and our goals turn less materialistic?

5. If you created a perfect life list right now, what five goals or qualities would you include?

6. During captivity, Katie's mantra was "That which is endured is conquered." Do you feel this is true? How can a strongly held belief such as this one keep hope alive? Many of us have a saying, motto, Bible verse or a phrase that captures our personal philosophy and serves as our talisman during times of trouble. Do you have one?

7. Katie and C.D. have a strong bond from working closely together in a difficult environment. Through mutual respect and trust, they come to love each other. But at first they are not "in love" with each other. In your life, have

you loved and not been in love? Been in love and not loved? Does including the element of a sexual relationship add to or cloud this issue? Given a choice, would you rather "be in love" or "love" someone?

8. As one would expect, given her circumstances, Katie suffers many of the challenging symptoms of post-traumatic stress disorder (or syndrome). One of the most disturbing symptoms is repeated nightmares involving her captivity. Reportedly, the best treatment for these nightmares isn't medication, but a mental technique where the sufferer changes the ending of the nightmare while awake, so that the ending ceases being upsetting. Do you think this kind of healing takes a great deal of personal determination and concentration? Does a person's self-esteem affect this kind of challenge?

9. Could Katie have defeated her dream demons any earlier? How? Did defeating those demons take becoming involved in a stable, loving relationship with C.D.? Did Katie have to first determine her children were safe before she could allow herself to heal?

For more information on this subject, go to www.ncptsd.va.gov/facts/index.html.

10. Katie is angry with the doctors trying to help her. Anger and blame—unreasonable and unearned—is normal in these situations. The person often feels betrayed—in Katie's case, by her military peers for leaving her behind. Have you ever experienced these emotions in this way?

11. Katie refuses to talk about her experiences as a prisoner, including being raped. Because rape is a crime not of sex but of violence and control, it's a very common reaction for rape victims to refuse to discuss the rape. For many, each time they do discuss it, they relive it, and that makes it impossible to go on and live a "normal" life. Yet it's equally important that they deal with the issue and not slide into denial, which is emotionally unhealthy. Katie refuses to give her captors another second of her life by dwelling on that which cannot be changed. In her position, would you feel compelled to talk about the experience, or not? Why?

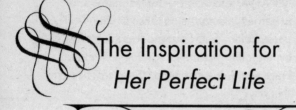

The Inspiration for
Her Perfect Life

As a writer, I'm often asked what inspires my books. I'm ashamed to admit it, but the truth is it's often anger. That was the case for my military novels in general, and for *Her Perfect Life* specifically.

At the beginning of the second war in Iraq, after the 9/11 attacks, I was watching a news broadcast—I am a news junkie, and have been all my life. One of the anchors said about the military that no man is left behind.

While that is a goal, and a fervent wish, it is not fact. Scott Speicher was left behind in the first Iraq war. His family believed he was dead, then maybe he wasn't, then he was and then maybe he wasn't. As a parent who also had a husband and son on active duty in two different branches of the military during the first Iraqi war, I rode that emotional roller coaster with them. I knew too well how I would feel at the seesaw of grief, the not knowing, and—God, forgive me—wondering if I should pray my child was dead rather than alive because of what could be happening to him if he were captured and had been taken prisoner of war. Hussein's regime was notorious for torture—the kinds of torture so inhumane that a mere mention of his tactics curdle the blood of even the most hardened, battle-worn soldiers in the world, much less those of a mother.

During the second Iraqi war, in a prison cell, soldiers found evidence scratched into a wall that Scott Speicher could have been there. And once again, I thought of him and his family, his wife, Joanne Speicher-Harris, and the unavoidable gauntlet of emotions they had to be feeling. Once more hope and grief and open wounds and the endless torment of haunting questions. Where is he? What's happened to him? Is he dead? Alive? Hungry? It's endless. Scott Speicher is the only soldier unaccounted for from the first Iraqi war. As of the date of this writing, his fate has not been determined.

So it was with an empathetic wife-and-mother's heart, that I began exploring as a writer. What if a female soldier had been captured? Some were. What happened to them? What if one had been in Scott's position—believed dead, reported dead. What if eyes-on-the-ground intelligence had verified her to be dead? And what if she wasn't?

Men are physically stronger than women, but women have emotional strength, and history proves that mothers move mountains to get to their children. They will endure anything, sacrifice anything, do anything—including that deemed impossible—for their children. The bond that makes love unconditional is stronger than any other. And so, of course, the captive in *Her Perfect Life* had to be a mother, a wife, a woman with everything to live for and everything to go home to when hostilities ended.

Yet I didn't want to write a story of her despair during captivity. It is all too easy for us to imagine the horrors and nightmares there. Instead, I found myself wondering, what if after a long time she came home? What if Scott had been in that cell? Nine years had passed for the world, but his world had stopped the day he'd been taken captive. What if she were rescued? What would she find in her world, then? What had happened in the interim with her family, her home—all that she'd known and loved?

That is the story I wanted to write. About her coming home. About what she found there, and how she coped with all that had happened to her during captivity and all that had changed by the time she returned. The adjustments she willingly made, and those thrust upon her. I wanted to write about Captain Katie Slater rebuilding *Her Perfect Life*.

And as her story unfolded to me, I wept along with her, through the highs and lows and the memories, and I laughed along with her as she tackled challenges, expected and unexpected, and made mistakes and failed and triumphed. And through it all, I remembered Scott Speicher and his family, and I continue to pray that one day he too has the opportunity to rebuild.

Vicki Hinze

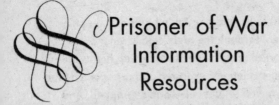

Prisoner of War Information Resources

The willingness with which our young people are likely to serve in any war, no matter how justified, shall be directly proportional as to how they perceive the veterans of earlier wars were treated and appreciated by their nation.

—George Washington

1. **Federal Research Division: POW/MIA Databases**
   www.loc.gov/rr/frd/powmia-home.html
   In December 1991, Congress enacted Public Law 102-190 (the McCain Bill). The statute requires the Secretary of Defense to make available to the public all information relating to the treatment, location and/or condition (T-L-C) of United States personnel who are unaccounted for from the Vietnam War.

   The facility chosen to receive this information was the Library of Congress. The Federal

Research Division created the POWMIA Database, the online index to those documents.

2. **Former American Prisoners of War**
   www.vba.va.gov/bln/21/Benefits/POW/
   U.S. Department of Veterans Affairs (VA) Web site for Former Prisoners of War (POWs).
   This site is designed to assist Former POWs, their families and survivors in obtaining needed VA benefits and VA health-care services.

3. **Geneva Convention Rules for Treatment of Prisoners of War**
   www1.umn.edu/humanrts/instree/y3gctpw.htm

4. **Defense Prisoner of War/Missing Personnel Office**
   www.dtic.mil/dpmo/
   The DPMO is responsible for the oversight of policy on the rescue of Americans who are isolated, captured, detained, or missing in a hostile environment and the discovery and identification of the remains of those who have not returned from foreign battlefields.

5. ***U.S News* Magazine article:** Personal account of an American woman army surgeon captured in Iraq in 1991.
   www.usnews.com/usnews/doubleissue/heroes/cornum.htm

Cornum's stalwart conduct helped reshape the debate on women in the military. The possibility of capture was often cited to keep women out of combat. After Cornum testified about her experience in 1992, many combat posts were opened to women.

6. **Women POWs through history to the present era**
   userpages.aug.com/captbarb/prisoners.html
   Short articles and references concerning women held as prisoners of war from the Civil War to the present conflicts.

7. **Post Traumatic Stress Syndrome**
   Support Services
   www.ptsdsupport.net/index.html
   PTSD Support Services specializes in combining personal experiences of post-traumatic stress disorder and practical application skills learned during workshops, counseling and resources from all over the Web. A PTS victim produced this site.

8. **National Center for Post-Traumatic Stress**
   Disorder—Department of Veterans Affairs
   www.ncptsd.va.gov/
   The National Center for post-traumatic stress disorder (PTSD) was created within the Department of Veterans Affairs in 1989, in response to a Congressional mandate to address the needs of veterans with military-related PTSD.

This Web site is provided as an educational resource concerning PTSD and other enduring consequences of traumatic stress.

9. **Post-Traumatic Stress Disorder Resources**
   A medical viewpoint—symptoms, treatments, causes.
   www.medicinenet.com/ posttraumatic_stress_disorder/article.htm

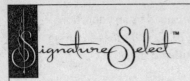

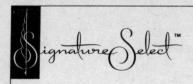

For three women, the right time to find
passion is BEFORE their time…

PERFECT TIMING

USA TODAY bestselling authors

Nancy Warren

Julie Kenner

&

favorite author
Jo Leigh

What if the best sex you ever had was 200 years
ago…or 80 years ago…or 60 years ago? Three
bestselling authors explore the question in this
brand-new anthology in which three heroines
travel back in time to find love!

May 2006

Signature Select™

Take a trip to the sensual French Quarter with
two favorite stories in

NEW ORLEANS NIGHTS

USA TODAY bestselling author

Julie Elizabeth Leto

The protector becomes the pursuer in two
editorially connected tales about finding
forbidden love with the bodyguard amidst
murder and mystery in New Orleans.

"Julie Elizabeth Leto always delivers sizzling,
snappy, edgy stories!"—*New York Times*
bestselling author Carly Phillips

May 2006

If you enjoyed what you just read,
then we've got an offer you can't resist!

Take 2 bestselling love stories FREE!
Plus get a FREE surprise gift!

Clip this page and mail it to Silhouette Reader Service®

IN U.S.A.
3010 Walden Ave.
P.O. Box 1867
Buffalo, N.Y. 14240-1867

IN CANADA
P.O. Box 609
Fort Erie, Ontario
L2A 5X3

YES! Please send me 2 free Silhouette Bombshell™ novels and my free surprise gift. After receiving them, if I don't wish to receive any more, I can return the shipping statement marked cancel. If I don't cancel, I will receive 4 brand-new novels every month, before they're available in stores! In the U.S.A., bill me at the bargain price of $4.69 plus 25¢ shipping & handling per book and applicable sales tax, if any*. In Canada, bill me at the bargain price of $5.24 plus 25¢ shipping & handling per book and applicable taxes**. That's the complete price and a savings of 10% off the cover prices—what a great deal! I understand that accepting the 2 free books and gift places me under no obligation ever to buy any books. I can always return a shipment and cancel at any time. Even if I never buy another book from Silhouettte, the 2 free books and gift are mine to keep forever.

200 HDN D34H
300 HDN D34J

Name _____ (PLEASE PRINT)

Address _____ Apt.# _____

City _____ State/Prov. _____ Zip/Postal Code _____

Not valid to current Silhouette Bombshell™ subscribers.

Want to try another series?
Call 1-800-873-8635 or visit www.morefreebooks.com.

* Terms and prices subject to change without notice. Sales tax applicable in N.Y.
** Canadian residents will be charged applicable provincial taxes and GST.
All orders subject to approval. Offer limited to one per household.
® and ™ are registered trademarks owned and used by the trademark owner and or its licensee.

BOMB04   ©2004 Harlequin Enterprises Limited

COMING NEXT MONTH

Signature Select Spotlight
ANGEL EYES by Myrna Mackenzie
Her special clairvoyant ability has led to painful betrayal for Sarah Tucker, leading her far from home in search of peace and normalcy. But an emergency brings her back, throwing her headlong into her past—and into the passionate but wary arms of police officer Luke Packard.

Signature Select Collection
PERFECT TIMING by Julie Kenner, Nancy Warren, Jo Leigh
What if the best sex you ever had was two hundred years ago... or eighty years ago...or sixty years ago? Three bestselling authors explore the question in this brand-new anthology in which three heroines travel back in time to find love!

Signature Select Saga
KILLING ME SOFTLY by Jenna Mills
Brutally attacked and presumed dead, investigative reporter Savannah Trahan assumes a new identity and a new life—but is determined to investigate her own "murder." She soon learns how deep deception can lie...and that a second chance at love should not be denied.

Signature Select Miniseries
NEW ORLEANS NIGHTS by Julie Elizabeth Leto
The protector becomes the pursuer in two editorially connected tales about finding forbidden love with the bodyguard amidst murder and mystery in New Orleans.

Signature Select Showcase
ALINOR by Roberta Gellis
Ian de Vipont offers marriage to widow Alinor Lemagne as protection from ruthless King John. His offer is sensible, but Alinor cannot deny the passion that Ian arouses within her. Can their newfound love weather the political unrest within England?

Fortunes of Texas Reunion, Book #12
THE RECKONING by Christie Ridgway
Keeping a promise to Ryan Fortune, FBI agent Emmett Jamison offers his help to Linda Faraday, a former agent now rebuilding her life. Attracted to him yet reluctant to complicate her life further, Linda must learn that she is a stronger person than she realizes.